# smoke

# Also by Ellen Hopkins

*Crank*

*Burned*

*Impulse*

*Glass*

*Identical*

*Tricks*

*Fallout*

*Perfect*

*Tilt*

*Rumble*

# Ellen Hopkins

**Margaret K. McElderry Books**
NEW YORK  LONDON  TORONTO  SYDNEY  NEW DELHI

MARGARET K. McELDERRY BOOKS • An imprint of Simon & Schuster Children's Publishing Division • 1230 Avenue of the Americas, New York, New York 10020 • This book is a work of fiction. Any references to historical events, real people, or real places are used fictitiously. Other names, characters, places, and events are products of the author's imagination, and any resemblance to actual events or places or persons, living or dead, is entirely coincidental. • Text copyright © 2013 by Ellen Hopkins • Cover design and illustration copyright © 2013 by Sammy Yuen Jr. • All rights reserved, including the right of reproduction in whole or in part in any form. • MARGARET K. McELDERRY BOOKS is a trademark of Simon & Schuster, Inc. • For information about special discounts for bulk purchases, please contact Simon & Schuster Special Sales at 1-866-506-1949 or business@simonandschuster.com. • The Simon & Schuster Speakers Bureau can bring authors to your live event. For more information or to book an event, contact the Simon & Schuster Speakers Bureau at 1-866-248-3049 or visit our website at www.simonspeakers.com. • Also available in a Margaret K. McElderry Books hardcover edition • Book design by Mike Rosamilia • The text for this book is set in Chaparral Pro and Trade Gothic Condensed No. 18. • Manufactured in the United States of America • First Margaret K. McElderry Books paperback edition February 2015 • Manufactured in the United States of America • 10 9 8 7 6 • The Library of Congress has cataloged the hardcover edition as follows: • Hopkins, Ellen. • Smoke / Ellen Hopkins. • p. cm. • Sequel to: Burned. • Summary: After the death of her abusive father and loss of her beloved Ethan and their unborn child, Pattyn runs away, desperately seeking peace, as her younger sister, a sophomore in high school, also tries to put the pieces of her life back together. • ISBN 978-1-4169-8328-6 (hardcover) • ISBN 978-1-4424-2358-9 (eBook) • [1. Novels in verse. 2. Grief—Fiction. 3. Emotional problems—Fiction. 4. Sisters—Fiction. 5. Runaways—Fiction. 6. Mormons—Fiction.] I. Title. • PZ7.5.H67Sm 2013 • [Fic]—dc23 • 2012038452 • ISBN 978-1-4169-8329-3 (pbk)

This book is dedicated to the far-too-many victims of abuse—physical, sexual, and emotional—on this planet. If we can, in fact, change the world, this would be an excellent place to start.

# Acknowledgments

This book was a long time coming, a sequel I never intended. But far too many of my readers needed closure to the story I told in my second novel, *Burned*. And, because I truly love this book, I want to thank those readers who kept insisting until I caved and wrote it. You were absolutely correct. Pattyn deserved closure, and while it may not be the soap opera ending some of you requested, I believe I've done right by her in these pages.

I have previously thanked my family for their unwavering support. But it feels like a good time to do so again. Topping the list is my husband, John, who has spent countless hours babysitting, serving as parent-school liaison, transporting kids and pets, grocery shopping and cooking, running even more mundane errands, and otherwise allowing me the hours I need to write. FYI, *Burned* remains one of his favorite books of mine. He's such an incurable romantic!

smoke

*Pattyn Scarlet Von Stratten*
## Some Things

You can't take back, no
matter how much you wish
you could. No matter how
hard you pray to

                    **some**

all-powerful miracle maker.
Some supposed God of Love.
One you struggle to believe
exists, because if he did,

                    **things**

wouldn't be so out of control,
and you wouldn't be sucked dry
of love and left to be crushed
like old brittle bones that

                    **are**

easily ground into dust.
Hindsight is useless
when looking back over
your shoulder at deeds

                    **irreversible.**

# Dear, Sweet God

Forgive me. I don't know what to do.
Where to go. How to feel. I'm perched
on the precipice, waiting for the cliff
to crumble. No way to change what

happened. What's done is done and I . . .
I can't think about it. If I do, I'll throw up
right here. Bile boils in my gut, erupts
in my esophagus. I gulp it down, close

my eyes. But I can still see him, lying there.
Can still hear the gurgle in his throat.
Still smell the rich, rusty perfume of blood
pooling around him. I so wanted him dead.

My father. Stephen Paul Von Stratten.
The bastard who beat my mother. Beat
my sister. Beat me. The son of a bitch
who was responsible for the accident

that claimed my Ethan—catapulted him
wherever you go when you die. Our unborn
baby rode into that wilderness with him.
Dear, cruel God. Why couldn't I go, too?

# Eye for an Eye

If ever a person deserved to die,
it was Dad. But when I saw the bullet

hit its target square, watched him drop,
surprise forever branded in his sightless

eyes; when his shallow breathing went
silent, I wanted to take it back. Couldn't.

The Greyhound shifts gears, cresting
the mountain. Donner Pass, maybe.

Can't tell, leaning my head on the cool
window glass. It's dark. After ten. Escaping

into the night. Into the unknown. It's warm
in the bus, but I can't quit shaking. I think

I'll be cold forever. Frozen. Soul-ripping
sadness ice-dammed inside of me.

I shouldn't have listened to Mom. Shouldn't
be here. Shouldn't be free. I should be in

handcuffs. Behind bars. Locked away
forever. That's what I deserve. Instead,

I'm on my way to San Francisco.
I want to see something I've never

seen—the ocean. They'll find me,
sooner or later. Put me away in a cement

box without windows, where I belong.
I want to carry a memory with me,

bury it inside my heart, treasure, to be
exhumed when I need something

beautiful. Peaceful. Pacific. Of course,
I'll probably never feel at peace again.

Dad had ghosts who visited him often,
demons he tried to drink away. Now

he'll be my ghost. A ghost, filled with
demons. Haunting me until I'm a ghost, too.

# The Bus Is Crowded

I chose a seat near the back, away
from the driver. Mistake. Too close
to the bathroom. It stinks of urine

and worse. Every now and again
someone goes in there and then it
smells like marijuana, though smoking

is prohibited on all Greyhounds.
At least that's what the signs say.
Not like the driver cares. Easier not

to interfere with derelicts, dopers,
failed gamblers, and crazies. Oddly,
I feel safe enough among them.

Like freeway drivers in separate cars,
all going the same direction at the same
time, each passenger here has a unique

destination. A personal story. I try
not to listen. Try to tune the voices
out. Don't need other people's drama.

# But Some I Can't Miss

Somewhere behind me, a couple
has argued for an hour. Seems
he was up two hundred dollars
at Circus Circus. But she dropped
that, plus three hundred more,
which explains why they're:
> *riding a piss-smelling bus home*
> > *'stead of getting a little cooch*
> > > *in a cozy motel room before*
> > > > *catching the morning Amtrak.*

Kitty-corner and a couple rows
up, two blue-silver-haired women
talk about their husbands, kids, and
grandkids. One of them got lucky
on dollar slots. Now she can pay
her electric bill and have enough
> > > > *left over to put some back into*
> > > *our savings. Shouldn't have*
> > *took it out for this trip, but I*
> > *just had one of those feelings. . . .*

# Behind Me

The guy takes up two whole seats.
        No one wants to sit near him, mostly
because he smells like he hasn't had

a shower. Ever. Probably homeless and
        put on the bus by law enforcement. They
don't much like finding people frozen

to death in riverside cardboard boxes.
        Lots of homeless take up residence on
the banks of the Truckee. Wonder if one

of them will notice the metallic glint
        of a 10mm. The gun that killed Stephen
Von Stratten. Wonder if the cops will

check the river. After . . . it . . . Mom
        told me to take Dad's car and go far
away. Fast away. She gave me her money

        stash, packed a few clothes. *Once
                the cops come,* she said, *they'll
        look for the car. Dump it soon.*

Driving into Reno, it came to me—
          a scene from an old movie—to park
the old Subaru in the airport garage.

I took the overhead walkway, down
          the escalator, out the front doors,
carrying the tatters of my life in

an overnight bag. Walked the couple
          miles to the bus station, much of it
along the river. Seemed like a good

place to lose the gun Ethan gave me
          for protection. It did protect Jackie
from another fist to her face. But, oh,

the price was dear. For Dad. For me.
          For the entire family. What will happen
to Mom and the kids now? Tears

threaten, but I can't let them fall.
          Can't show weakness. Can't show
fear. Can't look like a girl on the run.

# Smelly Homeless Guy

Doesn't only stink. He's sick, too,
coughing a death cough. After a long
phlegm-infused hack, the girl across
the aisle and one row forward turns

> and says to him, *You is disgusting,*
> *man. Di'nt you mama teach you to*
> *put you hand over you mouth when*
> *you cough?* She is Hispanic, not much

older than me. Maybe a year or two.
Pretty, under heavy eyeliner and
a waterfall of shiny black hair, but
tough-looking. Not someone I'd want

to make mad. Better to keep my eyes
fixed out the window, my thoughts
to myself. If I were the guy behind
me, I'd do the same. He says nothing.

> But lets go a chest-heavy cough,
> punctuated by a loud, totally gross
> fart. The girl jumps into the aisle,
> fists raising. *Listen here, you*

*piece ah shit. You do that again,*
*I'll kill you. Right here. Right*
*now. And nobody gonna care.*
*Nobody gonna say a word, yeah?*

Several people agree, *Yeah.* A couple
actually clap. The girl draws down
on Homeless Guy. *Did you hear me*
*or what? 'Cuz I sure wan' ah answer.*

When he continues his silent
not-a-reply, she advances toward
him, back turned to her own seat
and the creep lurking across the aisle,

right in front of me. Her backpack
sits unguarded on the floor. The man
checks to make sure her attention
is totally focused on Stinky Man.

Once he's satisfied she's not looking,
he reaches across, slips a hand under
the flap of her bag, rooting around
until he finds something he wants.

I can't see exactly what it is,
but he palms it with a satisfied
expression as the girl goes off
on homeless guy one more time.

> *I don' wan' you goddamn*
> *germs an' I don' wanna smell*
> *you shit. I think maybe you should*
> *move up front now. Okay?*

She reaches into her jeans pocket,
pulls out a switchblade, opens it
for effect. The guy has nothing with
him but a thin coat. He grabs it, pushes

past her, hurries forward. The back
of the bus breaks out in cheers.
The front turns around, wondering
what's up. They'll find out soon enough.

# When the Girl Turns

Back toward her seat, she finds me
staring at her. Admiring her, really.

> *Wha' you lookin' at?* Anger blankets
> her like perfume. Somehow it makes

her even prettier. "Nothing. Sorry . . ."
Should I mention the thief who stole

whatever? I could just mind my own
business, I guess. Not like she'll appreciate

it if I tell her. But I'd want someone to tell me.
I gesture for her to lean closer, and for

some reason, she does. I lower my voice.
"Uh, you might want to check your stuff.

That man across from you was in your
backpack." Hope she doesn't knife him.

> Her eyes, black as nighttime water, jab
> mine, searching for truth. She shrugs. *Okay.*

*Thanks.* She slides back into her seat.
Without a glance at the man next to her,

she lifts her pack up onto her lap, nods
at the open flap. She turns to him.

*Did you find what you was lookin'*
*for? I think maybe you should give*

*it back, then move on up front with*
*the sick dude.* Her hand runs down

over the outside of her jeans pocket.
Still, the man tries to deny it.

> *I don't know what you're talking*
> *about. You're not threatening me . . . ?*

*Two seconds, or I scream rape.*
It takes one for her wallet to reappear

and the guy to disappear up the aisle.
She looks at me again. *'Preciate it.*

# I Return

To my personal interior hell.
   One thing I grabbed as I left
      the house was a notebook. Not
         my nice denim-bound journal,

the one holding all my secrets
    and memories I must never
       lose. I left that book in Caliente,
         secure in the care of Aunt J.

This is the one I was supposed to
    write in for seminary. The one
      I never bothered with. But Ms. Rose
        was right. Keeping a journal helps

you put things in perspective. I could
    use some of that now. I reach up, turn
      on the reading light. Dig into my
        battered little backpack for notebook

and pen. I suppose I shouldn't put
    anything incriminating in here.
      Then again, if they catch me, it
        won't make much of a difference.

## Journal Entry, October 27

*Dad is dead. I thought it
would feel good to say that,
thought it would make things
right. But nothing will ever
be right again. I had planned
to kill all the people I thought
responsible for Ethan's death.
But after Dad, I couldn't.*

*I am not the hand of God.*

*Ethan! I am hollowed out
with you gone. Those people
deserve to die. But it wouldn't
bring you back. Wouldn't give
back our baby. And when I
witnessed death at my feet—watched
the fragile light of life go pale—
I lost all will for vengeance.*

*I am a coward. And so, I run.*

*Jackie April Von Stratten*
## Some People

        Are worthy of a bullet straight
        to the heart because that is where
        cruelty evolves into evil.
Some
        humans aren't human at all,
        despite how they appear.
        Humanity is what lives inside
people,
        harbored beneath skin, flesh,
        and bone. A soul, if you like.
        A glimpse of God. The spark
        that continues, should you
deserve
        an afterlife. Faithful Mormons
        believe every Latter-Day Saint
        continues on, transitioning either
to
        heaven or hell. But I think
        those who have no hint of life's
        light within are completely
        snuffed out when they
die.

# Violent Death

Has a stink. Blood. Poop. Pee.
And something else, something
I can't find a name for, but it's
mixed up in the sewer smell
leaking from Dad's empty shell.

              He has vacated the premises.

Whatever made Dad "Dad" is gone.
I don't think he had a soul. A life
force maybe. But not anymore.
What's lying there, cooling and stiff
on the shed floor, has nothing inside it.

              He can't hurt me anymore.

Pattyn saved my life. Dad would
have killed me for sure, one slow
fist fall at a time. I was halfway
there, and ready to give up my own
spirit. Instead, it's Dad who's dead.

              I should feel bad. All I feel is numb.

# Our Tiny House

Is overflowing people.

>Cops.
>Kids.
>Ladies from church.
>Bishop Crandall.

Is a cacophony of sounds.

>Questions.
>Crying.
>Shushing the crying.
>Comforting the new widow.

Is a chaos of feelings.

>Confusion.
>Anger.
>Fear.
>Dread.
>
>Relief.

# The Last Hours Blur

All I wanted was a minuscule taste
of love—to be rewarded with even

the vaguest ghost of what Pattyn
experienced with Ethan, as short-lived

as that was. All I wanted was, for one
blink of time, to feel needed. Desired.

Desire, become lust, become fear.
Fear, become pain, become terror.

Terror, become release. And I am
frozen there. People talk all around

me. Their voices inflate inside my head
until it thuds and I can't quite make

out what they're asking me now.
What happened? I don't know. I'm not

sure. It was all so fast, so slow motion.
Someone in a uniform—a woman with

> warm hazel eyes—tells me, *Relax.*
> *Take your time.* A cop. She's a cop, and . . .

19

## Who Invited the Cops?

Mom didn't call them. She called
Bishop Crandall. I remember that.
Remember her standing over me,

> phone in hand. *Hurry, please.*
> *I think . . . I think Stephen's dead.*
> *I'm not sure. I can't touch him.*

Our bishop lives less than five
miles away. In the short time it took
him to get here, Mom had covered me

with a blanket. I could feel it sponging
blood, but it couldn't hide the damage
to my face. Bishop Crandall looked

at me with disgust. In fact, my father's
cooling corpse seemed to bother him
less. He kneeled on the floor beside

> Dad, put a finger against his wrist.
> *I'm afraid he's gone, Janice.*
> *What in God's name happened?*

Through my swelling eyes, I saw
Mom shake her head. *I don't know.*
*I don't know. I was just getting out*

*of the shower when I heard gunshots.*
*I threw on some clothes and came*
*running, just in time to see the Subaru*

*roar out of the driveway. It was . . .*
She paused, trying to make sense
of what she'd seen. *Pattyn was driving.*

"She saved me," I wheezed, the act
of sucking in air so excruciating
that I could barely catch breath at all.

Darkness snatched at me. My head
throbbed and my brain refused
to process any more information.

But I knew one thing, and it was
worth the searing effort of repeating
it. "Pattyn saved my life."

# Next Thing I Knew

I swam up into muted yellow
       light and found myself here, in
       Dad's shabby recliner, wrapped

in a clean blanket. People had
       started to gather—LDS sisters,
       to help care for the little ones

and Mom, who is propped up
       on the sofa across the room,
       Samuel on her lap, peering up

at her pasty face. Bishop Crandall
       must have made the calls, and he
       continues to direct operations,

instructing his wife to please
       pack some clothes for the girls,
       who are being divvied up among

the church faithful, and have no
       idea why. The exception seems
       to be Ulyssa, who sits in a corner

with Georgia, who sucks her thumb,
       though she gave it up weeks ago.
       'Lyssa's eyes scream that she knows.

# The Hazel-Eyed Cop

Knows, too. And she wants
to know why Dad is dead
and why I look the way I do.
That's what she's asking.

I think really hard. Try to say
the right thing. "Dad was . . ."
I can feel the shadow of his fist.
". . . doing this to me. Pattyn

came in, I don't know from
where, but she was holding
a gun. She told him to stop,
but he just kept on . . ."

I can see the iron of his jaw,
the determination in his eyes.
*What are you going to do,
little girl? Shoot me?* he said.

*You don't have the balls. . . .*
My face heats beneath the cuts
and bruises. "She warned him
again, and this time he stopped.

Then he moved toward her.
I knew he'd take the gun away,
hurt us both, so I screamed
for her to shoot. God, it was so

loud. And then he just dropped.
And then . . . I don't know . . ."
There's more, and it's important,
but I can't remember. "It's all

fuzzy and strange and I think
I must have blacked out because . . ."
The deputy stops me with a hand
laid gently on my forearm.

> The gesture, unexpected, is tinged
> with compassion. It stings, and I
> can't hold the tears in anymore.
> *Okay, honey. That's enough*
>
> *for now. I've called an ambulance.*
> *They'll take you to the hospital*
> *for an examination. We need to*
> *know exactly what he did to you.*

# I Can't Go

They'll find out our dirty family secret.
The one we're never supposed to confess.

Everyone will know now, won't they?
About what Dad does. Did. And then,

there's the other shameful thing. I should
tell, make Caleb pay for what he did. But

no one will believe me. Caleb, the not-so-
saintly Mormon boy, said so, and it's true.

No one at church. No one at school. Even Dad
didn't. Why, Dad? Why didn't you? Oh,

if only he would have! "I don't think . . . ,"
I try. "We don't have much money."

> *That's okay. We can work that out.*
> *I'm going to talk to your mom now.*
>
> *Are you all right here by yourself*
> *for a few?* I nod and she leaves

me as alone as I can possibly be in
this simmering cauldron of people.

# It Seems Like Forever

But finally, the deputy lady
         returns. *The ambulance is here
now. Don't be afraid. They're
         friends of mine and I told them
to take real good care of you.*

She lifts me to my feet. Slides
         an arm behind my back, holds
on. Good thing. My legs shake
         so hard, I don't think I could
walk on my own. She steers me

         out into the iced October night.
                  A million stars dance in the sky.
         Beautiful. And I am ugly. My teeth
                  start to chatter. *Bring a blanket,*
         the cop tells her paramedic friend.

                  He is dark haired, good-looking,
                           and I can't believe that's what
                  I'm thinking as he wraps me in
                           warm thermal. *I've got her now.*
                  He lifts me up into the back

of the ambulance, sits me
        on the gurney. It is only now
I notice the crowd of neighbors,
        bracing themselves against
the chill to see what's going on

at the Von Strattens. It isn't
        the first time they've heard
the yelling, or even shots fired.
        Dad's regular benders resulted
in shed target practice on more

than one occasion. But tonight
        the place is swarming with cops,
using flashlights to comb for
        bullet casings. They'll only find
one. That's all it took. A white

van, unmarked, but clearly from
        the coroner's office, has backed into
the yard, close to the shed door,
        barely blocking the view of the sheet-
covered stretcher being loaded inside.

# I Can't Tear My Eyes Away

*Here now,* says the paramedic.
*You need to lie down, okay?*
He covers me with another
blanket, straps me to the gurney.

*I need to do a couple of things
before we go. Let me know if I
hurt you.* He reaches for my arm
to check my pulse. *What's this?*

He coaxes open the fingers
of my left hand and I realize
I've been clutching something.
"Pattyn's locket," I say, and for

a second I don't know what that
means. But then I remember.
I accidentally grabbed it when . . .
*Should I give it to your mom?*

"No!" I don't know why, but I
feel an overwhelming need to
keep it with me. Pattyn will want
it back. The paramedic—Kent,

28

according to his name tag—nods.
*Okay. You hang on to it.* Gently,
he closes my fingers around it again.
Then he proceeds to take my blood

pressure. Air pumps the cuff tightly
around my very sore arm and I wince.
*Sorry,* he says, releasing the air again.
Now he uses a small penlight to scan

my pupils. Hard to do with
my face swollen up around them.
Finally, he puts a stethoscope
to my chest, tells me to inhale.

I don't know what it sounds
like amplified. But to my regular
ears, it sounds like a pathetic rasp.
Kent scowls, asks me to repeat

the paltry performance. No better
than the first time. He jots some
notes, looks at me with sympathetic
eyes. Jade eyes. Green eyes.

# Green Eyes

Started this. Green eyes
are to blame. Not Kent's.
Caleb McCain's. God!

How could he? I wanted
him, but I didn't want
that. Not yet. I thought

he was nice. Thought
he was lonely, too, with
his mom gone so long.

At school he doesn't act
that way, but at school
you have to pretend to be

all stuck up if you don't
want to get picked on. But
at church I'd see him sitting

alone, staring off into space,
as if, if he concentrated hard
enough, he might find a psychic

line to his mom, wherever
she is. Wherever she vanished
when she decided to leave.

All I wanted was to soothe
him, to tell him I'm lonely,
too, despite the ever-present

bustle of my extremely large
family. All I wanted was to
wind myself into his arms,

take comfort in each other's
warmth, and we were warm.
All I wanted was to kiss him,

let him kiss me back, and
understand the meaning of
a shared kiss. We kissed, and

at first it was everything
I expected. But then, I don't
know. It all changed with

a yank of my blouse, and
his hand was underneath it,
touching me, pinching me.

And his kiss turned rough,
and I pleaded with him to stop.
But he wouldn't. He wouldn't.

# Next Thing I Knew

I was on the floor with my arms
pinned over my head, and a hand
jammed between my legs. "Please,
Caleb. Stop. Don't do this."

    *Ah, c'mon,* he said. *Pretend that*
    *you don't, but you know you want*
    *this more than I do. All girls do.*

Then I felt it, hard behind his jeans.
"No!" But it came out a harsh whisper.
I was petrified Dad would hear. Maybe
even more scared of that than of what

was happening to me—one wicked
thrust and Caleb drove himself inside
me. Something ripped. Something
pried. I thought he would tear me apart.

    But I didn't dare scream, and he
    pretended that made it okay. *See?*
    *You like it. I knew you would.*

All I could do was go limp, tears
streaming and soaking my blouse,
until he shuddered his finish,
punctuated with a disgusting grunt.

# And His Amen?

*Jesus. Look at all the blood.*

Then outside, heavy footsteps.
All the thrashing had brought
Dad looking. Caleb heard his
drunken stumbling. Jumped up.
Zipped up. Ran right by Dad,

       whose reaction was Johnnie
       Walker slow. *Wha . . . ?*

Then he saw me lying there,
skirt hiked up, fluids trickling
from between my legs. I tried
to tell him it wasn't my fault.
Caleb stole what he wanted.

       But Dad wouldn't listen. *You
       came out here to meet him,
       you goddamn whore. What did
       you expect? Cookies and milk?
       You're ruined now. What man
       will ever want you?* And then

he started to teach me a lesson
I won't forget until the day I die.

# Vitals Duly Noted

Kent goes to talk to Mom. After a few,
she climbs into the ambulance.
"You're coming with me, aren't you?"

> She kneels beside me. *I can't.*
> *The police want a statement.*
> *And I have to feed Samuel.*
>
> *He woke up with all the . . . noise.*
> *I'll come as soon as I can, though.*
> *It shouldn't be too very long.*

What can I say, but, "Okay." I peer up
at Mom's doughy face, seeking some
hint of emotion. But I don't see sorrow.

Don't see fear. She is a glacier.
Totally expressionless. Probably
in shock. "Are you okay, Mom?"

> *I have to be, don't I?* Her voice falls
> to a near whisper. *How could she do*
> *it, Jackie? What happened to Pattyn?*

# Dad Stole Everything

From Pattyn. Every tiny taste
of love she'd ever known. Gone.
She came for revenge. But that
wasn't what made her shoot.
"If it wasn't for Pattyn, I'd be dead."

> Her head twists side to side.
> *Stephen wouldn't have killed*
> *you, Jackie. He was your father.*

"You're wrong." I reach for her
hand, bring it to rest gently against
my cheek. And it comes to me
that my mother hasn't touched
me in years. "I love you, Mom."

> Tears fill her eyes, reflecting
> a trace of something left alive.
> *I love you, too, Jackie girly-girl.*

The last time she called me that,
I was maybe seven. Sadness knots
itself around me. Squeezes hard.
Mom backs out of the ambulance
wordlessly. Leaves me in Kent's care.

# The Doors Close

Behind her. The engine starts.
       No lights. No sirens. No fanfare.
I'm whisked away. At least

I can't see the neighbors.
       Gawking. Rumoring. Small-
town gossip is like sewage.

How far has it crept by now?
       Does Caleb know about Dad?
Does he realize he played

a very big role? Everyone
       in seminary will be privy
first thing in the morning.

How long will it take for all
       the people at school to find
out, make me an even bigger

pariah than I am now? Or . . .
       what if they feel sorry for me?
Is such a thing even possible?

# Not Speeding

It's a twenty-five-minute ride
to Renown. It used to be called
Washoe Med. I was born there,
and so was Samuel, and all of my
sisters except Pattyn. She came

      early, the story goes. Always
      did have a mind of her own, so
      Mom ended up having her in
      the bathtub. *No different from*
      *any pioneer woman,* Mom says,

whenever she repeats the tale.
And just like all the early Mormon
settlers who found their way to
Nevada, one of Mom's LDS sisters
helped her through that birth.

Tonight, they're helping her sort
out the postscripts of death. I'm glad
she has someone to do that. If it
were up to me, I'd tell them exactly
what to do with Dad's body—burn it.

# At the Hospital

They wheel me into emergency,
leave me lying there while they look
over the consent form Mom signed.
I'm still holding Pattyn's locket.

Here in the light I can study its
intricate etchings, and carved on
the back are the words that changed
her life forever, for better and so

much worse. *I love you.* Poor Patty.
I work at the catch tentatively.
Pain permeates even the smallest
movements. The oval opens and

inside is Ethan. He's smiling,
but his eyes hold a vague notion
of trouble. Almost like he knew.
And yet, he loved her anyway,

lifted her up on a pedestal so high
what was left but for her to come
tumbling back down again? Was
it worth it? I have to believe it was.

# After What Seems

Like a very long time, a doctor
    comes over. His hair is gray
        and he has a scraggly beard.

    Nothing like the docs on TV.
        *How are you feeling? Any pain?*
            Well, duh. Just look at me, Doc.

I nod. "I'm sore everywhere,
    but hurt the worst on my left
        side. Something feels broken."

He pulls up my blood-soaked
    blouse. Pokes around at my ribs,
        and just underneath them. "Ow!"

    He nods. *Broken ribs. Maybe more.*
        *We'll do a CT scan. And Detective*
            *Crow asked us to do a vaginal exam.*

"What? No! Dad never would . . .
    He never touched me like that."
        He didn't. But someone else did.

*Pattyn*
# Someone Touches Me

In a most remarkable way,
and though I understand
I'm mired in a quicksand of

          dreams,

I am comforted to know
all that separates us is a thin
veil of consciousness. His lips

          are

still warm from the far side
of the grave. And even in sleep
I wonder what I'm waiting

          for,

why I'm here if he is just
there. Why do I insist on
remaining among

          the living

when life means struggle
and death is only a door
to easy street?

# A Sudden Bump

Jerks me from sleep, pulls me out
of Ethan's arms. Ethan? Don't go.

But as the bus squeals to a stop,
he's gone. I reach for the locket

I wear close to my heart, where
Ethan still lives. But it's gone, too.

No! Please, no. Where could it be?
It must have happened . . . Now it

all comes crashing back into me.
I'm on the bus. Where are we?

A sign outside the window tells me:
Sacramento. Up in front, the driver

> confirms, *Sacramento. Fifteen*
> *minutes to stretch your legs.*

People get to their feet. Fully half
the bus empties. I stay put. Nothing

out there but trouble. It is late, close
to midnight, so I'm a little surprised

when I hear people boarding again.
Better use the bathroom. I start toward

the far corner of the bus and the girl
across the aisle warns, *It's nasty.*

I shrug. "Got to pee." But when
I open the door, I scoot back like

there's a snake inside. No reptiles.
Only crap, kind of sprayed all over

the toilet seat. I spin around and
the girl laughs. *Tol' you. Disgusting.*

The driver has started the bus,
closed the doors. "Wait!" I head

up the aisle, clutching my bag.
"I have to use the bathroom."

He looks at me like I'm crazy.
*Fifteen minutes are up. I've got*

*a schedule, you know. We stop in*
*Vacaville. Twenty-five minutes. Hold it.*

# What Can I Do?

Make a scene? I think about
sitting up front, closer to
the door, and so a quicker
dash to the bathroom when
we get there. But Stinky

  Homeless Guy is still up
  here. And so is the thief. I go
  back to my original seat,
  hoping twenty-five minutes
  goes by quicker than I think

    it will. Not only do I have to
    pee, I need a fresh sanitary pad.
    The doctor said no tampons
    until I resume my normal cycles.
    I have no idea when that will be.

    I haven't stopped bleeding since
    I lost the baby, and that was two
    weeks ago. I'm still cramping, too.
    That's getting better, but I wish
    I had some Tylenol. Then again,

      I wish a whole lot of things.

# I Manage to Hold It

All the way to the next stop.
*Vacaville*, announces the driver.
It's a small station, but a much
anticipated one. I hurry up the aisle.

Passing by the thief, I'm glad
I remembered to grab my backpack.
I find the restroom, take the nylon
mesh money pouch from my bag.

Much of it is coin, thank God. The sanitary
supplies dispenser wants quarters. I've got
a dozen rolls, so I buy a couple extra.
Who knows when I'll get to a store.

I'm still in the stall, adjusting a clean
pad, when the bathroom door opens.
Someone goes into the cubicle
nearest the door, which opens again

a few seconds later, followed by
the sound of a fist—or foot—hitting
metal. *What the fu . . . ?* It's the Latina
girl. *Get the fuck out of here!*

*Oh, I don't think so.* It's a man.
*You want to scream rape? Try*
*it, with this in your mouth.* There
is the sound of a struggle, and now

I hear a choking sound. Bad.
Really bad. What do I do? I get
up, pull up, zip up. Open the stall
door quietly, move in behind . . .

The thief! His pants are down,
and his body is leaning into the girl,
and I have to do something. I've still
got the money pouch in one hand.

All those quarters are heavy.
I swing the thing hard as I can
at the back of the thief's head. My
aim is good. It hits with a *crack.*

*What the . . . ?* The guy pivots, one
hand going up to the back of his
skull. *You! I'll kick your fucking ass.*
I back away as he starts toward me.

45

# Except He Has Forgotten

His pants, now twisted around
his ankles. Down he goes, in a belly
flop onto the dirty linoleum. The girl

       is on her feet. She looks down at
       the guy's exposed butt cheeks. *¡Cabrón!*
       She gives the guy a vicious kick,

              straight south of the pimply white rounds.
              Her aim is good, too. The guy's face
              blooms, red with pain. *Oh,* is all he can say.

I realize suddenly that I need to
get out of here before some random
security person decides to investigate

the noise. I head for the door,
walking quickly. The girl is right
behind me. When we reach the waiting

room, I turn to look at her. Her throat
is swelling up around purpling finger
marks. "You should call the cops."

She shakes her head. *Nah. I'm okay.*
*Besides, they'd probably say I asked*
*for it. Oh, hey. There goes your bus.*

I look out the window in time to
see a big belch of exhaust smoke.
"Perfect. Now what'll I do?"

*First thing we should do is get out*
*of here before that son-a-bitch gets*
*to feeling better. Come on. There*

*be another bus tomorrow.* She starts
for the main entrance, where a man
in a black uniform stands munching

a burger. When I hesitate, she says,
*Don' worry. He's just a night security*
*dude. Useless.* I follow her right past

him and we exit into the fog-muted night.
She keeps on walking. I don't know
what else to do but keep walking, too.

# No Sign of the Thief

Behind us, we push forward
      along a mostly deserted boulevard.

Finally, I get up the nerve to ask,
      "Where are we going?" She seems

      to have a destination in mind,
            and she does. *Home. I live close.*

I don't understand. I don't know
      her at all. And she doesn't look

like the type to help out a stranger.
      "You're taking me to your house?"

      She shrugs, keeps on walking.
            *You got someplace better to go?*

"No. I . . . uh . . ." I could be
      a murderer. "It's just . . . why?"

      *You help me, I help you. That's*
            *all.* I expect her to head toward

the lights. But every step pulls us
        away from town. Finally, she turns

down a rutted gravel road flanked
        by big open fields. Fog curls up off

them, like tongues licking the night.
        It's warmer here at low elevation, but

I'm chilled, not just to the bone,
        but all the way through to marrow.

And it has nothing to do with
        the weather. The mist-paled moon

illuminates our way toward
        a thin amber glow in the distance.

        *You're on the run.* A statement.
                It's obvious, then. I should deny,

yet I respond with a blunt, "Yes."
        I wait for the obvious question.

# It Doesn't Come

Finally, I can't stand it. "Don't you
want to know why?" I would. I think.

> *Makes no difference to me.*
> *People run for many reasons.*

True enough. But only a few,
I'd guess, for the exact reason I am.

As we close in on a small cluster
of lights, the girl slows a little.

> *What's your name?* she asks.
> Then she adds, *I'm Adriana.*

I hesitate. Am I an official fugitive
yet? Is my picture on every newscast?

> *It's all right. You can make one up,*
> *but mis padres—my parents—will ask.*

"Patty." The name slaps. Only Jackie
ever calls me that. Jackie. God.

# What Am I Doing Here?

I should be there. Making sure
Jackie is okay. How will I know?
And how do I dare stay here?

How can I put any sliver of trust
in this stranger? In her family?
"Are you sure this is okay?" I ask,

half hoping she'll reconsider,
send me back out into the obscurity
of late autumn darkness. But she shrugs.

> *People come, people go. Sometimes*
> *there is no room, but many of us have*
> *followed the crops south for winter.*

> *Mi mamá, she works cleaning house,*
> *and mi papá prunes the almond trees*
> *in the cold months. So we stay here.*

We reach the source of the lights—
a half-dozen elderly mobile homes,
situated haphazardly around a sort

of courtyard made from cement pavers.
Three seem deserted. Two look asleep.
Adriana opens the door of the last.

> And though it is the earliest hours
> of morning, someone is awake and
> waiting up for her. *Hola, mamá.*

> She gestures for me to follow her
> inside. *This is Patty. She needs
> a place to stay tonight. Bien?*

Her mother is pretty, but weathered,
too many years spent baking like fruit
in the California sun. She turns

> suspicious eyes in my direction. Adriana
> is quick to explain, *She missed her bus
> because of me.* She moves into Spanish.

I assume she's relaying pertinent details
because the woman's eyes lose a measure
of wariness, gain a hint of gratitude.

# Whatever Adriana Said

I am given permission to stay for the night.
I even have a bed—her brother, Angel,

is currently elsewhere. The mattress
is narrow and hard, and the blankets thin,

but three are warm enough to fight the cool
air inside the austere room. It is tiny, barely

bigger than a closet. An afterthought.
Perhaps one part of a larger room, divided.

The only furniture besides the bed is a small
nightstand with a couple of drawers, apparently

all he needs for his clothing. There are no
pictures or books or mementos. Nothing

to make the room his except for the ghost
of some soapy scent. It is strongest

on his pillow and when I lay my head against
it, I inhale memories of Ethan. Will they bring

us close in my dreams? Can they carry me
to wherever my forever love has gone?

## Journal Entry, October 28

*Are you there, Ethan? Somewhere?*
*Anywhere? I'm crazy scared, and*
*I need you with me more than ever.*
*Can you feel the race of my heart?*
*Emptied of love, still it reverberates,*
*echoing in the pulse at my throat.*

*Can you hear me when I call out*
*to you? Will you sleep with me*
*tonight, and will we share this*
*unfamiliar bed with our baby?*
*Are you cradling him even now?*

*My eyes catch sight of the ring*
*you put on my left hand. A trio of*
*small diamonds struggles to glimmer*
*in the low lamplight. One for me.*
*One for you. One for the two of us.*

*That, you said, was the promise*
*of this promise ring. What do I call*
*it now? How do I wear it now, when*
*every time it catches my eye, all I can*
*think of is you, and who you allowed*
*me to become for such a short time?*

*And now, who am I? A criminal.*
*A fugitive. A murderer. Words that*
*should not—cannot!—apply to me.*
*How is it possible that they do?*

*I'm here, somewhere near Vacaville,*
*in the Promised Heartland of*
*California, where they grow nuts*
*and grapes and cotton in the summer.*

*I'm here, in a foreign house, with*
*strangers, people who tend those*
*crops for other people I don't know.*
*I don't deserve their kindness, and*
*why would they choose to take me*
*in? Such compassion is a rare gift.*

*I want to disappear into soft folds*
*of sleep. I wouldn't care, really,*
*if I never woke up again. Outside,*
*the wind has risen, whining across*
*naked fields. The sound is death,*
*humming its autumn dirge.*

*Stalking me. Waiting impatiently.*

*Jackie*
# Autumn Leaves

Trails behind a brittle wake,
auburn, plum, and gold.
It is the saddest of

seasons,

all of spring's green
promise pleated into
summer's flowered skirts
and spread beneath the sun to

wither.

Harvest gathered,
processed, ladled
into jars and stored
on cellar shelves,

dreams

of yesterday preserved
behind glass, to be recalled
in chill days of winter
as memories of growing things

fade away.

# Hospitals Stink

Of alcohol and antiseptics and the weird
sweet smell of oxygen through the tubes
in my nose. And beneath all that are
definite traces of sickness and death.

How could anyone ever be a nurse?
The nurses here have sympathetic
voices and warm, gentle hands
that touch me with the certainty

that every inch of me would scream
pain except for the drugs they've
pumped into me. My body is almost
as numb as the inside of me. I hear

Mom's voice in the hall. Hear
a stranger's voice explaining,
*It's protocol, Mrs. Von Stratten,*
*and we really must insist, if only*

*to eliminate rape as a possibility.*
*Or a motive. If your daughter*
*was protecting her sister, well . . .*
Well, what? Would they let her off?

Mom quits arguing and that makes
me uncomfortable. A nurse breezes
into the room, no smile, all business.
"Wh-where's Mom? Can I see her?"

> *In just a few minutes.* She tears open
> a plastic bag, removes a long Q-tip—
> looking thing. *I'm going to take a swab,*
> *okay? I promise I won't hurt you.*

"But why? I already told the deputy
Dad never, ever touched me like
that. Please . . ." Caleb didn't use a condom.
What, exactly, will it show, other than

> I'm not a virgin anymore? *Look,*
> *honey, we need to be certain. I know*
> *it's embarrassing, but vaginal exams*
> *are part and parcel of being a woman.*

She calls me honey, but offers no
real sympathy. Is that part of being
a woman, too? I grit my teeth,
open my legs. But I refuse to cry.

# My First Vaginal Exam

Doesn't take long. The nurse gives
no comment. I have no clue what

she thinks, or what the swabs will
or won't prove, other than Dad never

visited there. His cruelty did not
take the form of incest, although

his deviant satisfaction in inflicting pain
might well have been substitute sexual

pleasure, or maybe even an aphrodisiac.
How many nights did we hide our heads

under our pillows, trying to dampen
the sound of his beating Mom into

submission, followed by the rhythmic
creaking of their bed, Mom's whimpers

of pain turning to moans of whatever?
Never again, Dad. Never again.

# Finally, Mom

Comes into the room, followed
by the doctor who first examined
me. "Can I go home now?" I try

> to sit up, but everything starts to spin.
> Doctor I-Can't-Remember-His-Name
> shakes his head. *The lung puncture*
>
> *isn't deep, but we want to preclude*
> *any chance of collapse. And your*
> *spleen is ruptured. It probably*
>
> *won't require surgery, but we need*
> *to keep an eye on you for a couple*
> *of days.* He smiles. *You don't mind*
>
> *missing a few days of school, do you?*
> *Sorry, but trick-or-treating is definitely*
> *out this year.* He, of course, has no idea

that the Von Strattens don't observe
Halloween. No costumes. No candy.
No carved-up pumpkins. Nothing.

# The Doc Pats My Leg

Leaves me alone with Mom.
She waddles closer, taut-postured
and blank-eyed. "Are you okay?"
I ask again, as if she's the injured one.

    Most people would think she is,
    I guess. Ask me, though, I'd tell you
    she's lucky. *Good as can be expected.*

Why do I want to apologize?
Does it matter at all that I'm here,
swollen and broken and wheezing

    back pain every time I try to breathe?
    *They took him away. To the morgue.*
    *It's a homicide, so they'll do an autopsy.*

Stupid. I can tell them how he died.
It was a bullet, dudes, straight through
the chest. He bled out. But his lack
of heart killed him. *Thump-thump. Shh.*

# Mom Slumps into a Chair

Sits staring at me for a few until
whatever she sees makes her look

away. Is it death, a concrete reflection
in my eyes? She starts to say something.

> Stops. Finally, she asks, *What now?*
> *I don't know what to do. How will*

> *we survive? How can I live alone?*
> Alone? The word initiates an electric

jolt of anger. It crackles in my head.
"I hate to break this to you, but there are

still seven of us there with you." Seven kids
stacked like nesting eggs and wedged into

that dilapidated manufactured three-bedroom
home. The only one of us she worries about,

maybe the only one she really notices,
is baby Samuel. Her first—and probably

only—son. The boy Dad wanted more
than anything, now fatherless. Amen.

# Poor Samuel

I know that's what people
at church will say.

and,

A few might feel sorry for
the rest of us. But it's the baby
they'll think about first.

Just like Mom did. Does.
Not,

And most definitely
not,

No, that will never happen.
Instead,

*Poor Samuel.*

*Poor Janice.*

*Dear, little Samuel.*

*Poor, dear Jackie.*

*Poor, confused Pattyn.*

*First pregnant, now
this. Can you believe
it could happen here,
among LDS faithful?*

# The Crackle Gets Louder

"Didn't Dad have life insurance,
Mom? And you'll get his retirement,
won't you?" He worked for the state
of Nevada ever since he left the army

in the late seventies. He could have
retired already, but too much time
at home with all us kids was beyond
his consideration. He probably would

have worked until the day he died.
Oh, wait. He did. A trickle of glee
threatens the somberness of this
occasion. "You'll be okay, Mom.

We'll be okay." In fact, we'll be
a whole lot better off without him.
I don't say that last part out loud.
Good thing, too, because she says,

> *You don't understand, do you?*
> *Your father was not a kind man,*
> *I know that. But he was my husband.*
> *And, believe it or not, I loved him.*

64

# She Plants Her Head

In the cushioned earth of her hands,
allows herself a small breakdown.
Too tired to argue, I watch her cry.

Finally, my patience disintegrates.
"Unkind, Mother? He was cruel.
No, that's not right. He was vicious.

I don't understand how anyone could
love someone like that, or how a woman
could stay married to a man who takes

such pleasure in inflicting pain. What
if things had gone differently? Would
you still love him if he'd killed me?"

*B-bu-but, he could never have . . .*

"You don't know, do you? You really
don't get it. He could have. He wanted
to. I looked into his eyes, Mom. Know

what I saw? Lust. There was lust there.
Not sex lust. Bloodlust. When my ribs
cracked, he heard it. And he smiled."

# I Want to Fall Apart

Want to scream.

He was a monster
who needed to die.

If it wasn't for Pattyn,
it would be me, bloated
and white, on that cold
morgue slab right now.

I know you're hurting,
but not nearly as much
as I am, with two broken
ribs and a punctured lung,
bruises, abrasions, loosened
teeth. Plus wounds you
can't see, not even with
X rays or probes or scans.

Yes, you're scared, but
so am I, and what about
Patty, banished to some
nameless place—wherever
you go when you don't
dare show your face.

Look at me, Mom!

Look at me, Mom!

Look at me, Mom!

Look at me, Mom!

Look for us, Mom!

## But What Good

Would screaming do? Mom would
be the only one who didn't hear.
And even if she actually bothered

to look, she wouldn't see me any
more than she looked at me and saw
what Dad had done when she first came

running after the *BLAM* of the gun.
God, it was impressive, bouncing off
the shed's metal walls. Jars—dozens of them,

foodstuffs stored against End Times—
rattled and the cabinets shook, and for
about ten seconds it seemed the Apocalypse

might, in fact, have begun. Dad went
down and Pattyn cried, *No*, but that
couldn't stop the tide from crashing

against the rocks. By the time Mom
got there, took in the carnage, and dropped
to her knees beside Dad, he was gone.

A wave of nausea sweeps through
me. I choke it back, look to Mom,
hoping for some reaction to what

I just said. She just sits there, shaking
her head. Disbelieving. As if I would
lie about something like that. "Go home,

Mom. Take care of the kids." Like
she can. Like she has any idea how to
manage that without Pattyn or me

helping out. How will they all get
ready for school? Oh. She'll probably
keep them home for a day or two.

That's what a murdered man's wife
should do. Keep them home. But
she can't. They'll drive her crazy, and

she's already soft around the edges.
My thoughts blur. "Are the girls all
right? Have you told them yet?"

> *It's after midnight, Jackie. The girls*
> *are asleep. I'll tell them in the morning.*

# She Stands to Leave

And I'm so tired.
                              And I'm so confused.
          But I've got to know,
                    "What are you going to say?"
My eyelids are heavy and
                              my brain is scrambled
          from drugs and trauma
                    and the need to escape.

But from somewhere distant
                              like a cave or a bunker
          I think I hear Mom answer,
          *I'll tell them God called their father*
                    *home. That he's traveling now to*
*the Celestial Kingdom, and we'll see*
                    *him again when our time comes.*

My breathing falls shallow
                    against the stiff pillow. I'm pulled
          inch by inch toward sleep and
                    as I let go, I see Dad, a slow spin
of energy away from God, not toward.

          A soundless, formless scream
     somewhere in the outer darkness.

# All I Want

Is the blessed nothingness
    of dreamless sleep. I never
        get what I want. Several times
           during the night some nurse
               or an approximation thereof—
                  she appears like a wraith and
                     the cool of her hands is cadaver-
                        like—comes in, wakes me to ask
                     how I'm sleeping, then denies me
                        sleep by checking my blood pressure.

I free-fall back toward slumber,
    touch down in a world defined
        by barely subconscious visions.
            I feel like I'm half in, half out
               of the real world. Half hospital,
                  half hallucination. Caleb. He's
                     here, and he coaxes me into his
                     arms. Kisses my battered face.
                        It hurts, but when I struggle to pull
                        away, he denies any chance at escape.

*I'll never let you go,* he says, but
the voice doesn't belong to Caleb.
It's Dad, and I'm in *his* arms, and
the eyes looking down at me are
filled with anger, crazy anger, and
now it's Dad squeezing. Viselike.
Iron-muscled. Breath! I can't find
breath, and I can't scream. Air! No
air. *You didn't think I'd leave, did
you? You can't get away from me.*

My mouth is still fighting to scream
when my eyes jerk open, wrench me
into the soft, gray light of not quite
morning. Hours since my last pain
pill, every nerve ending screeches.
Fear clings to me like high meadow
muck, wet and heavy and smelling
of rot. But as the window blossoms
with sunlight, trepidation fades. I'm
here. Alive. And my father is dead.

# I Wrap Myself Up

In that thought like a blanket,
warm and comforting and safe.
But now Caleb is on my mind.
Dad said he ruined me. That no
one will ever want me again.
Maybe that's a good thing.

I can't change what happened.
Was it God's way of punishing
me for wanting to know what love
feels like—the physical side of
love? In seminary we're told sex
should be saved for procreation:

making babies, within the confines
of marriage. But in whispered
confessions, Pattyn convinced me
sex is rightly an outpouring of love,
with or without some cheap gold ring.
And that marriage scrubbed of love

is ownership. I find no trace of love
in the marriage I've witnessed firsthand. And my one taste of sex held
no hint of love. Only a glimpse of hell.

*Pattyn*

# People Have Got It Wrong

There's probably a scripture
somewhere that references

                hell

as some fiery place where bad
souls smolder forever. But for
that, the requirement

                is

death and after that, who cares?
No, you have to be

                alive

to take the rides at the devil's
amusement park. Bring a coat.
Turns out brimstone is,

                in

fact, more dry ice than briquette
and even the warmest

                hearts

cannot escape freeze-over.
When your existence is

                emptied

of hope, drained dry of belief,
you can stare to the far horizon
and find not a single remnant

                of love.

# I Creep from Sleep

Startle awake, awash
in a tide of unfamiliar.

Strange pillow,
perfumed in some
unrecognizable way.

Strange window,
leaking pallid light
through a swirl of mist.
This is not my home.

A bold rush of anxiety
yanks me out from beneath
the threadbare blanket,
just as memory slaps
my face. Sits me back
down on the narrow bed.

The shed.
Jackie.
Dad.
The bus.
The thief.
The girl.

# I'm Somewhere in California

No longer Pattyn Von Stratten.
I'm playing the part of Patty Carter.
"Patty" because the name is familiar.
"Carter" because it belongs to Ethan.

"What now, Ethan?" I whisper into
the gray. "Where do I go? Please.
Tell me what to do." I am answered
by a crush of silence. Nothing more.

First thing I need is the bathroom.
I tiptoe to the door, open it quietly.
No movement. No noise at all. I find
the proper room. Pee. Change my pad.

But what do I do with the used one?
Can't flush it. . . . An old memory strikes.
The hallway was soggy, soaked with a river
from the plugged toilet. Dad stood, fists

clenched, screaming for a confession.
It wasn't mine to give, but I shouldered
the blame to save my sister 'Lyssa from
the barrage, the pain of unbridled rage.

# I Took the Blame

But I refuse to revisit what happened
next. I swaddle the bloodied pad with
toilet paper, try to forget its meaning.
Wash up as best I can in cold tap water.
I don't dare change. My clothes aren't too
offensive yet, and who knows when I'll be
able to launder them. I vacate the bathroom,
locate the trash, push the Stayfree as far
as I can beneath what's already there.

Now what? Should I leave? I have no idea
how to find the bus station, but it can't be
that hard, right? But shouldn't I say goodbye—
and thank you—to Adriana and her family?
I go back to her brother's room. Sit quietly
on his bed, considering my life from here
forward. How do people dive into an unknown

future without hesitation, without forward
planning, without a hint of what's to come?
I should be petrified. Instead, I mostly feel dead
inside. What does it matter, really, where I end
up, even if that happens to be prison? Maybe
I should turn myself in. Accept the inevitable.

# A Soft Creak

Of the unsteady floor lures my attention.
It's Adriana at the door. "Good morning,"
I say, and it sounds ridiculous, like a doctor

> greeting you in such an ordinary way right
> before telling you he needs to operate.
> Adriana is gracious enough. *Buenos días.*

> She slinks closer, and when she notices
> the ring on my finger, gestures toward it.
> *Is that what you're running from?*

Involuntarily, my head begins to shake
and without thinking, I say, "He's dead."
There. Conceded. Ethan is dead.

> She stares at me and the black pools
> of her eyes light with sudden sympathy.
> *Lo siento. I'm sorry. You loved him.*

All the love I have ever known balls
up in my throat and I choke on it, but
manage to say, "He was everything."

# I Think She Might Touch Me

In the way people do when empathy
floods them suddenly. Instead, she sits

       on the floor, too far for physical contact,
       close enough for the emotional. *I lose someone,*

       *too. Not dead. Deported. Seven months ago.*
       *Luis will come back to me in summer. I think.*

Not sure why I tell her. Maybe because
I need to acknowledge, "My baby died, too."

Now I lie, but only a little. "I'm running
away from the man who killed them."

Her eyes grow wider. Darker. She starts to
say something. Changes her mind. Finally

       offers, *Are you hungry? I think you*
       *must be, no?* She gets up off the floor

and I follow her into the small kitchen.
She is reaching into the refrigerator when

the front door bursts open. *Adriana!*
*¿Dónde está tu mamá?* The woman, who

is maybe twenty, clutches an obviously
sick baby. The infant is flushed,

and a familiar rash covers her exposed
arms and legs. *Teresa tiene fiebre . . .*

A *fever,* says Adriana. She reaches
the baby, whose chest rattles loudly.

"Wait! Have you been vaccinated
for measles?" Adriana shakes her head.

"I wouldn't touch the baby, then.
I'm pretty sure that's what she has."

Adriana translates, and the two women
talk for a minute. *María—my cousin—says*

*Teresa got sick yesterday. In the night*
*she became very hot. And now, she coughs.*

"Measles are really contagious. I know.
My father didn't believe in immunization.

My sisters and I passed it around. Has anyone
here had measles? You can't get it again."

> *I don't think any of us had them. Not me,
> for sure.* The baby starts to cry, and that

makes her cough. "Teresa looks
very sick. She should see a doctor."

> Adriana says a few words to María, who
> shakes her head. *No. No puedo hacer.*

> *She says she can't do that,* explains Adriana.
> *It used to be okay. But not anymore.*

"You mean, because she's . . ." I don't have
to say "illegal." "Here. Let me take the baby."

María hesitates, but when Teresa wheezes
in a heavy breath, she reluctantly hands her over.

# The Baby Is on Fire

I know what to do. I've nursed my sisters
through measles, flu, even pneumonia.
"Do you have any baby Tylenol?"

They don't, which doesn't surprise me.
"Aspirin, then? Or ibuprofen? Anything.
We need to get this fever down. And do

you have baking soda? Measles itch like
crazy." Adriana searches the cupboards,
and I direct María to run a sink of lukewarm

water. As the basin fills, Adriana hands
me the baking soda. I dump a bunch into
the water, watch it dissolve, then gently

lower Teresa into the sink. She wails,
but that's okay. "María . . ." I put one
of her hands under the baby's head, tell

her to keep pouring water over her body.
It's English, but she understands. Adriana
has returned from the bathroom with a bottle

of Bayer. I find a knife, cut one aspirin
into quarters. "It won't taste good. Do you have
something sweet? Juice? Or maybe jelly?"

The commotion has roused Adriana's mother.
Her father, it seems, is already at work. "Tell
your mom to stay back from the baby unless

she's had the measles. You should stay away,
too. It's airborne—you can catch it from her
coughing. I'm afraid María is going to have it

soon, and it's harder for adults." I remember
the doctor telling Mom that. She caught a mild
case, but Dad never did. He bunked with a friend

from church until the bug finished making
the rest of us itch and our house was declared
measles-free. I crush a piece of aspirin, mix

it in a small spoonful of grape jam. Teresa
has quit crying. The baking soda must be
working. When I urge the spoon into her mouth,

she starts to complain, but when she tastes
the jam she thinks again. It can't be great,
but maybe she knows she needs it because

she swallows most of it. Purple drools from
the sides of her mouth and when I wash it away,
I notice the water is cooling. That's exactly

what we want. Her temp should cool right along
with it. Still, "She should have baby aspirin, and
baby cough syrup. Can somebody go to the store?"

> A detailed discussion in Spanish follows.
> Finally, Adriana explains, *My mama must go
> to work. Her . . . empleador—um, employer—*

> *wants her never to be late. I do not drive.
> So María must go. But she shouldn't
> take Teresa, so I will have to care for her.*

"I can do it. I mean, if you want me to."
Another conversation ensues, this time truncated.
The consensus: They're grateful for my offer.

# I Send a List with María

Keep it as short as I can. I'm pretty sure
money is an issue, though the baby has
plenty of diapers and decent clothes.
On my list:

> Baby acetaminophen or aspirin
> Baby cough syrup
> Calamine lotion
> Adult flu medicine
> Maxi pads

I count out too much of my meager
cash for that last one, but I need to stay
as clean as I can. I don't ask how María
can drive when it's obvious any license
must have been procured creatively.

Neither do I ask:

> Why she speaks no English
> Where the baby's father is
> How she came to live next door
> Why Teresa can't see a doctor

# By the Time María Is Ready to Go

The baby's fever has dropped. I wrap
her in a towel, sprinkle a little baking

soda on her lesions, dress her in a loose
nightie, sit with her on María's sofa.

No use spreading the measles germs
any wider than we already have.

I lay her on her side to ease her cough,
cover her with a teddy-embossed quilt.

She looks up at me with obsidian eyes,
tries hard not to close them. But when

I start to sing age-old lullabies, she drifts
off within a few minutes. Poor little girl.

I coax her silky black hair away from
her face. It's long, for a baby her age.

My sisters never had much hair until
they were toddlers. What are they doing

right now? Eating breakfast? Mourning?
I think about them, all named after

generals, Dad's immense conceit, of course.
Youngest to oldest: Georgia (after George

Patton, also my namesake, or Washington
if preferred); Roberta (Robert E. Lee); Davie

(for Jefferson Davis); Teddie (Roosevelt);
Ulyssa (S. Grant); Jackie (Pershing).

Six sisters, all raised to be good Mormon
girls—keepers of the family hearth until

some perfect LDS boys carry them over
distant thresholds to procreate more fine

Mormon children and start the cycle again.
So, what happened to Jackie? What happened

to me? The answer, always, was Dad. Now
that he's gone, the omnipresent threat

of annihilation vanished cold, can our psyches
be reconstructed? Are we even a little fixable?

# A Term Comes to Mind

Post-traumatic stress disorder. Usually
you hear it in reference to soldiers returning
home from war. Often the aggressors,
awaiting retribution, real or imagined.

Dad was our war, Jackie's and mine, and
we were innocent casualties. You *were*
innocent, right, Jackie? I can hear her scream,

>        *No, Dad! Please! Please stop!*

Can hear her crying. Denying.

>        *It wasn't my fault! He raped me!*

I don't know who raped her, or if that was
the truth. But why wouldn't Dad listen?
Why didn't he help her? No. He beat her.
I can still hear the heavy thud of his fist

>        against her flesh. Can still hear him rasp,
>        *. . . goddamn whore. What did you expect?*
>        *Cookies and milk? You're ruined now.*

# Ruined?

Because some horrible guy strong-armed
her, stole something that wasn't his? Even
if she did go out there to meet him, the Jackie
I know was only looking for someone who
would make her feel loved. Loved. Not abused.

Ruined. The same way Dad insisted Ethan
damaged me, like I was property ordained
to fall into disrepair. But Ethan's love
gave me value. He was like a magic wand,
turning a small pile of rubble into treasure.

Ruined. Like our family. Bruised. Broken.
Beaten down and all because of Dad's
shriveled heart. It was already empty.
So why couldn't he find room inside it
for me? Anger foams up suddenly.

And I'm back in the shed, yelling for Dad
to, "Stop! God help me, stop right now or . . ."
When he turned, saw the gun in my hand,
all he did was laugh and dare me to do it.
You dared me, Dad. And who's ruined now?

# Something Moves Beside Me

I jump from my stupor and the baby cries. Baby?
Teresa. Oh. I reach over, feel her skin,
starting to heat again. I'd like to take her
outside, let the morning air and damp cool her.

But if I remember correctly, sunlight
isn't good for measles. Hurts the eyes.
I peel back the blanket, pick her up.
"It's okay, little one. Mommy will be

home soon." Her crying escalates, so I walk
with her, pace the floor, recite nursery rhymes.
In English, not that it matters. The rhythms
should soothe her. But they don't, and it

strikes me that she's probably hungry.
I don't know what to do about that. I look
in the kitchen, but find nothing like formula
or bottles. María must breast-feed, and the way

Teresa has turned her face into my body,
tiny lips sucking at my shirt, confirms that.
I offer my little finger as a pacifier, like
I used to do for my sisters. Might have done

for my own . . . Now it's me who's crying.

# A Tidal Wave of Grief

Crashes into me, floods the emptied
harbor inside my heart. How can I
so miss what never really was?

Ethan's death is a tangible loss.
We touched. We talked. We planned
our future together. He was a concrete

piece of me. Our baby was no more
than a flicker of light. A possibility.
A spark of Ethan. A whisper of me.

How can thinking about him initiate
such brilliant bolts of anguish? Not fair
that we never looked each other in the eye!

Not fair that he never drew breath,
never nursed. Never cried or laughed
or crawled or caught the measles.

Dear God, yes, I questioned you.
I was scared of what having a baby
would mean. To me. To Ethan. To us.

But even if I deserved punishment,
my baby didn't. How could you,
God of mercy, be so unmerciful?

## Journal Entry, October 31

*Been here with the Medinas for four
days. María got the measles, and it
hit her pretty hard. I'm helping her
with the baby so she can try to sleep.*

*Teresa is a lot better. The itching
doesn't seem to bother her as much,
and we've managed to keep her fever
down. She doesn't cry very often now.
In fact, she's smiley and all about
the coos. With those huge dark eyes,
she's absolutely beautiful.*

*I had to convince María to let
me supplement her breast milk with
formula. Teresa wasn't getting
nearly enough. Measles, fevered
nipples, and a sucking baby make
a painful combination. Sad, though,
to interfere with such intense connection.*

*My Spanish is minimal and María
speaks almost no English. Yet we manage
to communicate. I know her husband,
Tomás, is somewhere to the north.*

*He was sad to leave her and Teresa,*
*but he must follow the work. She and*
*the baby are safer here with family—*
*Adriana "es su prima," is her cousin.*
*It's difficult to be without Tomás,*
*María says, but their love is strong.*
*It will bring him home again.*

*Home. What can it mean to people*
*so far from their native country,*
*and living in temporary, tenuous*
*circumstances?*

*Home. What does it mean to me?*
*Will I ever know home again?*

*Jackie*
# Aeries

Small against the mountain,
an afterthought of time, I climb
this sacred place built of

granite

spires and tremor-strewn boulders.
The mist has lifted, revealing
beneath the drowsing sun,

sky

the color of pale lilacs. A knife-
edged cry demands attention
as two eagles rebuild their aerie,
sheltered by a canopy of

feldspar.

How immense, this intricate weave
of brushwood and sharp-scented greens,
quilted with the raptors' own feathers—a

cushion

for fragile shells and April fledglings.
I watch the goldens' hushed rise,
harmony on wing, envy their

effortless

drift beyond the undulating valley
below. I am here because my home
is down there—an aerie, woven
of secrets and feathered with

lies.

# Home from the Hospital

Just in time for the funeral. The viewing
is in an hour. Wonder what there is to
see. Wonder if we can smell brimstone.

No amount of makeup is going to disguise
the purple and yellow abstract of my face,
but my mother is determined to try.

> *That's a little better,* she says, looking
> every bit the black widow, rotund belly
> distending her shiny new funeral garb.

"I don't know why you want to hide
what he did. Everyone should know."
I'm sick of pretending. Sick of the lies.

> *His whole family is here. What good*
> *would it do to taint his reputation?*
> She looks at me with such sincerity

in her eyes it makes me want to puke.
"Like his family has no idea, Mom."
Aunt Jeanette, who will be there,

definitely knows. Pattyn confided
everything in her. Also there will be
Grandpa Paul—Dad's dad, whose

belt-wielding child rearing is supposed
to explain Dad's own. But why should
violence beget violence? Does that

mean I'm genetically predisposed to
beating my children, too? If I'm allowed
to have them, that is, being ruined and all.

> *Please, Jackie. Help me make it through*
> *today. Get dressed now, okay? It's time*
> *to go.* She makes a less-than-graceful exit

and I slip into my own shiny black dress,
the first brand-new clothes I've ever owned.
All the Von Stratten girls got them, cheerfully

supplied by our LDS sisterhood, so together
we'll look like an entire nest of poisonous
spiders. I think I can hear God laughing.

# What *Isn't* Funny, Really?

The cops found Dad's Subaru in the airport
parking garage, where Patty dumped it.

They impounded it to look for nonexistent
clues, leaving Mom with only her beater

Taurus to haul all us kids around in. Um . . .
not gonna happen. To get the eight of us

into Carson City requires a small parade
of cars, one or two Von Stratten girls riding

with each volunteer LDS driver. Maybe
Mom will buy a minivan with Dad's life

insurance money—seats for nine, in case
she finds a new man. I snort at the image.

> Sister Crandall glances in the rearview
> mirror. *You find something amusing?*

If only she knew. "No. Uh . . ." Jeez, think!
"I was just remembering a joke Dad told me

once. Wanna hear it? Knock, knock . . ."
Even if I actually knew one, I wouldn't

be able to pull it out of my brain
right now, so I'm overjoyed when

she says, *I don't like jokes.* Huge
surprise. The woman is humorless.

Beside me on the backseat, 'Lyssa
gives an amused look with wide, azure

eyes. But, wisely, she remains silent.
It's a short drive around the lake,

which is half emptied by this year's
hot summer and water-short winter.

The cottonwood fringe cheers its gray
mud shoreline with flounces of autumn

orange and lifts my spirits a little.
Enough, I hope, to get me through

this day of pretense. Of excuses
and lies, and knowing everyone

there will be trying to pry secrets
out of me with too obvious stares.

# Mom Limited the Viewing

To family members only.
She might have invited close
friends, except Dad didn't have
any. A small wave of sadness
sweeps over me. None of us
has any close friends. We only

have each other. And since
we're all shattered, that isn't
much, especially without Pattyn.
She was our glue. We file into
the small room behind the main
hall. The casket is open so we

can pay our respects to the hull
inside. It's dressed all in white,
which makes its waxy skin appear
even paler. Mom shouldn't have
spent all that effort putting makeup
on what's left of Dad. He looks

like the mannequin he's become.
Most of the kids have spent the last
five days with church members.
This is the first time they've seen
me, and I don't know whose face
scares them more—Dad's or mine.

# I Don't Recognize Everyone

Aunt J is easy. I haven't seen her
since I was little, but Pattyn told
me so much about her, I know who
she is right away. She's holding hands

with a tall man who looks very
much like the boy whose picture
I'm wearing inside a gold locket,
keeping it safe for Pattyn. This will

be the second funeral Ethan's dad
has been to in less than a month.
Ethan was buried while Pattyn
was still in the hospital. She didn't

even get the chance to say goodbye.
Kevin and Aunt J took Ethan's body
back to Caliente and laid him to rest
in the shadow of the mountain he loved.

Dad, on the other hand, will lie
beneath six feet of alkaline sand
in an ugly cemetery here in Carson.
The thought gives me a trill of pleasure.

# Grandpa Paul Isn't Alone

The woman on his arm is decades younger.
I've never met his third wife. He lost the first
to cancer, the second to divorce. Gossip had it
Number Two couldn't stand the Stump.
Grandpa Paul lost a leg at the end of World
War II and never bothered with a fake one.
I guess his "middle leg" kept working fine.

Dad was one of five children from Grandpa's
first wife. The second stayed long enough
to give him two more offspring. From the way
things look, Number Three will gift him with
at least one more. Disgusting. He's well into
his eighties. Artificial insemination? Grandpa's
oldest living son, Uncle Duke from Elko,

is here today, along with his own brood.
Two of Dad's brothers predeceased him, also
succumbing to cancer. Eastern Nevada
is rife with it, the result of aboveground
nuclear testing in the 1950s. The dreaded
disease has definitely culled a few Von
Strattens from Nevada's census counts.

A bullet recently deleted another.

# Everyone Walks Past

The dearly departed. A few stop
and say something. One or two
actually touch him. At the moment,
a man bends down, looks at him curiously.

I don't know who the man is, but there
is something familiar about him. In fact,
he looks like Dad in a way, so he must
be a relative. He straightens, moves

forcefully toward the door, and I can't
help but notice the perfect fit of his
obviously expensive suit. It must have
been tailored—so not Von Stratten.

My turn to view Dad, but I refuse to
look. I limp quickly by, then fade
against the back wall, watch everyone
say their farewells. That's the right word.

According to LDS doctrine, Dad has simply
journeyed on to the spirit world.
To be happy, he'll have to repent.
But Dad never once said he was sorry.

# The Casket Is Closed

With great ceremony. Now it will
be wheeled to the chapel where

our church brethren, plus a few of Dad's
coworkers, are seated. The family trails

the coffin. Everyone stands as we pass.
And more than a few stare at me. I wish

I was strong enough to toss defiance
back at them. Especially one—Caleb

McCain. His father is a church elder,
one who will give a short eulogy,

but I can't believe Caleb has the guts
to stand there, smiling at me. "You

did this to me!" I want to shout. "You
did this to *him*." But I am a coward.

There's even proof. The swabs came
back positive for semen, negative

for Dad's blood type. Caleb's would
match. But all that proves is we had sex.

How can I press charges, especially
when my mom doesn't want me to?

When the doctor said, *The vaginal
bruising indicates rape,* Mom acted

horrified. But once he left the room,
she said, *I think we need to leave*

*law enforcement out of this. I've got
too much to handle now without*

*thinking about more police reports
and judges and juries. We can let*

*Bishop Crandall take care of it,
right?* Right. Obviously, he went

straight for the jugular, which
is why Caleb dared show his face

here today. Which is why his father
is up in front of the gathering, talking

about the Plan of Salvation instead
of one word, pro or con, about Dad.

# Eulogies

Music. Admonitions. Music.
Pleasant stories about Dad—
apparently, a man I never
knew. Music. Revelations
about the Plan of Salvation.
Only, there's nothing new.

Everyone here knows this stuff.
Everyone here repeats this crap.
Everyone here is just as brainwashed

as the next. Except, I'm very
sure, Aunt J and Kevin. Why
did they even come? They don't
belong here any more than Pattyn
does. I'm glad she's gone, but
I wish I knew where she is,

and if she's okay. Will we ever
hear from her again? Will they
catch her, lock her away? Why
did she have to be so noble?
What's the point of being a hero
when everyone thinks you're a villain?

## The Real Villain

Is going to be interred now.
There will be a gravesite service.
But I'm sick of all this garbage.

I catch Mom, who's almost to
the door. "I'm not feeling so well.
Can I wait here, or find a ride home?"

> *I suppose. You do look pale.*
> *Don't forget about the luncheon.*
> *We should be there in an hour.*

The luncheon. Right. Turkey. Ham.
Potato salad. A regular picnic, prepared
by the sisterhood and served up at

the Crandalls' fine house on the hill.
I'm anything but hungry, and don't plan
to attend, but I say, "Okay," watching

the church empty. The man in the suit
walks up to Mom, reaches out to her
and says something. She takes a step

backward, studies his face, finally
accepts his hand before turning away
almost abruptly. Who is he, and what

was that all about? He watches Mom
retreat, following the people who have
peeled off, some to the cemetery, some

to the luncheon. Others, straight back
to their regular lives. Most of the Von
Stratten clan will witness the lowering.

Who can I get a ride from? A week ago,
I would've asked Caleb, who stands
with his father talking to Bishop Crandall.

Of course, a week ago there was no
funeral. How can life change so much
in a matter of seconds? Every now

and then, Caleb glances my way.
The smirk that seems cemented
to his face tells me there will be no

punishment, at least none that matters.
Or maybe Mom didn't even bring
it up. Seven days ago, I thought

I was in love with Caleb McCain.
Now, the sight of him makes my skin
crawl. How can things change so fast?

# A Voice

Falls over my shoulder.
*Hello, Jackie. It's been*
*a long time. How are you*
*holding up?* It's a mellow rasp,

unfamiliar. I turn. "Aunt J."
My face must say something,
because she opens her arms
and I fall into them, sniveling

like an idiot, "It's horrible.
Awful. Everything's all wrong,
and I don't see how it will
ever be right again. I'm . . ."

Soaking her blue silk dress
with tears, not to mention
makeup, that's what I'm doing.
I pull back. "I'm so sorry."

*Don't fret. Never did like this*
*dress much.* She has the eyes
of a doe—big and brown and kind.
*Everyone run off and leave you?*

"I . . . I just got out of the hospital,
and I'm still a little shaky. Another
hour on my feet at the cemetery
didn't seem like a good idea."

> *I'm as sound as a show pony,*
> *and it didn't seem like a good idea.*
> *How about if Kevin and I give*
> *you a lift back to the valley?*

"Oh, yes. I'd like that. Thank
you." Aunt J slips a hand under
my elbow, just enough support
to let me walk by the McCain men,

battered head tipped high. Caleb
smiles, predatory, but it's anger
that courses through my veins,
not fear. I think of an old saying,

*Revenge is a dish best served*
*cold.* White-hot revenge brought
us here today. I'll plan on
the chilled variety for Caleb.

# Kevin Waits

For Aunt J in the parking lot,
      leaning against an old Ford
pickup. Old, but immaculate.

           Aunt J introduces us, and he
                tips his black Stetson. *Happy*
         *to make your acquaintance.*

      *We might be a little tight, but*
            *it's not a long way,* observes
      Aunt J. *You can take shotgun.*

Kevin is a careful driver.
      Meaning he goes just under
the limit, maybe because this

spotless classic truck doesn't
      have seat belts. We are half-
way home when Aunt J tells me,

      *Pattyn learned to drive in*
           *this truck.* She hesitates, then
      *What happened that night?*

      *I know she was in a world*
           *of hurt—we all were. Are.*
      *But I can't believe she'd do it.*

I repeat the story, swearing
          one more time that Pattyn
was only protecting me.

          Aunt J tsks. *That's not what
                    some people are saying. They're
          calling it premeditated murder.*

"No! You know her better than
          that. I mean, the accident made
her a little crazy. But it didn't

change who she is inside. Part
          of her hated Dad. But in spite
of every horrible thing he did to

her, to me, to all of us, a big
          part of her loved him anyway.
You could see it in her eyes.

I don't understand it, but it's true.
          The last thing she wanted to do
was kill him. If not for me . . ."

I crash into the wall again, choke
          on my voice, and tears storm, this
time wetting my new black dress.

110

*Pattyn*
# A Storm Brews

To the west, somewhere over
the Pacific. I can't see it yet,
but I smell its approach, heavy
as dirt, on the thickening

         wind.

The scent of nearing rain
is different here, on the far
side of the mountain. No playa
forests where this zephyr

         blows,

only city and highway and
fallow field, the skeleton
trees of almond and peach,
branches in place of

         bones.

Clouds roll toward me,
eventually over me and on,
crowning the peaks above
my Nevada home. They

         rattle

memories, awaken desire
left sleeping there. Here,
among strangers,
I am alone.

# Nine Days

On the run, and all I've done
is sit. Well, except when I pace,

walking Teresa, who is ever
so much better, but can't understand

why her mama is too sick to hold
her. The measles nailed María

to her bed but she refuses to chance
an ER visit. It's her only choice,

Adriana says, since the clinics closed
their doors to illegals. By federal law,

emergency rooms must provide
for everyone. But María insists no little

fever (like, 103 at its peak) or itchy
sores are worth the risk of some crazy

Anglo trying to separate her from
her baby or husband, who'd have no

way to find her if she's locked up
or deported. And the idea of spending

even a single night in a metal cage,
like some hairless monkey, is too much

to consider. Funny. Half of me feels
the same way. The other half wonders

how bad it could be. Nine days. They
must be looking for me, but I haven't

heard a single thing out here, where TV
is accomplished with a small roof

antenna and no one turns it on
until prime time. Who wants to watch

the news? I've got split emotions
there, too. Half of me can't stand

the thought of knowing. The other
half really, really needs confirmation.

Nine days. Dad must be preserved in
the ground by now, buried in Mormon

white. Does anyone know the details
yet? Does anyone suspect why?

# If I Believed in Fate

I'd say it sent me here. I needed
somewhere safe to stay, and turns
out María and Teresa needed
me. This is a temporary situation,
though. I'm still trying to figure out
what comes next. Where will I go?

What will I do? It's November,
getting colder every day. Living
on the street wouldn't be easy.
It's hard enough here, with a roof
but scant heat. María can't afford
to keep the place very warm.

She's living off a small savings,
earned working side by side
with Tomás in the orchard before
Teresa was born. The owner
is more generous than some, and
her rent is not too high. But propane

is dear, so she keeps the thermostat
at fifty and makes do with Salvation
Army sweats and blankets. And I
thought my family lived humbly.
Still, María lives in hope of the future,
a more precious gift than she knows.

# Too Many Hours

Cooped up inside makes me
a little stir-crazy. Teresa
is napping, so despite the snap
in the air, I step outside to stretch

my legs for a few. It's early
afternoon, but the light is pale
with the approaching storm.
At least the wind has died down.

As I circle the trailer, I notice
Adriana walking up the road
toward home. I go to meet her.
"Do you walk everywhere?"

> She smiles. *Not everywhere.*
> *Only to the bus stop. Once*
> *I get there, I ride. There is*
> *good bus service in the city.*

"Where do you go? I see
you leave in the morning."
She gives me a funny look.
Have I overstepped? "I'm sorry.

115

I don't mean to sound nosy.
I'm just curious and . . . well,
I've only spoken baby and sign
language for the last few days."

> Now she laughs. *You must*
> *learn more Spanish. Por la*
> *mañana voy a la escuela.*
> *In the morning, I go to school.*

"School? I mean, escuela?
How do you say 'what kind
of school' in Spanish?" Thunder
rumbles in the near distance.

> *You say, "¿Qué tipo de escuela?"*
> *I answer, "Colegio comunidad."*
> *Community college. I'm studying*
> *fire technology. El fuego tecnología.*

"Fire technology? You want
to fight fires?" A black memory
swoops over me. Summer inferno.
Thick, acrid smoke across the playa.

# We Arrive

At the trailer. I listen at the door,
hear no telltale noises behind it.

Then I turn, expecting Adriana
to have gone on inside, but she's

> still standing there, watching me.
> *You take very good care of the baby.*

"I'm used to it. I've helped raised
lots of them. My mom . . ." I shake

> my head. She nods hers. *Too many
> women make too many children.*

> *Maybe one day for me. But first
> I want to do things. To accomplish.*

"Firefighting is dangerous.
You must be a brave person."

I wish I was. At the moment,
I feel like a mouse in the wall.

> But Adriana observes, *I think
> you must be brave, too. Valiente.*

117

I think back to that night on the bus,
the way she reached into her pocket

for a knife when she felt threatened.
"We have things in common."

It slips out and, as unlikely as it
seems, it's true. "One or two."

> *Una o dos. Excepto, usted usó*
> *una pistola.* She doesn't have

to translate. Despite the cold, I leak
a veil of sweat. "How do you know?"

> She shrugs. *I hear news at school,*
> *so I use the computer. The picture*

> *they show es vieja. Old. Your hair*
> *is lighter now, your skin more brown.*

Summer tanned and sun-bleached.
"I, uh . . ." I don't know what to say.

# Or What to Ask

One question does come to mind.
     "How long have you known?"
     I study her face, which hasn't so

much as twitched. Stoic. I think
     that's the word I'm searching for.
     Again, she shrugs. *A few days.*

"But you haven't said anything?
     Why not?" Surely she's wanted
     to. Surely she told someone?

She doesn't answer right away.
     First, she sits on the small landing.
     *I don't know what you did or why.*

*It's not my business. I know you take*
     *good care of Teresa. You gentle.*
     *Kind. I know your man is dead.*

*That is no lie. Some things you*
     *don't lie about. I think some other*
     *things. But what I think don' matter.*

# Actually, It Does

It matters a lot. "What do you
think? I'd like to know." Or,
quite possibly, I need to know.

> She considers for a minute,
> then says, *I think whatever
> happened, there were reasons.*
>
> *I think you are no danger and
> that culpa—guilt—is more
> punishment for you than jail.*
>
> *I see no anger in you, only
> sadness. I also see no fear in you
> and I think you aren't afraid*
>
> *because you have not much
> to lose. What was important
> is gone. These things I understand.*

It's the most she's said to me
since I've been here, and her words
touch me in a necessary way.

She understands, at least as much
as she needs to. "But what about
your parents and María? Do they know?"

> *There is no reason for them to.*
> *It is best if they don't so they*
> *have nothing more to hide.*

Everything she said steamrolls
into me, and she's right. Guilt
is the most painful punishment

of all, and it's forever, and now
it's heavier still because I have no
right to ask these people for a place

to hide. "I can't stay here long.
But I have nowhere to go. I thought
of San Francisco, to see the ocean.

But I never considered beyond that."
I can't go back. That would ruin
everything. But what lies forward?

# From Behind the Thin Metal

Of the trailer comes the sound
of María's deep, wrenching cough,
followed by Teresa's wail.
"Sounds like naptime is over."
As I reach for the door handle,

> she says, *There is no hurry*
> *for you to go, and when it's time,*
> *we will find a place. I will pray*
> *to María Santísima. The Blessed*
> *Mother will know what to do.*

I want to hug her, but I have
a feeling she's not the hugging
type. So I settle for, "Gracias.
Thank you, Adriana. I . . . Never
mind." I turn and go inside,

thinking about the Catholic
reverence for Jesus's mother.
Nothing like that in an LDS
temple. No Madonna statues.
No Virgin Mary worship. The idea

that a woman—even one chosen
by God as his vessel—might
have such power would never
be entertained. A woman's worth
is contained within her uterus.

Currently, mine is scrubbed free
of value. I reach for Teresa,
who immediately stops crying
and peers up at me with liquid
black eyes. "Such a beautiful

girl," I croon. Will she learn
a little English from me before
I leave? "You were born here,"
I tell her on our way to the kitchen
for a bottle. "You are American,

do you know that?" While I mix
the formula, I hum patriotism—
"America the Beautiful." "The Star-
Spangled Banner." "O'er the land
of the free and the home of the brave."

# I Might Be Unshackled

But freedom is beyond
my reach. And, while
fear isn't strangling me,
neither am I truly brave.

>>>Of course, how many
people live unafraid? To
truly embrace courage,
I think, requires one of two

>>>>>things—unshakable faith
that death is no more than
a portal to some Shangri-la
reunion. Or zero belief at all.

>>>I wish I still believed
in God, in the chance
to reunite with Ethan
and our baby one day.

But if there is a hereafter,
one my father has been
welcomed into, it must
be a godless wasteland.

# Bottle Emptied

Teresa gets all squirmy, signaling
the need for a diaper change. I locate

the Huggies, lay her on the couch,
little behind wriggling on a receiving

blanket, commence the procedure,
which isn't really all that bad. As I slip

miniature sweats back up over her chubby
legs, I glance out the window, where

an old white pickup precedes a dust dragon
along the dirt drive. It's the first strange

vehicle I've seen since I've been here,
but it doesn't look like law enforcement,

and I'm more curious than nervous
about who's inside it. The truck rolls

to a gentle stop and once the dust passes,
two young Latinos step down from the cab.

María's heard the activity. She comes
out of her bedroom, flushed and shaky,

peers out the window. *Angel,*
she says, and then, *y Tomás!*

Such joy! Adriana has come outside,
and I see her say something. One

of the men turns, concern evident in
his expression. Tomás starts toward us,

and María tilts her head, asking a silent
question. She looks awful, but I don't think

she's contagious at this point. I smile.
"It's okay." Like it would matter anyway.

Teresa squirms, wanting her mother.
I hand her over just as Tomás pushes

through the door. He stops, assesses
María's face, still covered with reddish

brown blotches. Then he laughs and
sweeps her into his arms, kissing back

and forth between her and Teresa.
I blush at the happy reunion, crimson

but green within. There will never
be such delirious reconnection for me.

A complete fifth wheel, I nod a hello
toward Tomás, step outside into the muted

light. Across the narrow yard, Angel
regards me cautiously and I return

the favor. He is tall, and resembles
Adriana—good-looking, with caramel

skin and angular features suggesting
Spanish ancestry. And his scowl—so

much like hers. Well, this is awkward.
They've obviously been talking about

me. Should I go over and say hello?
I guess it's either that or stand here

and look as ridiculous as I feel. I just
wish I knew what she's told him.

# Journal Entry, November 6

Tomorrow I leave Vacaville, and
the relative security I've found with
Adriana's family. Angel has been
working the walnut orchards north
of here, and the grower's wife is
looking for a live-in housekeeper/
cook. Not many people are anxious
to move to Butte County. It's isolated.
Insulated. Pretty much perfect for me.

I spent a little of my money stash
on some black hair dye and instant
tanner, for when the sun's handiwork
begins to fade. I don't exactly look
Mexican, but neither do I look much
like the girl who's wanted as a "person
of interest" in a Carson City murder.
No one but Adriana knows I'm that girl.

The story we told her family is simple.
My boyfriend abused me, so I ran. But
I have nowhere safe to go, and a need
to hide. I'm not sure anyone believes it,
but these people are immune to pointless
curiosity. They ask no useless questions.
Hope no one asks questions of them.

*Jackie*
# November Snow

Has descended on the valley
in great volleys of white, choking
the streets with impassable
drifts, too many for too few plows.

We

flounder inside, too many
for too few rooms, nothing but
television drone to soothe
our need for the oxygen we

can't

access, inhaling the furnace's
gas, not to mention that of six
kids, one baby, plus Mother,
too many for too few toilets. We

see

too many commercials, too few
shows worth watching, and all
that does is make us restless
for the clear azure days

beyond

our ability to conjure, and so
we dive into too many daydreams,
too few of them attainable, whittling
all hope of joy in the face of early

winter.

# So, Basically

I've been either hospitalized
or interned in our house since . . .
the exception being my father's
funeral, an emotionless tribute
to someone deserving castigation.

Aunt J and Kevin drove me home,
all of us wanting to question each
other, but feeling like that would be
improper. I wanted to know about
Caliente, the ranch, the horses, if

they were making wedding plans,
or if those had been swallowed by
sorrow. How sad, to rekindle forever
love, only to have it crushed by death.
Death. Death. I have to include Pattyn.

She's dead inside with Ethan gone, no
more than a compromised container
of blood and bones. How can love be
so fragile—paper-thin porcelain
awaiting the fall of a granite fist?

# I Did Ask

Aunt J if she knew who the man
at the funeral was—the one wearing
the tailored suit, the one Mom seemed
almost afraid of. The one who looked
like Dad. Turned out there was a reason.

> *That was Douglas. Your brother.*
> *Guess you've never met him, have you?*

"No." Douglas, the gay son who Dad
disowned? No wonder Mom reacted like
she did. "Dad never even talked about him,
except when he got drunk. Then he spewed."

> *Douglas is quite a success story.*
> *He put himself through law school*
> *and is a high-powered lawyer in*
> *Sacramento. You should know him.*

"I couldn't. Mom would kill . . ."
The word jammed in my throat. "I mean,
homosexuality is a sin." Right after
murder, the church has taught us.

> *Jackie, girl, the good Lord makes*
> *people just the way he wants them.*
> *Why would God bother to create sin?*

# With God's Grace

And enough strength of spirit, gays
can go straight. That's what Brother Prior
says. But I wasn't about to argue the point.
I changed the subject instead, asked what
was probably a totally inappropriate question.
"So, do you and Grandpa Paul ever talk?"

> At the funeral, I couldn't help but notice
> how they barely glanced at each other.
> Aunt J answered me unflinchingly.
> *I haven't spoken to my father in more*
> *than forty years. I'm sure he's fine with that.*

Pretty sure it had something to do
with Kevin, who tensed noticeably
during our short exchange. He and
Aunt J were together in high school,
then something happened—something

bad enough to convince Kevin to leave
Ely. Eventually, he married someone
else—Ethan's mom. After she died,
Kevin and Aunt J found each other again.
As fragile as it is, love can also be stubborn.

# I Wish I Knew the Details

But Aunt J and I aren't close
        enough, not like she and Pattyn
                were. Maybe one day we can be.

She came very near to being
        Pattyn's salvation. Can she be
                that for me? Can anyone? Pattyn

told me the little information
        I have about Aunt J, during
                the narrow span of days between

her returning from Caliente
        and the accident. If she and
                Ethan had only made it across

the mountain, everything would
        be different. Better for them,
                and for Kevin and Aunt J. For

the rest of us, I'm not sure.
        Today, snowed in, Dad would
                be raging. Probably against me.

## Snowed In

At least I'm spared pretending
any sort of normality at seminary
or Mutual. Thank God I'm spared

that, not to mention school. My body
is healing slowly. The bruises have
faded to pastel, and I can breathe

better. But I'm forbidden to lift
the little ones yet, which leaves
that burden to 'Lyssa. Luckily, we're

mostly sitting around. Besides TV,
we play board games. Wonder
what it's like to have a PlayStation

or Wii. The phone rings and when
Mom answers, she takes it back
to her room. But from here, I can

> hear her say, *I submitted the death
> certificate and insurance policy
> last Friday. . . .* Only six days

after Dad died. Their insurance
agent is LDS. He's making sure
to move the claim right along, and

that's a good thing. I have no idea
how much Mom will get. I hope
it's enough to ease the stress level

around here. Mom's voice rises
in back. *What about Stephen's
retirement? He put in thirty-three*

*years.* Too proud to retire at age
fifty-eight, and still stout enough
to look formidable to someone

willing to risk Security at the state
capitol building. Dad wanted to be
a cop, but something in his Vietnam

war record precluded that, a huge
disappointment only mentioned
when he was waltzing with Johnnie.

# LDS Faithful

Spurn alcohol, along with tobacco,
coffee, and tea. Some even refuse
chocolate or Coke. Anything with
caffeine. But whiskey, well that's

something Mormons don't risk.
Dad, however, had an overly
friendly relationship with Johnnie
Walker Black since way before

I was born. Weekdays after work,
he'd drink just a little—enough
to help him sleep, I guess. But once
Friday afternoons rolled around,

his dance with Johnnie lasted until
he passed out Saturday nights. Yet,
almost always, he made it to church
Sunday mornings, wearing a thick drift

of cologne and deodorant to try
and mask the faint reminder
of Johnnie in his spit, in his sweat.
And in the bruises Mom often sported.

# With Luck

Mom won't ever again have to
go to church black and blue.

      One ear tuned toward the hall,
      I hear her finish, *I'll pull all that*

      *together and bring it along on*
      *Sunday. You* will *be at services?*

      *Good. And, Josiah, thank you*
      *for all your help. See you Sunday.*

Josiah? The only Josiah I know
is . . . In the back of my skull, just

above my neck, a low buzz begins,
growing steadily louder. I wait for

Mom to emerge from her room,
and when her face appears it wears

a satisfied smile. Despite the billion
bumblebees inside my head, I push

my voice low, struggle to keep it
pleasant. "Who was on the phone?"

> *Josiah McCain. He's a lawyer,*
> *you know, and he's helping me*
>
> *through all this paperwork. He's*
> *such a dear man, and without him—*

I explode. "Josiah McCain!? Well,
I guess that explains things, doesn't it?

Like why Caleb looks at me so smugly?
He totally got away with it, didn't he?"

Sold out. "Does Mr. McCain even
know what his son did? Does he?"

> *Well, of course he does. I told*
> *Bishop Crandall everything, and . . .*

She turns her eyes to stare at the floor.
Oh my God. "They bought you off."

My voice is a razor-edged keen,
scaring Roberta and Georgia into

blubbery tears, and I bite down hard
not to join them. "Look at me, Mom."

138

# But She Can't

Or won't. 'Lyssa tries to soothe
the little ones. That should be my job,
but right now, all I want to do is yell.
I try to chill, but the annoying hum
has amplified inside my head until

it pounds. "Damn it, Mom!" Now
her eyes lift to my face, brimming
disbelief. I've never cussed before,
at least not so anyone could hear.
I whisper, "Don't you care?"

> This is when she should hug me,
> promise to make things right.
> But, no. *Of course I care. But it's*
> *your word against his, and he swears*
> *it was consensual. Besides, as Bishop*
>
> *Crandall said, what's done is done.*
> *We can't change that, but maybe*
> *some good can come from it. If not for*
> *Josiah, I'd be lost right now, Jackie.*
> *I'd have no idea what to do.* Pathetic.

"You do realize if not for what
happened, Dad might still be alive?"

# Her Body Language

Murmurs defeat. But then she
hardens and what comes out
of her mouth is screamed denial.

> *Well, he is dead! But we're still
> here, so we have to move on, and
> we can't do it without resources.*

> *I don't know why you're acting
> so indignant. It was your fault,
> too. Accept that and get over it.*

"Is that what the great Bishop
said I should do?" I already know
the answer. I just need to hear it

> from her. *He said guilt applies
> equally to the two of you, and that
> God is an evenhanded adjudicator.*

So, not only do they want me
to wait until the afterlife for justice,
but they would put me on trial, too.

"You believe that?" Her eyes tell
me no, which means she doesn't
care. "Have you ever cared, Mom?"

Is the amount of love one's heart
can hold finite? Did each subsequent
baby chip away at Mom's supply?

My skull feels like an anvil beneath
the sledge's steady fall. "I have
a headache. I need my meds, okay?"

She shrugs and I go to the bathroom
for the Percocet they sent home
with me. The instructions tell me

one or two tablets every six hours.
My doctor warned me about
dependency, liver damage, etc.

I usually take one, but since two
won't kill me, I swallow a pair
with a tumbler of water. I want sleep.

# It's Late Afternoon

When I lie on my bed, the light
through the small window tinted
flat and gray by falling snow.
My head still thumps, and now
it's spinning. If I close my eyes
I might get sick, so I stare at the ice

etching the glass, forming intricate
patterns, until the swirling motion
begins to slow and the anvil quiets.
I remember nights lying here beside
Pattyn, talking about everything
and nothing at all. Boys. School.

The future. When she came back
from Aunt J's, our conversations
changed a little. We didn't talk boys.
We talked Ethan. We didn't talk
school. We talked alternatives.
We talked the future. Beyond

classrooms, seminary, and sacrament
meetings. Beyond Dad, Mom, and
this poor excuse for a home. Beyond
sadness worn like a second layer of skin.
Beyond here. See where that got us.

## Something Pushes Me

From sleep into uncertain time—
night? Early morning? It's dark beyond
the window, and the bedroom is filled
with the noises of my sisters' slumber—
'Lyssa's low, even breathing, Teddie's
regular snores. My head is thick with

Percocet residue, no pain but the lingering
ache in my side. I lie still as I'm able,
grasping for memory. What woke me?
A pale vestige of nightmare threads
through me, quickens my pulse. I've almost
got it. But do I really want to remember?

How could I have a bad dream when
the drug should have quieted my brain
activity? But no, I'm positive. If I just . . .
It's a flash, nothing more, but enough
to make me fight slipping back into sleep.
I remember a hulking form blocking

the sidewalk ahead of me. I was scared
to get close, but it kept walking slower.
I knew it wanted me, but I was drawn
to it, had to know what evil looked like.
Suddenly, it turned. And its face was mine.

# I Slip Out of Bed

Tiptoe down the hall to the bathroom.
On my way to the toilet, I trip over
a couple of towels, kick a small pair
of shoes. That would never have

happened with Dad here. His absence
hangs heavily, an incense of malice
reminding us of his regulations, the threat
of his punishment. Will that ever dissipate?

The air is colder than even November
should dictate. When I wash my hands,
I run the water as hot as the aging heater
will warm it. I splash my face, lace wet

fingers through twists of reddish hair,
wishing it hung in long, blond waves
like some of the girls at school have.
Why can't I be like them—blond and pretty

and thin? Why was I born with such
stunning mediocrity? Why can't I be
somebody special—someone people
notice? I'm sick of being forgettable.

*Pattyn*
# Barely Noticeable

In a corner of the pitted
windshield, hiding in
plain sight, really, but

        caught

by a random pause
of my scanning eyes

        in a

fortunate slant of light,
a miniature white spider
has woven an impossible

        web

of filaments so thin
they are almost invisible.
They remind me

        of

the threads that bind
me to Ethan, this world
to the next, the

        shadows

of yesterday with
the promise of tomorrow.

# In a Regular Car

The trip from Vacaville to Butte
County would take around two
and a half hours. By wheezing
pickup, in the driving rain, it will
take longer, which is fine. Angel

and I have some planning ahead.
Last night we settled on what to
say to Craig and Diane Jorgensen,
who own five hundred prime
California acres, many of them

growing walnuts, plus peaches
and cherries. Between the trees,
they run cattle, so year-round
employment is available for some,
including Angel, who has proven

himself invaluable to the operation
in the three years he's been there.
Other workers, like Tomás, move
seasonally, as fewer are required
during the cool months of winter.

# The Highway

Is straight and smooth, so Angel
doesn't have to concentrate too hard,
despite the downpour beating against

the windshield. His English is good,
so communication isn't difficult.
"What are they like? The Jorgensens?"

> *I don't know much about the missus.*
> *But the mister, he is a fair man. Works*
> *hard, right beside his crew. The land*
>
> *belonged to his father, and his father*
> *before that. Mister says there will*
> *always be trees, not houses on the land . . .*

He doesn't quite finish the sentence,
but rather leaves a question dangling.
"And do you doubt he means that?"

> *No. Not him. But the land, it goes*
> *from father to son, and the mister*
> *has no son. Only two daughters.*

Deirdre is fourteen years older
than her little sister, who is not quite
four. Apparently, the missus, as Angel

calls her, had a surprise visit from
Mr. Stork. Or someone. Angel says
little Sophie doesn't much resemble

> her sister, who is her father's image,
> despite being a girl. Personality-wise,
> however, not so much. *The mister is good*

> *to his workers. The girl not so much.*
> *I do not like to speak badly of her. But*
> *I think she is trouble. Her friends, too.*

Good to know. The last thing
I need is more trouble. I plan
to keep my head down, work hard

and invite as few questions as
possible. God, this is like living
a movie. Or a very bad dream.

148

# A Big Concern

Is having no ID, no social security
number, and an invented name.

Patty Medina. When Angel called
the Jorgensens to tell them the good

news—that he knew someone who
was interested in the housekeeping

position—that someone was his
"cousin." Me. According to our story,

my Irish-American mother went
south of the border to teach English.

There in Guadalajara, she fell in love
with Angel's uncle, my fictional

Mexican father. Which, we hope,
will explain why I don't exactly look

Hispanic, despite my (dyed) raven
hair. As for having no passport or visa,

seems there are avenues around that.
On our way through Sacramento,

we detoured down a suburban alley,
stopped by an understated tract house

where a friend of a friend of Angel's
snapped a quick photo. It cost me

most of my stash, half down and half
when Angel picks them up, but in a few days

I'll have the documents I need to apply
for an individual taxpayer identification

number, which is what you use to file
· tax returns if you don't qualify for a social

       security number. *Some growers don't*
       *bother with taxes,* Angel explained.

       *But the mister, he pays into the IRS.*
       *His undocumenteds must have ITINs.*

       *Most people don't know many illegals*
       *pay taxes, too. Most don't think about it.*

# I Never Thought About It

But then, I had enough of my own
       problems to worry about. Even when

Dad would go off on a rant about
       illegal aliens and how they drained

our limited resources, stole our jobs,
       and poisoned our minds with drugs,

I never bothered to consider the truth—
       or untruth—of his warped ramblings.

Not like his opinion wasn't shared,
       not to mention broadcasted widely.

I've never had Hispanic friends.
       In fact, the only "relationship" I ever

had with a Latina resulted in me
       breaking Carmen's nose, defending

my hold on a guy who was only
       interested in easy sex—so not me.

Okay, she might have been snotty.
       But I totally was out of my head.

It's weird because, even as I
          questioned the tenets of my faith,

I hated the way people typecast
          me because of my religion. So how,

especially considering the disdain
          I had for my father's judgment,

could I so easily stereotype
          every Latino, legal or not, the same

way Dad did? I inhale, exhale,
          inhale again, and it comes to me

that when Adriana and I needed
          each other, we cast away doubt

within the overarching bond
          of sisterhood and, defying all logic,

reached across some indefinable
          no-man's-land created by . . . who?

# And Now, Here I Am

With Angel, who doesn't know
      me at all, and yet has taken me under
      his wing only because I needed help.

A cynic would say he must have
      an ulterior motive, but the only one
      I can find is that his sister asked him to.

As I think about it, I really want
      to tell him again, "Thank you.
      I didn't know what I was going to do."

      He smiles. *Hey. No problem. The missus*
            *will be happy with me. And if she's*
            *happy, the mister, he will be, too.*

I find myself relaxing, and reason
      tells me I'm stupid. "Why has it been
      so hard for the Jorgensens to find someone?"

      *It's very lonely so far from town.*
            *Young women want to go out.*
            *Old women don't want to work hard.*

*Also . . .* He pauses. *Also, I think*
      *the missus might not be so easy*
      *to please. You will not be the first*

*to try. The others chose the fields.*
      We reach Gridley, and Angel asks,
      *Is there anything you need? There*

*aren't many stores where we go*
      *from here. I must get gasoline*
      *before we leave town, too.*

I ask him to stop at the market
      I don't have much cash left, but
      I should pick up a few essentials—

shampoo (Suave will do) and
      toothpaste and feminine hygiene
      stuff. I've mostly quit bleeding,

thank goodness. But better to be
      prepared. Only a few things worse
      than being surprised and unprepared.

# Stocked Up, Gassed Up

Angel turns east out of town,
toward the Sierra. We cross
the Feather River and Highway
70, then wind back into a part
of California few tourists ever
explore. Every mile brings

trepidation, but also, strangely,
reassurance. Who would look
for me out here? Now, if we can
just pull off our story. We. Our.
Totally unfair of me to be doing
this, in so many ways, to so many

people. And yet, here I am, trying
to make it happen. It's sort of like
I'm on autopilot. Plodding through
each day, one foot forward, and then
the other. It's the nights that are bad.
Trying to sleep in strange beds,

on unfamiliar sofas. Fighting bad
dreams. But even those are better
than the memories that track me,
waiting for the perfect moment
to pounce, wind their fingers
around my throat and choke.

# I Glance at Angel

Who is doing his best to avoid
the big puddles disguising potholes
beneath them. Curiosity bubbles up.

"Can I ask a personal question?"
His shrug reminds me of his sister.
"Adriana is legal, yes? But you aren't?"

He chances taking his eyes off
the road long enough to give me
an assessing look. But I've got

> nothing to gain by his telling me
> the truth. *Adriana was born here.*
> *I was not. My father came across*
>
> *first, and when he was settled,*
> *my mother came, too. I was little.*
> *Two years old. We have lived here*
>
> *many years. We work here. We pay*
> *taxes here. We have families here.*
> *California is our home. Not Mexico.*

# Downpour Turns to Drizzle

Just about the time we pull off
the pavement onto a long gravel
driveway between two huge stands
of trees, all lacking leaves. Some
are obviously older, bigger, with
wide spaces between them.

> The smaller trees are planted
> closer together. Angel explains,
> *Walnuts produce best when they*
> *get older, and they need more space.*
> *We start them near each other, then*
> *thin them as they grow. What we cut*
>
> *the mister sells for firewood and*
> *lumber. Walnut is beautiful wood.*
> *And it burns very hot. When the trees*
> *get too old, we cut them, too, and*
> *the younger trees replace them.*
> Pride edges his voice. He is part

of this, even though he'll never
own the land. No wonder he worries
about what will happen here in
the future. But the future isn't static.
Not much use worrying about that.

# We Start a Slow Creep

Along the wet gravel toward
the main house. Angel points
to a row of small cabins near
some big sheds or barns.

> *I live there. Second house*
> *from the left. And here is my*
> *cell phone number in case it*
> *is important to talk to me.*

My stomach is aflutter and
I do my best to quiet my nerves.
I'm glad he's not too far away,
and I don't even know what that

means. I take a deep breath as
Angel drives around to the back
of the big house—an old California
standard. Long and low stucco with

a red tile roof. Big trees will shade
it in the summer. Now their skeletal
branches are emptied of leaves. Yet
I can't see a single one on the ground.

Someone keeps this yard spotless.
I suppose it will be up to me
to keep house the same way.
We get out of the truck, go to

the back door, and Angel rings
the buzzer. Eventually, a woman
answers it. She looks to be about
forty, yet she carries those years

very well. She is shorter than I,
and slender, though her shoulders
and arms look like she works them.
When she sees Angel, she smiles,

       reminding me of the way a cat
       grimaces. Her pale eyes travel
       over me, absorbing information.
       *Hello. Patty, right? Come in,*

       *come in. I'm Mrs. Jorgensen.*
       *Thank you, Angel.* He has been
       dismissed, and knows it. He gives
       me a quick wink before he leaves.

# A Pair of Tricolored Dogs

Comes running around the side
of the house, barking. I freeze,
unsure of what they have in mind.

>    *Don't worry about them,* says
>    Mrs. Jorgensen. *Otto! Milo!*
>    *Be nice!* Almost in unison, the two

slow, come over to say hello. Other
than Aunt J's, I don't have much
experience with dogs, but when their tails

wag, initiating a sort of full-body
wiggle, I relax. "Which one is
which?" I hold out my hand for

>    them to sniff, and both do. *Otto*
>    *is the one with two blue eyes.*
>    Milo has one blue eye, one brown.

I pet the dogs and as I follow
the missus inside, feel four eyes—
three blue, one brown—watch me go.

# The Lady of the House

Leads me through the back door.
We pass an immaculate laundry room
that's almost as big as my bedroom
at home, and the clean perfume
of detergent is somehow comforting.

I trail her through the big, bright
kitchen, the sound of our footsteps
against the tile all that breaks the silence
except for the muted noise of a television
somewhere beyond the far doorway.

Past a formal dining room and living
room, both empty and spotless white,
as if rarely used. What is being used
right now is a family room, where
a little girl is watching Nickelodeon,

sitting cross-legged on a faux-fur white
rug beneath the huge flat-screen TV on
the wall. We catch her attention and
she jumps to her feet, comes running
our way, making Mrs. Jorgensen tense

> noticeably. *Slow down, Sophie. How*
> *many times have I told you not to run*
> *in the house? You'll hurt yourself.*

The child screeches to a halt, proceeds
at a pace her mother will appreciate—
one sure step at a time—until she reaches
my side. She tugs on my hand. *What's
your name?* The eyes staring up at me

are a stunning blue, accented with
a fringe of ultra-long lashes. "Patty,"
I say, and she echoes the word quietly.

*Will you play with me, Patty?*
Her entreaty is so heartfelt, it makes
me wonder if she ever gets to play.
*And can I have a cookie?*

I bend so I can look her in the eye.
"I hope we can play. That would be fun.
You have to ask your mama about the cookie."
When I straighten, I find Mrs. Jorgensen
assessing our interaction. She clears

her throat. *Okay, Sophie. Patty and I
have to talk now. I'll ask your sister
to get you a snack. Go watch TV.
Deirdre!* she calls. *Come here, please.*

# No Immediate Response

Mrs. Jorgensen ushers me into a small
office. *Have a seat. I'll be right back.*

I settle into a leather chair in front
of a knotty pine desk, count the small
cracks on the armrest to still my nerves.

Farther up the hallway, knuckles flurry
against wood. *Open the door, Deirdre.*

I hear the request met, words traded.

*What do you want? I'm busy.*
*Doing what?*
*Research.*
*For what?*
*Are you dense? School.*
*Have you been smoking?*
*Why do you care?*
*Deirdre Joy! Not in my house.*
*Fine. How about the barn?*
*Are you insane?*
*Probably. It's genetic, I hear.*
An audible huff.
*Are you finished, then?*
*Would you please get Sophie a cookie?*
*That little twerp can wait on herself.*

# It Takes a Threat

To gain Deirdre's cooperation—
no boyfriend, no date, no dance.
She stomps down the hall, stops
long enough at the office door
to give me a solid once-over with

> critical eyes. *Who's that? The new*
> *maaaaaaaid?* The way she draws out
> the "a" makes it sound like a dirty word.

> Her mother comes up behind her.
> *We'll see. She's here for an interview.*

> *Yeah, right. Like anyone else would want*
> *this job.* She addresses me, *You're hired.*
> *Just so you know, working here sucks.*

Wonder why. I keep my mouth shut,
and she heads toward the kitchen,

> yelling to Sophie to follow, *if you want*
> *a goddamn cookie so bad.* Wow.

Mrs. Jorgensen offers a weak apology
for her daughter's behavior, and
the interview, such as it is, begins.

## Journal Entry, November 7

Mrs. Jorgensen must have noticed
Angel wink at me because one of
the first things she asked was if we
were a couple. When I insisted no,
we're just cousins, she said, "Cousins
often marry. It's legal in California."
I let her do most of the talking and
she didn't ask too many questions
except had I ever cleaned house or
taken care of toddlers before. Uh, yeah.

So, we agreed on a trial period until
the first of the year. Room, board, and
$150 a week under the table, working
seven a.m. to seven p.m., Monday
through Friday. Part of that time
I'll have to myself, if the missus and
little Sophie do something together.

Saturdays, I'm sort of on call until
noon, with Sundays completely free
so I can go to Mass and spend time
with Angel. Guess she didn't believe
me when I said we're not in love.
I didn't correct her again. But here's
what I know—I will never love again.

*Jackie*
# The Truth

Is a product of perception.
One person's mountain
is another's hill. Your river
is someone else's creek.
In the end, it doesn't matter.

A lie

is different. Oh, you might
claim a small white one is
really a positive, but a lie,
no matter where it falls
in the spectrum,

corrodes

gently. Relentlessly.
Confess it, you'll regret
the pain it causes.
But choose to keep
it a secret, and the longer

you

do, the deeper it gnaws,
through skin and flesh,
sinew and bone, all the way
to your heart. And there
you'll carry it always.

## Holding a Lie

Inside is caustic enough
when it's your own, but when
it belongs to someone else,
it makes you crazy. Mom argues

that staying silent about what
happened that night isn't the same
thing as lying. I disagree, and if
you ask me, it's her lie I'm holding.

It's gnawing at me. Especially
now that I'm back at school, where
some of Caleb's friends know,
I'm sure. I can see it in their ugly

grins when I walk by. Especially
now that I'm back at seminary,
where I'm confronted by him every
day before school, not that he has to

say one word. All he has to do is look
my way. I wish I could meet his eyes,
blind him with a hate beam from mine.
I wish I could just go ahead and ask

Brother Prior to explain how
the top officials in our church
not only looked the other direction
but actually colluded, manufacturing

the perfect way for Caleb to walk
away, penalty-free, while I will
be punished for the rest of my life.
Pattyn would ask. But she is fearless,

and loved to make Brother Prior
squirm with questions he wasn't
prepared to answer. Questions like,
*Are we responsible for our dreams?*

And then she went on to pester
him, asking how God would feel
about someone whose dreams
were soaked with sex. Brother

Prior said he couldn't speak
for God, then returned to serving
as his mouthpiece, through scripture
recitation, the irony totally lost on him.

168

# If I Could Only Find

A tiny percentage of Pattyn's courage,
I'd wipe the stupid grin right off
Brother Prior's face with a question

about what a suitable mourning period
might be before a widow takes up with
someone new. Especially if that someone

is a church elder whose wife walked out
on him, and the church, some time ago,
causing a huge scandal, one played

out quite publicly, front and center
at Sunday services. Not that Mom
is exactly playing kissy face with Josiah

McCain, but if you ask me, the two
of them are way too friendly. Yeah,
yeah, I understand that he's giving

Mom free legal advice and she's grateful
for that. But this goes beyond simple
gratitude. And yes, I get that as a church

muckety-muck he feels somewhat
responsible for her well-being with
Dad gone and all. But talking on

the phone pretty much every day?
Stopping by, just to see if she needs
anything? Holding Samuel and cooing

baby talk to him, just like a daddy
would? Not acceptable. But even if
I could get past all of that, I could never

accept a couple of things. The biggest
one is that, as Caleb's dad, Mr. McCain
is a daily reminder of that night, and of

the silent victim's role I've had forced
on me, not only by Josiah McCain and
Bishop Crandall, but also by my own

mother. The second thing is that when
he and Mom talk within easy earshot,
I can hear the way he makes her laugh.

Like a girl—a giddy, infatuated teenage
girl. *That* should be my role. She should
still be playing the part of grieving widow.

# I Make People Laugh, Too

And not in a good way.
Everything about me has
changed. I thought it was
bad when no one noticed
me at all. Now people stare
and snigger when I walk by.

The hallways have never
seemed so narrow. Crowded
with eyes. I turn from my locker,
bump into Derek Colthorpe,
and my biology book crashes
against the ochre linoleum.

"Sorry," I mumble, not sure
why I'm apologizing. The stench
of marijuana clings to him, and
he stares at me with droopy
red eyes. Man. Smoke much?
Finally, the connection he's

     reaching for sinks through
     the haze. *Hey. I remember you.*
     *You're Pattyn's sister, right?*

I remember him, too. He was
Pattyn's first kiss. First real crush.
He got her drunk on tequila and
if Dad hadn't gone looking for her,
might very well have stolen
her virginity, coercing her with

alcohol instead of brute force,
the way Caleb stole mine. My
pulse picks up speed and it hurts
to wheeze shallow breaths. I reach
for my book, but Derek grabs it first.
He offers it, but before I can accept,

       someone pushes my shoulder.
       Hard. *You're not talking to my man,*
       *are you, bitch?* It's Carmen, and

Derek stutters, *N-n-no. I bumped*
*into her and she dropped her book.*
*That's all.* He rushes past me, grabs

       her hand, and as they hustle off,
       I hear her say, *You heard her crazy*
       *sister killed their father, yeah?*

# Everyone's Heard

It was all over the news for three days,
until some disgusting Nevada senator's

affair became the bigger story. We were
on TV, in the newspapers, on the radio

and the Internet. I'm sure by now some
sicko has made a YouTube about us.

Probably echoing the tabloid theme:
Patricide—This Is Not Your Everyday

Good Little Mormon Girl. Featuring
interviews (okay, more like twenty-

second sound bites) with a few kids
from school, faces blurred to avoid

identification. But I knew who they
were. Justin Proud. Derek Colthorpe.

Carmen Vargas. Justin and Derek
mentioned Pattyn's obvious affection

for guns. Carmen called her violent,
told the story about Pattyn breaking

her nose. And for nothing, Carmen said,
except she was jealous over a boy. And

while everything they said was technically
accurate, the impression viewers came away

with was anything but. No one spoke up
to correct that. Not even Mom.

People see. People talk. Everyone knows
the basic facts, if not the dirtiest little

details. My teachers seem sympathetic.
They speak to me with gentle voices,

ask if I'm doing okay. The kids either
stare and whisper behind my back or

pretend I'm not here at all. Pattyn's old
friends, if you can call them that, stick

their noses in the air, act all high-and-
mighty like their backstabbing gossip

played no part in this drama. They have
to know it did. I hope guilt eats them alive.

# Holding Everything In

Is hard. But I have no one
to confide in. Pattyn is (was?)
my best friend. Everyone else
is just a classmate. I've never
invited anyone over. Our house
is too small, too crowded, too
messy. And then, there was Dad.

When Pattyn and I used to lie
in bed, whispering into the earliest
hours of morning, we'd talk about
beyond high school and AD—after
Dad. Before Patty met Ethan, our
plan was to move away for college,
live together. Finally make friends,

find boyfriends, celebrate life
beyond fear. Now she's gone,
maybe forever, so where do I go
from here? If I want college, I have
to elevate my grades, work toward
a scholarship. And right now I'm so
behind! How will I ever catch up?

# I Do My Best

To concentrate in biology, but
I'm pretty sure everyone's staring
at me, and even if they're not,
I have no clue what Mr. Lindquist

is talking about. Science has never
been my best thing anyway, but
having missed so many classes,
I'm seriously in the dark. The more

he goes on, the more I feel like
I'm stuck in a bad dream. I glance
down and am happy to see I've
got clothes on over my underwear.

Still, this panicky sensation sucks
at me, threatens to pull me under.
I take some deep breaths, work very
hard not to run screaming from

the classroom. When the bell rings,
I approach Mr. Lindquist, who is at
his desk punching numbers into
his computer. "Um. Excuse me?"

When he looks up, the irritation
in his eyes immediately softens
to pity, which bothers me. *Oh.
Jackie. How can I help you?*

"I, um . . . It's just, I've fallen
behind in this class and I'm
worried. I was wondering if
there's a way to get some help."

He's nodding before I even
finish talking. *It's good that you
asked sooner rather than later.
We do have a program available.*

*Some of our AP students tutor as
part of their community service hours.
Lynette Rose coordinates that. When
is your study hall? Ask to take it*

*in the library and I'll let her know
you're coming.* He consults his screen
again. *You've missed two tests, but
I'll let you make them up next week.*

# The Library

Is a safe haven. Not sure if
    it's the same in every school,
        but here, the stacks are fortresses.

I love the smell of books,
    even old ones, as most of
        these are, at least the nonfiction.

Ms. Rose collects young
    adult novels, so there's a wide
        selection of fiction. Everything

from vamps to vampires,
    she likes to say, and that's
        an apt description. Pattyn's

a huge reader, and she passed
    that passion on to me. Books
        were her escape, and they are mine,

too. The best, I have to hide,
    or at least I did while there was
        any chance Dad might find them.

# My Study Hall

Is last period, which is awesome
because the library is pretty much
deserted. When I come through the door,

one or two kids sitting way in back
look up from their work, but only
for a second. Ms. Rose actually stands

as I go toward her desk. She is tall,
slender, and so, so pretty. *Hello,
Jackie.* Her voice is honey.

*How are you holding up? This must
be awful for you.* Hmm. Dad's dead,
Pattyn's on the run. I was raped, but

can't tell anyone because, apparently,
my mom thinks I'm to blame. Awful?
Uh, "Yeah." I know she wants to ask

about Pattyn, whom she mentored, in
a way. So I answer without the question:
"We haven't heard anything. I don't know

where she is, or even if she's o-k-kay."
The way the last word sticks in
my throat, you'd think I'd actually

  choked on it. My eyes water, and
  so do Ms. Rose's. *I have faith*
  *in your sister. She's a special girl.*

  Zap! She changes the subject. *Okay,*
  *then. Mr. Lindquist says you think*
  *tutoring will help you catch up.*

  *Your past grades tell me your situation*
  *is mostly circumstantial. Mostly.*
  *Let's talk about your weaknesses. . . .*

Math and science. Yep. They always
have been. I got through freshman
algebra with a lot of help from Patty,

who for some reason liked it. But
geometry? Can't figure a reason
for it, other than I need it to graduate.

# We Spend an Hour

Discussing weaknesses.
>> Last year's algebra.
>> This year's geometry and biology.
>> Next year's chemistry and algebra two.
>> My need for senior-year calculus.

Discussing strengths.
>> English, forever my favorite.
>> Spanish, a no-brainer.
>> World history, a window toward today.
>> My determination to succeed.

Discussing goals.
>> Advanced placement next year.
>> SAT prep.
>> Scholarship pathways.
>> My need for community service.

Discussing dreams.
>> College, anywhere but Nevada or Utah.
>> Travel, perhaps a semester overseas.
>> Career—what, exactly, do I want to do?
>> My desire to see my sister again.

# We Do Not Talk

About mission work.
My church expects it—
going out into the world
to spread the word of God,
not to mention Joseph Smith.
Guess I'll disappoint them.
        Neither do we talk about
        getting married young and
        having lots of children, my
        mother's example, and one
        she thinks her girls should follow.
        Guess I'll disappoint her, too.

        We do talk about the best
        time to work with my tutor.
        Can't do it after school, so
        it will be during this study
        hall. *Do you want to start*
        *tomorrow if he can?* she asks.
"The sooner the better,"
I say, adding my promise
to work really hard toward
the goals and dreams we
outlined together. I only hope
I don't disappoint her, too.

# Self-Confidence Bolstered

At least a little, I use the bus ride
home to dive into the list of makeup
work I've been avoiding. I'll start
with Spanish, and three paragraphs

I need to write on *"Lo que 'hogar'*
*significa para mí."* What home
means to me. I think about that for
a while. Discard all the corny stuff—

*mi familia feliz* (we're so not a happy
family) and *calidez, el confort y el*
*amor* (warmth, comfort, and love) in
favor of exterior landscape—*las altas*

*montañas nevadas y de alto desierto*
*de playa.* The tall, snowy mountains
and high desert playa are the truest
description of "home" I can offer

without coming clean about *la*
*verdadera fealdad de mi casa,*
the true ugliness of my home.
Who wants to hear about that?

# The Bus Drops Me Off

At the corner. I have to walk—
slide, really—about a quarter
of a mile on the slick shoulder,
and as I approach the house,
I think I must be seeing things.

Someone is pounding, or trying
to, a FOR SALE sign into the front
of our lot. By the time I get there,
he has accomplished his deed,
and is carefully backing his car
out of our driveway. When I go

inside, Mom looks up from a mound
of paperwork, shakes her head like
she can't quite believe what she just
did. "You're selling the house? Isn't
this kind of a sudden decision?"

> *Too many memories here. Anyway,*
> *we need a bigger place, and we won't*
> *be going far. I put in an offer on a four-*
> *bedroom over off Lakeshore. They accepted,*
> *and as long as the loan is approved,*
> *we should be moved in before Christmas.*

*Pattyn*
# Holidays

Are gathering days,
family and friends around
the hearth or table. How

             I

long for such communion
as the season arrives
with its usual blush
of activity. Most people

             don't

value the anxious
flurry as much as they
should. It isn't enough to

             want

a special celebration.
Working, preparing, even
stressing about making
it absolutely perfect happens

             to be

the only way to assure
success. A stellar holiday
is not the product of wishing

             alone.

# Last Thursday in November

I find myself in a stranger's kitchen,
stuffing a turkey for her family's
Thanksgiving. The prep work
is nothing new. I've helped with it
many times. But once the bird is roasted,

all that lovely dressing steaming in
a bowl, the potatoes mashed and dripping
gravy, I will not be sharing the dinner
table. This will be the first time in
seventeen years I've spent T-day

away from my own family. T-day—
that's what Davie called it from
the time she was about three. Sadness
sits on my shoulder, a gigantic vulture,
waiting patiently to dig its talons into

my heart. The busywork helps some.
Listening to the sound of television
football in the family room, I can
almost pretend it's Dad watching it,
rather than Craig Jorgensen.

Except the TV in our house is
only a few feet from the kitchen
counter, and instead of taking up
half the wall, it's the size of a very
big book. Except . . . Dad is dead.

I slam head-on into that wall
for about the billionth time. It's been
a month, but it feels like a decade.
It's been a month, but it feels like
only moments ago. Most of the time

I don't think about it. Busywork
helps with that, too. This big old
house never lacks for something
to do, and I make every effort to
stay on top of things. I want to be

indispensable. It definitely isn't easy.
Angel was right. The missus is hard
to please. She's rather strict, in fact,
and insists on having things done
a certain way. But, hey, I'm used to that.

# Right Now

She and Sophie are napping.
The little one takes a bit after
her mother. She can be demanding.
Of course, she's only three, and most

three-year-olds want their own way.
The difference is, not all of them
get it. My sisters never had a quarter
of the toys that Sophie does, and

she's tired of hers already. The only
one she really clings to is a soft
rag doll with big blue eyes and
pink flannel clothes. Sophie points

at her and says, *Me*. The doll does
look like her, except for the clothes.
The missus would never dress Sophie
in pink flannel. She wears smart

denim skirts with tights underneath
or miniature designer jeans. Her
pajamas are silk. When the missus
is occupied, Sophie comes to me for hugs.

# A Roar Lifts

In the family room. Touchdown! The clock
says two p.m. We planned dinner for four.
Turkey's in. Pies—apple, cherry, and pumpkin!—

are cooling. The rest can wait a little while.
I go to let the mister know where he can find
me, and am surprised to see Deirdre beside

him on the couch, watching the game.
"Sorry to interrupt, but I'll be in my room
for an hour or so if you need anything."

> Mr. Jorgensen turns quite specifically
> my way. *Make sure that turkey's done,*
> *now. I like my beef rare. Not so my poultry.*

I smile. "I'll remember that. Beef, rare.
Poultry, not." Despite the gentle exchange
of humor, Deirdre totally disengages.

She's probably said ten words to me since
I've been here. Her face is very much
her father's. Angel was right about that, too.

But though her eyes are the exact same
shade of gray-blue as her dad's, somehow
they are less alive. Every now and then

I catch her staring sideways at me with
those grave cold eyes and it totally
creeps me out. But with her father

sitting right there on the creased
leather couch, Deirdre's gaze never
leaves the screen. I turn away, head

toward my bedroom, which is the only
one on the east side of the house.
Three others—the family's—catch

the setting sun. The guest room gets
full southern light. This a pretty place,
though Mr. Jorgensen's conservatism

is obvious when it comes to furniture,
which is well-kept but not so new,
the exception being in the master bedroom.

The furniture there is sleek chrome
and glass, all the missus's choosing,
and a regular nightmare to keep clean.

Still, polishing off fingerprints
isn't the worst job in the world. Right
now, it's the best job in the world.

# Some People

Would consider my bedroom, accurately
dubbed "The Maid's Room," small.

Yet it's larger than the one I grew up
with, and I don't have to share it with three

sisters, two of us per double bed. I have
an entire full-size bed all to myself,

plus a little writing table with chair,
matching pine dresser and nightstand,

and even a "smart" television, wifi-
enabled. I had no idea they made

TVs with built-in Internet. My room
at Aunt J's was lovelier, with its quilts

and adornments. But this one, though
embellishment-free, is the most modern

I've ever been able to call my own,
and I've got a private bathroom, too.

I know it's ridiculous, but a piece of
me is starting to feel comfortable here.

# That Piece

Is the Patty Medina piece,
and because she's completely
invented, I allow her a measure
of comfort. If she spent all day
every day worrying, it would
be obvious to everyone here.

Her more anxious alter ego, Patty
Carter, is put on display only on
Sundays, when she visits Angel
and his roommate, Javier. She's
the one who's hiding from her evil ex,
something I struggle to remember,

and so I don't let her say very
much. She would be quiet anyway.
Abuse victims generally are.
I do enjoy getting her out of this
house for several hours and it's weird,
but I find myself liking the Catholic

Mass with all its customs and
trappings. I don't think God is any
more present there than he is in
an LDS chapel. But the anonymity
there allows a more introspective
search for some trace of a higher power.

# The Final Third

Of my personal triumvirate
        is mostly a creature of the night.

Pattyn Von Stratten surfaces
        when my hands are finally at rest,

and my brain tries to shut itself
        off from the horror movies archived

inside—the ones that replay in
        infinite loops and always end red

with bloodshed. Killing, not
        death, because one thing this part

of me has learned beyond all
        doubt is that the dead don't lie still.

They walk. They talk. They laugh.
        They come sprinting after you, and

there's no way to outrun them,
        so you might as well embrace them,

hope all the love you hold inside
        coaxes them back to sleep again.

# A Little After Three

I baste the turkey, which browns
nicely. Then I heat the lower oven
for the crescent rolls, start some water
simmering for the green beans before going

        to set the table in the formal dining
        room. I am placing the forks when
        a little hand tugs the back of my blouse.
        *Watcha doin', Patty?* It's Sophie, plus

her baby doll, Me. "I'm setting
the table. Do you want to help?
The knives and spoons go like this."
I demonstrate and Sophie sits the doll

in her designated chair before trying
to place the silverware correctly.
It's a little crooked, but still I say,
"Very good. Let's just straighten—"

        *Are you stupid? She could cut*
        *herself! Give me that, Sophie!*
        Deirdre stomps over and grabs
        a butter knife out of her hand.

Sophie's eyes fill with tears
and she ducks behind me,
hiccuping. "I-I'm sorry," I say.
"But I don't think she can cut—"

> *Shut up. How dare you argue*
> *with me?* She breathes hard, and
> the smell of stale tobacco hangs
> heavily in her exhale. *Well?*

"I'm very sorry," I repeat,
wishing I could tell her how
I really feel. "But don't you think
she should learn how to do this?"

> She looks at me like I'm a total
> idiot. *What for? It's* your *job.*
> *Get away from her, Sophie.*
> Deirdre grabs her hand, tries to yank

her out from behind me. That
makes Sophie yell, *Stop it, Dee Dee!*
*I wanna help. Stop it. You hurtin'*
*me!* She pulls away. *Mama!*

# But It Isn't the Missus

Who comes to the rescue. *Enough!*
*What the hell do you think*
*you're doing?* Mr. Jorgensen

directs the question toward
Deirdre, who just stands there
glaring at me. Sophie runs and

jumps up into her father's arms.
*Daddy! Dee Dee's being mean. I*
*wanna help Patty set the table.*

*Shh now,* he answers. *You can*
*help. Of course you can. And*
*what a good girl to want to.*

Deirdre storms off, no chance
for her father to smell her breath.
Of course, maybe he already knows.

I'm not about to tell him. Sophie
squirms out of her daddy's grasp.
*Show me! Show me!* she pleads.

I glance at Mr. Jorgensen, asking
silent permission. He nods and I
give Sophie a stack of napkins.

"See how the napkins go under
the forks?" Sophie rushes around
the table, not bothering to fold

anything. I follow, correcting her,
and Mr. Jorgensen smiles. *I must
apologize for Deirdre. Don't know*

*what gets into that girl sometimes.*
He watches Sophie show Me her napkins.
*Girl's got one helluva mean streak.*

*Yeah,* agrees Sophie. *Hella mean.*
Her father snorts and I struggle
not to do the same thing. Instead,

I put a hand over my grin. "Thank
you for helping, Sophie. The table
looks beautiful. Dinner will be

ready soon. In fact, I'd better check
on the turkey. We want it done, not
burnt." As I leave the room, I hear

Sophie echo the words "burnt" and
"beautiful." They come out *brund*
and *booful*, but we all get the picture.

197

# The Pop-Up Timer

Informs me the turkey is done.
I put it on the counter, slip the rolls
into the oven, and drop the green
beans into the bubbling water.
I don't know if I should slice
the bird, so I start toward the door

          to ask. Behind it, I hear the mister
          say, *I don't understand what's going*
          *on with her, Diane. I think it must*
          *be those hooligans she runs around*
          *with.* . . . Not a good time to interrupt.

I back away silently, open a can
of cranberry sauce, and as I slide it
onto a plate, the missus comes into
the kitchen. She barely even glances
my way as she goes to a tall cupboard,
removes a familiar-looking bottle.

          As she pours half a glassful of
          Johnnie Walker Black, she notices
          the turkey. *Looks like it's about time*
          *to eat. I'll let everyone know. Can you*
          *carve the beast?* She takes a big gulp

of scotch, releasing the sickening
sweet rot smell into the air. I fight
to keep from gagging. "I can handle
the turkey. I'll have everything on
the table in ten minutes." Anything
to get her—and Johnnie—out of here.

I find a big platter, remove the legs,
use the sharpest knife in the drawers
to carve perfect slices. Spoon stuffing
and potatoes into bowls, drain the beans,
pour gravy into the sterling silver boat
I found hiding in the cupboard. Start carrying

everything into the empty dining room.
Suddenly, on the far side of the door,
Mr. Jorgensen yells, *You will get your ass
out of there and join us at the table or lose
the keys to your truck! Do you understand?*

At least it isn't just me she wants
nothing to do with. I go about my
business, saving a plate for myself
in the kitchen. The table truly is
beautiful. Too bad no one really
appreciates it. My family would.

199

# Thanksgiving Smells the Same Here

But it doesn't sound the same.
Our table wasn't always a happy one
at home, but it was rarely silent.

And even Dad tried to make holidays
celebratory, at least until he escaped
outside to his own stash of Johnnie WB.

We never ate quite this well. Our turkeys
were the frozen Costco kind, and we had
one pie for dessert, not three. But we

gave thanks, broke bread, and when we
finished, our stomachs had no empty
space. I sit here, alone in the kitchen

breakfast nook, picking at my plate
of fat-breasted Butterball, thinking
about what my family might be doing

right now. Are they sad because the table
has two empty chairs? Or do the extra
helpings make up for our absence?

## Journal Entry, November 28

*You can see it in movies or on TV,*
*or read about it in books, but until*
*you've actually experienced a holiday*
*totally alone and unrecognized, you*
*can't even imagine how that feels.*

*I'm under a roof. Well fed. Despite*
*the bone-bruising chill outside, I'm warm.*
*Clothed. Clean. And yet, I am homeless*
*because a house isn't a home unless*
*you share it with someone you love.*

*I don't understand, God. If you are real*
*and I am truly your child, how can you*
*be such a cruel father? What did I do to*
*deserve this endless punishment? Was it*
*only because I dared to question my place?*

*I swore nothing could be worse than*
*serving as a baby factory, than having*
*a man in charge of every phase of my life,*
*and yet, what I wouldn't give to have*
*Ethan here today, telling me what to do.*
*Oh, my love, please tell me what to do!*

*Jackie*
# What Do I Do

To become invisible again,
to melt into the background
like a crayon in the sun?
How do I outmaneuver the

whispers

that wait around every
corner, and more, how do
I silence the voices that

speak

inside my head, an accusatory
rumble belonging to
the dead? If only they'd talk

louder

perhaps I could understand
the intention of the drone.
Is it meant to flip me crazier

than

I already am, a healthy
dose of lunacy wrapped
up in this isolation? My heart

screams

for forgiveness, cries
out for love.

# Monday, Post-Thanksgiving

Seminary is all about—huge surprise—
thanks. What are we thankful for? What
about us might God be thankful for?

       Brother Prior offers personal examples.
       *I'm thankful for my wife and children.*
       *God is thankful for my obedience.*

Yeesh. How cliché. Is that really
the best he can do? Everyone here
is pretty much thankful for the same

things: their family. Their friends.
Getting good grades. Scoring the winning
touchdown. That would be Caleb, who

       also thinks, *God is thankful because*
       *when I scored the winning touchdown,*
       *I gave it up to his glory.* Not sure what

gets into me but I actually say out
loud, "How humble." Which draws
unnecessary attention and derision

       from Brother Prior. *Don't you believe*
       *God would appreciate getting credit*
       *where credit is due?* Oh, man. What

did I do? The last thing I need is to
be engaged this way. I lower my eyes.
"Of course. As long as it's honest credit."

Maybe there's more Pattyn in me than
I thought. But I'm sick of Caleb playing
hero when he's such a jerk. No, not right.

　　　　　He's a criminal. Wonder if Brother Prior
　　　　　is in on the cover-up, too. *What about you?*
　　　　　he asks me. *What are you thankful for?*

The smug tone of his voice initiates
a slow crawl of anger. It starts at
the tip of my tailbone, creeps up along

my spine to the base of my skull.
"I can't even be lame like everyone
else. My family is a total mess, and

I have no friends to speak of. My grades
suck right now and I don't play football.
Hmm. Oh, I know. I'm thankful for all

the support we've gotten from Caleb's
dad, who, for no discernable reason, keeps
going way above and beyond for Mom."

# I Only Hope

The innuendo is obvious to everyone
here. My boldness builds unreasonably,
and I dare to look directly at Caleb. For
once, he isn't smiling. But now I am.
"As for what God's thankful for about me,

it's probably that I always tell the truth."
Two long beats. "Sooner or later."
That probably went way too far and I'm
pretty sure I'll hear about it later from
my mom. But it makes me feel good for

the moment, especially when Caleb squirms
noticeably in his seat. Brother Prior changes
the subject. *Yes, well, that's very good.*
*The truth shall set ye free. And what else*
*is freeing?* He goes on to talk about how

rules can actually free you because
it's easy to make the right choices.
His logic, as always, is lacking, but
I think I've said enough for one day.
Maybe enough for a lifetime.

# What's Freeing

Is to have actually spoken my mind,
          or maybe more like a small piece of it,
          for once. And for once it wasn't just

to my sister. Half of me is giddy.
          The other half is terrified that I'll pay
          for it before too very long. At least

I probably won't get beaten. That
          end result is off the table for now,
          and buried in the frozen ground.

It's a short walk from Brother
          Prior's house to school. A layer
          of snow, trampled down into ice,

makes the sidewalk slippery, so
          I'm taking my time, looking down
          at where I should place my feet, and

I notice a shadow behind me,
          growing larger. Getting closer.
          Closing in. It's tall and broad and

I don't have to turn around to
          know it's Caleb. Suddenly, a large
          hand clamps down on my shoulder.

# He Hasn't Said a Word

> To me since that night. Not. One. Word.
> Now he says, *Wait.* He spins me around.

Instinctively, I duck, expecting a fist.
Instead, his hand falls away. "Wh-what

do you w-want?" Other kids are headed
this way, so I really don't need to be scared.

Except they cross the street, veer away
and around us. I start to shake, and not

> from the cold. Caleb notices and smiles.
> *I just wanted to know what you meant*

> *by that crack about my dad. I'd say your*
> *mom needs all the help she can get. Right?*

"Not from him." Legal advice. Cosigning
for the new house. A loan, even. "Not from

anyone who's close to you." Because that
brings me close to him, too. "I hate you."

Oh my God. Did I say that? No, I think
I just screamed that. People are now staring.

I gulp in air, notch down my voice.
"I can't believe you got away with it."

He pulls himself up very tall and his smile
vanishes. *Got away with what, bitch?*

"You know what!" My voice has risen
again. I force it lower. "You raped me."

*That's a lie. You know you wanted to.
You invited me out to that shed and*

*basically attacked me.* Attacked
him? By sliding my arms up around

his neck and parting my lips just a little,
asking for his kiss? My cheeks burn and

my eyes feel like someone pricked them
with needles. "All I wanted was a kiss,

Caleb. And if you ever say anything
different, I'll . . . I'll . . ."

*You'll what? Kill me?* He pushes me
and I slip backward, falling hard on my butt.

208

# He Stalks Off

And other people walk wide around
me as if I'm a pile of dog poop, or
something else that should be avoided.

> I collect my scattered stuff, scramble
> to stand on the smooth ice. *Here.*
> *Let me help you.* A hand reaches down

and I look up to see if someone's
trying to trick me. But no. It's Gavin
Stromberg, my tutor. I take his hand

and he pulls me up. I mumble, "Thanks,"
but it kind of gets caught on the lump
in my throat. Not sure he heard it.

> *You okay?* His gentle voice holds
> concern. It's one of the things that
> strikes me most about him. How soft

his voice is, compared to how big
he is—six foot three or so, and maybe
two hundred pounds. "I'm fine."

> *That guy is such an asshat. I thought*
> *he only picked on gay guys. Now he's*
> *pushing girls around, too. Very nice.*

"He's not nice. Not at all." We start
to walk, cutting across the parking lot
and reaching the door just as the bell rings.

> Gavin holds it open. *See you last period.*
> His hazel eyes study me from behind wire-
> framed glasses. *You sure you're all right?*

My butt's bruised, and so is what
little pride I've ever had, but I say,
"I've been worse," and I mean it.

He goes straight down the long hallway,
and I turn left toward my locker,
wondering what he meant about Caleb

picking on gay guys. I'm pretty sure
Gavin is straight, but even if he isn't,
he's big enough to play defense.

Caleb was suspended for a hazing
incident last year. I don't know all
the details, but heard it happened

in the locker room. Was that guy
gay? Did Caleb claim he was attacked?
And was that all covered up, too?

# We Have a Sub

In English. The lazy kind who gives
us free reading, which I usually like.
But today, too many thoughts swirl
around in my head. Too many words.
*Bitch.*
      *Lie.*
             *Invited.*
                      *Attacked.*

The only other person who has ever
called me a bitch is my father.
He said what happened was my fault,
too, and so did Bishop Crandall.
*Whore.*
      *Ruined.*
             *Guilt.*
                    *Judged.*

And then, those last words Caleb
said to me before he pushed me to
the ground. There's something in them,
trying to escape me. Some dark thing.
*You'll*
      *what?*
             *Kill*
                  *me?*

# Maybe I'm Crazy

I feel like it sometimes, and I am
        related to Dad, who was totally
                off his proverbial rocker. Is insanity

genetic? Big swaths of memory
        have gone missing, especially
                scenes from that night. I know

I blacked out when Dad was
        pounding on me. That's not
                crazy. It's just mental self-defense.

My brain jumped into the present
        when Pattyn came through the door.
                I remember how calm she was, and

how angry that made me, even
        though I was ecstatic she was
                there. But then, it's all a huge jumble.

I also remember the joy of kissing
        Caleb, my body's amazing reaction.
                And then. Pain. Struggle. Pain. Nothing.

Is it possible I encouraged him?
        Was there something in the nothing?
                Is my disturbed psyche covering up, too?

# It's on My Mind All Day

In classes,

I'm distracted.
I stare out the window.
I miss major lecture points.
My notes are useless scribbles.
The books I need are in my locker.

Thank goodness

there are no labs.
We have no quizzes.
No one calls on me to answer
questions I didn't hear in the first place.

Thank goodness

I can sit in the back,
where all the losers sit,
not caring that they're losers.
I can sit in the back, behind other
losers, where no one notices me at all.

# PE Defines Humiliation

We're in the gym, girls on one
side, boys on the other, Caleb
and his friends among them.
Usually I'm good at volleyball,
but today I miss every spike and
can't for the life of me defend the net.

> Finally, our teacher, Ms. Panetta,
> taps me on the shoulder. *Maybe*
> *you should sit down for a while.*
> *No need to push too hard, too soon.*
> *In fact, why don't you go shower?*

Topping this stellar day off, when
I arrive at the locker room, I discover
I've started my period early, and have
no supplies. At least no one else
is here to watch me wash off what I
thought was only unearned sweat,

fold up several layers of toilet paper,
and hope that holds things in check
until I can find some change for
the embarrassing machine on the wall.

# At Least I'm Not Pregnant

Thank you, God, for one little hint
      of sanity amid all the rest. But I do
      have a question for you. Did you really
have to go as far as a monthly bleed?

Okay, Eve might have disobeyed you.
      But come on. For one thing, you created
      that bastard serpent. Ooh. I just thought
the word "bastard." Am I on my way

to hell? Or was I already on my way,
      considering I'm ruined? It's all just
      so confusing. Anyway, back to Eve.
How old was she when you first made

her bleed? How old was she when you
      popped her into Eden? Why does Genesis
      not address the basics? I hate books that
don't give you necessary backstory

before diving into the action. I mean,
      you're all-knowing, right? So how is it
      possible you did not understand that
teenagers aren't equipped for this stuff?

# This Teenager Isn't, for Sure

I mean, I get outcomes. Wrong time
of the month plus sex equals pregnancy.

Just look at the fabulous example set by
my mother. Ever heard of birth control,

Mom, whether or not it's frowned
upon by LDS doctrine? Yeah, I get

that the Church celebrates procreation.
More little Mormons means more big

Mormons, equating to in-the-black
tithing. Other religions expect monetary

donations, and some would no doubt
like a percentage of their parishioners'

incomes. But how many demand that
ten percent come off the top before

the bills are paid? The LDS church claims
it's God's law. You're supposed to pay it

faithfully and happily because obedience
to the law brings rewards from God.

But would God really ask for money?
What if that means those few-too-many

offspring go a little hungry, a little cold?
What about the concept of overpopulation?

And not just worldwide, Mom. How
about overpopulating our home with too

many kids to care about properly?
I know you claim to love us equally.

But the truth is, Mom, the little ones
get more attention, and if I mentioned

it, you'd tell me that's only fair. Maybe
so. But I'd argue that as hard as diapers

and potty training might be, easing us
into adulthood is a much more difficult

job and that's why you refuse to do it.
Why have we never, not even once,

discussed how sex works—the details
every girl needs to play the game smart?

# I Don't Want to Figure It Out

On my own. But since I have no choice,
I forget it, make my way through the rest
of the day, to last period. When I get to
the library, Gavin is already there, geometry
book open. I wave to Ms. Rose, slide into
the chair next to him. He turns to me,

> grins, and I notice a tiny gap between
> his two front teeth, the only flaw
> in his otherwise perfect smile. *How's
> your day been? Hope it got better.*

That makes me laugh. "Actually, no.
But that's a very long, boring story,
so let's change the subject to something
really interesting. Like geometry."
Which, I have to admit, is becoming
a lot more interesting simply because
he's the one teaching it. He's smart

and cute, in a kind of intelligent geeky
way. Plus, he smells really good, like
gingerbread. And I don't know why
I'm thinking any of this. All I know
is, for the first time in a long time, or
maybe even ever, I feel almost normal.

# We Work

For almost an hour and I think
some of it is actually sinking in.
"It's kind of scary, but this stuff
is starting to make sense. Wow."

> He closes the book, puts down
> his pencil, takes mine from me.
> *Well, I certainly hope so. It's my*
> *job to make it make sense, you know.*

"Yeah, but I just never thought
it would. I mean, I've never been
good at it, and then I got so behind
because of my dad and . . ."

> *I'm sorry about what happened.*
> *I know what it's like to lose a parent.*
> *One of my moms died last year. Oh,*
> *in case you didn't know, I had two.*

"I didn't know. I'm sorry, too."
For some stupid reason, I reach out,
touch his hand. For some unknown
reason, he doesn't jerk his hand away.

# It's Such an Intimate Moment

What do
I do?
Move?
Don't?
　　Wait
　　for him
　　to move
　　his first?
　　　　This is
　　　　crazy. Good.
　　　　Bad. No, nice.
　　　　Very.
　　　　　　Wrong.
　　　　　　Right. No,
　　　　　　more. Important,
　　　　　　somehow.
　　　　No fear.
　　　　No pain, no
　　　　hint of those. No
　　　　promises.
　　And yet
　　a hint of more,
　　a flicker through
　　the fog.
A spark
of hope that
love might not be
a lie.

# The Tender Moment

Shatters almost immediately.
Outside the big plate-glass window—

the one Pattyn sent her book bag
through last year—Caleb walks by

with his arm around Tiffany Grant,
who leans against him like she might

> fall down without his support.
> Gavin notices, too. *Huh. What's up*

> *with that? I thought she and Justin*
> *were permanently attached at the groin.*

Justin Proud is a jerk, but Caleb's worse.
Even Tiffany doesn't deserve him.

"Hope she doesn't mind being attached
to Caleb's groin instead." It's a whisper,

but Gavin hears. He shoots a curious
look, but doesn't comment right away.

> Finally, very quietly, he tells me,
> *Some secrets will eat you alive.*

*Pattyn*
# Whispers

In the night,
provocative and pale
as the winter-

               shadowed

moonlight trickling
through the window.
What can these

               creatures

be, whose voices
pull me from dreams
into uncertainty? They

               speak

of yesterday, that
which can't be altered.
They sing of time

               beyond

tomorrow, a fluid
space, though influenced
by the past, still

               the door

to what might yet
be changed for better
or worse.

# Sleep Comes Hard

Some nights. I don't know what
invites the ghosts that gather like
smoke at my windows. But they're
out in force. I sit up in bed, blanketed
by darkness. The clock tells me it's
a little after two a.m. I'm sweating,
so I've been running in my dreams.

I think what woke me tonight,
though, was the spin of big tires
on gravel, the slam of a truck
door. Beyond the window,
illuminated by muted moonlight,
Deirdre stumbles toward the kitchen
step. Wasted again. And home very
late on a Friday night, not even
aware enough to be thankful
she managed to make it safely.

That girl is all kinds of trouble.
I do my best to stay well out of
her way. The anger that seethes
inside her reminds me of Dad,
and just like Dad, no amount
of booze or other substances can
do anything but soften its edges.

# I Settle Back

Into the big fluffy pillow, close
     my eyes, hope sleep will swallow me.
          But Dad is firmly on my mind now.

It's easy to picture him ugly.
     Fists raised. Red-rimmed eyes
          brimming crazy. Curses foaming

from his mouth. Liquor sweat
     popping from his pores, stinking
          up the house as he stalked, room to

room, seeking the proper outlet
     for the rage he carried locked
          away inside. No, not hard to see him

like that. But if I reach farther
     back, try very, very hard, I can
          tap into a well of deeper memories.

There's one I love, but I can't find
     it often. It hits me powerfully now.
          I am the only Von Stratten girl, and

Daddy opens his arms for me
     to crawl into. I put my ear against
          his chest. *Thump . . . thump.* I hear

him tell me, *I love you, little*
    *girl. Put away your bad dreams.*
        *Daddy's here.* Oh, Dad. How I wish

I could put away my bad dreams.
    But I'm living a nightmare, one
        you star in, aren't I? Now I remember

one night: Mom had sent me to the shed
    for spaghetti sauce. Dad was out
        there, drunk, talking to his first wife—

the one who had committed suicide.
    *Goddammit, Molly, go away. Please . . .*
        *you didn't have to do what you did!*

They lost one son in a firefight
    in Somalia. Dad disowned their
        second son when he came out. With

both her boys gone, Molly put
    a .357 into her mouth and pulled
        the trigger. Dad blamed himself and

now I hear him say, *Don't you know*
    *how much I miss you?* Suddenly,
        I see he was living a nightmare, too.

# I Get

How that chews you up inside,
corrodes you like acid. I wish
that understanding could make me
forgive my father. Because as much
as I can relate, and as horrified as I am
about how far things went, nothing
can bring back Ethan. That saber-
sharp pain has dulled a little. Now
it's more like a persistent throb.

Oh, Ethan! What I wouldn't give
for more time with you! We were
just getting to know each other.
What's it like, there in heaven? Is
our baby with you, or did he even
possess enough of a soul yet to move
on? I hate these unanswerable questions.
Is there a heaven? Is there a God?

Is there still an Ethan, in whatever
form? Sometimes I think Molly
got it right, that I should quit
asking questions, quit holding on,
quit struggling to live when dying
would be easier. Except, what if
suicide was the thing that kept me
from being with Ethan forever?

# LDS Doctrine

Is a little watery on the subject.
Basically, it says the commandment
*Thou shalt not kill* most definitely
applies to offing oneself. But, as always,

there are exceptions, like being
under "great stress," which supposedly
mitigates accountability. And in
the long run, brothers and sisters, only

God may judge whether or not a suicide
was insane or, more simply, vain. Amen.
So if you delve deeper into LDS belief,
which of the three Kingdoms of Glory

might a crazy self-killer find herself in,
postmortem? To attain the Celestial Kingdom
you have to be downright overqualified—
have an intimate relationship with Jesus,

be baptized, repentant, and carry legit
testimony with you throughout your life.
Even if you're eligible, to obtain equal
status with God, you must have been sealed

in marriage so you can procreate spirit
children for eternity. I suppose some
measure of insanity might actually work
for you there. Who wants to be a god anyway?

The Terrestrial Kingdom is reserved for
those who are basically good at heart,
but don't carry their testimony strongly.
Kind of good, kind of not. You don't get

to play God. If you're a liar or witch,
or you sleep around, tough luck, you go
to the Telestial Kingdom, a sort of spiritual
prison, for one thousand years before moving

up a kingdom. Hopefully a millennium
is long enough for you to learn your lesson.
But is there a Telestial Insane Asylum where
suicides are sent? Don't know. Don't care.

I prefer the notion of a single heaven where
you get to hang out for eternity with people
you love. I know how I spend "forever"
isn't up to me. But this is what I hope for.

# Little Hands

Shake me awake. I rise from the depths
of dreams into pallid morning light.

>    *I's hungry. Can I have some cereal?*
>    Technically, Sophie shouldn't come

into my room. Her mother frowns on it.
I don't invite it, but I don't chase her out.

"Okay. Go into the kitchen and wait
for me. I'll get dressed and be right there."

I slip into jeans and a soft flannel shirt—
clothes I've managed to buy with the small

pool of cash I've saved here. I don't make
much, but I don't have to spend much,

>    either. Sophie stands patiently in front
>    of the kitchen counter. *Guess what?*

>    *We gonna cut our Christmas tree.*
>    *Sanna's comin' soon if I'm good.*

"You've been very, very good. Santa
must have something special for you."

# Christmas Is Still

Over two weeks away. My family never
got a tree until just a few days before—
not enough room to keep it up for long.
Plus, Dad always waited for bargain prices.

Stupid movies and TV make it look like
everyone gets a big tree and decorates
the house with garlands and mistletoe.
Not so. Some of us make do with popcorn

and paper chains. On the other hand,
we girls did spend time together stringing
them. There was fear in our family, but
there was also love. It's hard to find a lot

of that here. The Jorgensens argue much
more than they laugh together. Deirdre hides
out in her room, if she's here at all. Little Sophie
makes do with whatever affection she can

gather in. Which is why she comes to me.
But I can't be her substitute mom. I don't
dare get close to anyone ever again. Losing
someone else I cared about would end me.

# I Sit Sophie

At the table with a little glass of juice.
"What kind of cereal do you want? Hot
or cold?" She's about the only kid I've

> ever seen who will pick oatmeal over
> Cap'n Crunch. *Oats. With cin'mon.*
> She thinks a moment, adds, *Please.*

I start the water, and as it begins
to boil, so do voices in the other room.
The mister and the missus again.

> Him: *She won't get up. What am I*
> *supposed to do? Kiss her ass?*
>
> Her: *Watch your language. She's*
> *a teenager. They need more sleep.*
>
> Him: *At her age I was up at daybreak*
> *helping my old man in the orchards.*
>
> Her: *She isn't you, Craig. Things*
> *are different now. Get used to it.*
>
> Him: *Goddamn right she isn't me.*
> *On her best day, she isn't* half *of me.*

# There's More

But I tune it out. Serve Sophie oats.
Start coffee, hoping the mister will
smell it perking and come looking
for his usual oversize mug.

> Eventually, he does exactly that.
> *We're going upcountry to cut*
> *our tree this morning,* he tells me.

He likes his coffee black, and
I pour it that way. "Sounds like
a nice family outing," I say.

> *It's been our tradition for years.*
> *Unfortunately, it appears Deirdre*
> *doesn't care to participate anymore.*
> *She refuses to get out of bed.*

I could tell him about her late arrival,
the state she was in. That she's likely
hungover. But all I say is, "I'm sorry."

> *Yeah. Me too. We had high hopes*
> *for her. Now . . . I really don't know.*
> *Anyway, take the day for yourself.*

232

# There's an Undercurrent

To his words. Some sort of implied
warning? Deirdre is here. They will
be gone most of the day. Maybe I
should make myself scarce? Barricade
myself in my room? Other than
bothering Angel, I have few choices.

The Jorgensens leave midmorning,
with Otto and Milo barking in the back
of their truck and Sophie waving
out the window. I go to my room, turn
on the TV, find an old holiday movie,
*It's a Wonderful Life.* Things are just

starting to go to hell for poor Jimmy
Stewart when yet another pickup—
this one totally old and gross and smoking—
skids up the driveway, braking wildly
in the gravel. The driver lays on the horn.
                              *Hey, honey, I'm home.*

He slams out of the truck, wobbles
across the drive to the back door and
would come right on in, except it's locked.
He rattles the handle, pushes the buzzer,
and when he gets no reaction, starts
pounding on the screen. What do I do?

# Now He Crabs Sideways

Along the back of the house until
he reaches Deirdre's bedroom window.

He seems to understand it's hers, because
he's a little more gentle when he raps

on the glass. I'm pretty sure he's drunk—
before noon!—but he's aware enough,

it seems, to realize he shouldn't poke
his hand through the shiny surface.

Apparently, Deirdre knows the guy
because the window opens and her face

appears, he leans into it, kissing
in a most obscene way, leading with

his extended tongue. Disgusting. But
she seems happy enough, kissing him

back like he's home from the war
or something. He doesn't look much

like a soldier, though. His hair is long
and sloppy, and his clothes look like

he slept in them. Probably in his truck.
I expect him to crawl over the sill,

into her room. Instead, she pushes
him back, says a few words, then

disappears inside, shutting the window
behind her. The guy backtracks to

his wretched vehicle, waits beneath
the steering wheel, hands drumming

against it to some obnoxious music
played way too loudly. I can hear it

from here, at least the thump of the bass.
Looks like Deirdre's going somewhere. No

wonder she didn't want to traipse
through the woods with her family.

After several long minutes, Deirdre exits
the house carrying a big hunting rifle.

Pretty sure deer season closed weeks
ago. Wonder what they're hunting.

# I Try to Finish the Movie

But I've seen it before and I know how
it ends—happily ever after. Right. Besides,
I keep picturing Deirdre carrying that rifle.
It reminds me of a certain day, tracking
a cougar who'd been killing Aunt J's cattle.

I wasn't paying attention, and would have
been that big cat's dinner, if not for Ethan,
who was watching out for me. He wasted
the mountain lion with a single shot.

That memory might be painful enough,
except the same cougar also interrupted
a very intimate moment with Ethan.
We had ridden our horses for miles,
stopped to rest them beside a stream.

Ethan and I kicked back on a bamboo mat
while Paprika and the black grazed.
We still hadn't made love, but our
kissing had brought us close, and that

day was no exception. So far away
from prying eyes, it brought us closer
yet. Drowning in love, I didn't want
to wait anymore, and promised him
I was ready to take that giant step.

I close my eyes, remember how his hands
felt as they lifted my shirt up over my head,
tenderly stroked my exposed skin. But just
as I thought the moment was at hand, a snarl
spooked the horses. Ethan and I jumped to our

feet, coming face-to-face with that big cat. We
had no guns that day. Our only weapons—
a big tree branch and a couple of solid rocks—
were enough to drive off the cougar.

The horses had headed for home, so Ethan
and I had to walk for miles until Aunt J
came bumping up the road in the old Ford
pickup and . . . Oh, Aunt J. I miss you.
And Ethan. Who am I without you?

Tears flow down my face and I don't try
to stop them. I haven't cried for Ethan
in weeks. I'm sick of pretending to be
strong. I'm weak. I'm lonely. I'm nobody.

On the TV, Jimmy Stewart's life has
been put back into order. His friends
have come to his rescue and he cries
happy tears. How Hollywood.
My tears are bitter. My tears are real.

# The House Is Empty

I have it all to myself, and while sometimes
that might please me, right now the silence
just makes me lonelier still. I have yet to buy

a jacket, something I must do very soon, so
I grab the thick sweatshirt I purchased last time
Angel took me into town. It proves almost

enough to fight the damp chill outside. I start
to walk, fast, faster, trying to outdistance
my omnipresent ghosts. As I get close to

the horse barn, I hear Angel and Javier
yelling. Hooves against wood. Whinnying.
Curiosity draws me to take a closer look.

The men are inside one of the stalls. A small
Appaloosa horse—or big pony—is backed
against one wall, kicking it rhythmically.

> Angel: *¡Maldita sea!*
>> Javier: *¡Cabrón!*

"What's up?" I ask, and when the men turn,
the filly comes toward them, nipping. "Careful!
Looks like the little horse has got the better of you."

Angel shakes his head. *This little horse*
*doesn't know what's good for her. We're*
*just trying to move her into the paddock*

*so she can run. We can't put her out in*
*the pasture or we'd never catch her again.*
*She's a fast one. And mean, too. The mister*

*believes Sophie will ride her. I say no one*
*will. This mare has a mind of her own.*
*Not such a good Christmas present.*

The filly whinnies again, and when her eyes
go wild, the white sclera becomes obvious.
"She's just scared. Aren't you, *caballito*?"

The caballito—little horse—pricks her ears
toward my voice. "There, there." She quiets
noticeably. "Want me to try?" I ask Angel.

He glances at Javier, who has no opinion.
*What do you know about horses?*

"I don't know a lot, but maybe enough.
Besides, I can't do a whole lot worse
than the two of you, now can I?"

# They Think I'm Crazy

And I probably am, but something inside
tells me the filly wants to trust someone.

Maybe even me. "Did she come with a name?
Can't keep calling her 'Caballito.' Too generic."

> *The man who brought her called her Shoshone.*
> *He said she's a wild horse from Nevada.*

"Shoshone," I repeat, moving slowly
toward her. When her ears go back, I stop.

"Can you give us a little room, please?"
Javier exits the stall completely. Angel

stands by the gate. Backup, I'm guessing.
Challenging the filly won't work. I need

to find a way into her heart. "Okay, pretty
girl," I say softly. "I know you're scared.

But you'll like the paddock." One step
in her direction. Two. She watches warily,

and when I see her tense, I stop. Drop
my eyes. No challenge here. She relaxes

and I start again. This will take patience.
"I've got all day, Shoshone." She paws

at straw on the stall floor. "Maybe we need
to buy her affection. A carrot, or grain?"

Angel translates and Javier disappears.
I stand very still, talking quietly to her,

letting her get used to my presence. Javier
returns with a bucket of molasses-sweetened

oats. When he comes into the stall with it,
Shoshone starts kicking the wall again.

"I've got a feeling she might have been
mistreated by a man," I say. "Vayase."

He goes, and I'm happy for the little Spanish
I've learned since I've been here. I hold

the bucket in front of me, letting her sniff
its rich scent. She nickers. "Ah. I think

we've found your Achilles' heel." Now
she comes to me, nose reaching toward

the oats and nuzzling into the bucket.
"There's a good girl. Don't be afraid.

No one here's going to hurt you." As
she starts to munch, I find a small well

of courage, reach my hand out to stroke
her neck. She doesn't protest, so I rub

all the way down to her shoulder,
no problem. All she does is chew grain.

I take a step backward. Shoshone follows
the bucket. Another. All good. "Lead rope?"

When we reach the gate, one slow step
at a time, Angel slips a nylon strap into

my free hand, and I manage to clip it
on the ring without so much as a nip.

> *How'd you do that?* demands Angel.
> *These girls, they stick together, eh?*

"It's all about trust," I say, running
my palm down the length of her nose.

# She Trusts Me or Likes the Grain

Enough to let me lead her to the paddock.
When I turn her loose, she kicks up her heels,
puts her nose in the air, and starts a fast trot
around the enclosure. Once she feels secure,
she breaks into a canter. Around and around.

> Angel and I watch her from outside
> the fence. *Where'd you learn about horses?*

I stay as vague as possible. "I lived
on a ranch in eastern Nevada for a while.
My aunt said I had a natural way with
animals." Aunt. Too much. I shut up,
and while we stand here, saying nothing,

> the filly trots up to us, snorting steam
> through the fence. *I think she likes you.*

I smile. "I think she likes the oats.
But I don't think she's intrinsically
mean. And I believe, with some work,
one day Sophie could ride her. What she
really needs is the Horse Whisperer."

> Shoshone's lips twitch into my outstretched
> palm. *I think you are the Horse Whisperer.*

## Journal Entry, December 7

*Memories hang like icicles—heavy and*
*sharp and dangerous. Memories, and regrets.*
*This would have been my first Christmas*
*with Ethan. We should be decorating*
*our tree, watching old holiday movies,*
*wrapping presents for each other that*
*we couldn't afford, but somehow did.*

*There are also memories in the barn,*
*but these, at least, are bittersweet—*
*the sound of horses eating; the smell*
*of their sweat, mixed with leather*
*and hay; the feel of bone beneath*
*muscle and hide. These remind me*
*of some of my very best days with Ethan.*

*And now there is something hopeful.*
*A wild Appaloosa named Shoshone.*
*Angel called her mean, but love and care*
*can turn that around. I'm sure of it.*
*I only hope I can be part of that. I need*
*something positive in my life, something*
*to look forward to, or how can I go on?*

*Jackie*
# Hope

Is holiday glitter. It shines
in the glass of ornaments, the foil
of tinsel, the trill of carolers.
And its source, Christians claim,

is

the iconic baby whose birthday
we celebrate on December 25.
The one represented by plastic
dolls lying in fiberglass crèches. It's

hard

to reconcile incense, gold, and myrrh
with Walmart cologne and candles;
dollar-store puzzles, yo-yos, and
coffee mugs. It's impossible

to

inhale the perfume of winter
forest beneath the branches
of even the most realistic
artificial trees. And you won't

find

the awe of angels
encased in a Hallmark card.

# Mom Got Her Way

We'll be in the new house
a few days before Christmas.

She made a deal with the devil.
His name is Josiah McCain.

> His end: expediting our move
> with money and his influence;
>
> pushing the insurance company
> to settle ASAP, filing everything
>
> that needed filing to accomplish
> that; ditto all the paperwork
>
> required by the State of Nevada
> so Mom can collect Dad's retirement;
>
> and topping it all off, the oh-so-murky
> (if you ask me) "emotional support."
>
> > Mom's end: over-the-top verbal
> > gratitude for his emotional support;
> >
> > choosing Caleb McCain's welfare
> > over her daughter's. That would be me.

# In a Way, I Understand

For the first time in her life,
Mom is sitting pretty. Our old
house is almost paid for. Once
it sells, she can pay off the loan
on the new one, a distressed
property bought relatively cheap.

The insurance payment has already
arrived, and that minivan I predicted
ended up being a Chevy Tahoe. It wasn't
straight from the factory, but as used
SUVs go, it was a steal—a one-owner
with only 32,000 original miles.

Dad's retirement hasn't kicked in
yet, but it will, and meanwhile there's
money in the bank. Mom is used to
living frugally, so she won't rush out
and spend it unnecessarily. And once
those monthly checks start coming,

she won't have to worry about
income. Especially as her kids grow
up and move out, one by one. So, yes,
I guess I get why she sealed her deal
with the devil. But I will always
resent being the price tag.

# If Mom Misses Dad

There isn't much evidence of it.
No cuddling up with one of his shirts.
No midnight tears against her pillow.

Right now we're busily packing,
and when I happen past her bedroom
door, I can see her cleaning out the closet.

Her clothes, she packs neatly into boxes.
Dad's clothes get stuffed into trash bags,
which she'll cart off to some thrift store.

> *Someone bring me a couple more
> boxes,* she calls. *And newspaper.*
> For the fragile stuff, such as it is.

A few pictures hanging on the walls.
Her mostly empty jewelry box, a gift
from Dad, though he never filled it.

Teddie ambles up, carrying a box
so big she can hardly see over it.
"I'll take that. How's the packing?"

> *Easy peasy. Not like we have so
> much to pack. 'Lyssa found a dead
> mouse in the closet, though. It stinked.*

"Stunk," I correct. "Oh, well. Hopefully
we won't have any mice in the new
house. Maybe we can even get a cat."

I take the box in to Mom. "Here you
go." She looks up from the picture
she's holding and her eyes are glittery.

> *What about the newspaper? I have
> to take care of this.* The photo is framed
> in a crystal heart. It's Mom and Dad

and baby Pattyn, just the three
of them, before life became too, too
complicated. "You okay, Mom?"

> *Of course! I just need the paper.
> Can you please get it for me?*
> Sitting pretty or not, a crack has

appeared in her not-so-invincible
armor. "Sure, Mom. I'll be right
back." I go after the requested packing

material. I'm glad she's crying. But
who are her tears for—Dad? Pattyn?
The three of them, pre the rest of us?

# Teddie Was Right

There wasn't all that much to pack
in the little room we've shared for
so long. I send her and 'Lyssa to help
our younger sisters box up their clothes
and few toys—well-used hand-me-downs.

I double-check all our drawers, and
accidentally push my dresser toward
the wall. The base bumps against
something underneath it. When I lift
it to investigate, I discover a hollow
space, and there I find the packaging

that once held Pattyn's gun, a 10mm
semiautomatic, according to the label.
The pistol isn't inside it, of course. But
neither is the box empty. When I lift
the lid, I find a cell phone. Where did

this come from? None of us have ever
owned a cell. (Well, except Mom,
who now has an iPhone, not that
she knows how to use it.) Obviously,
this is Pattyn's. But how did she get
it, and why is it here? The battery

250

is completely dead. I reach for
the charger, notice a piece of paper
folded neatly beneath it. It's a letter
in Pattyn's perfect handwriting:

> I hope you find this, Jackie. But to
> whoever happens to be reading this,
> I want you to know I love all of you.
> Even Dad, although right now I plan
> to kill him and everyone who made
> Ethan die. No one had the right to
> destroy my world. Why, God, why?
>
> Aunt J, thank you for allowing me
> a glimpse of happiness. And if you can
> find it in your heart, please forgive
> me for stealing your own. I'm so,
> so sorry. I'm scared to call you,
> scared to know what happened to
> Ethan, what happened with Kevin.
>
> I don't know what I'll do after

The note ends there, abruptly.
She must have been interrupted.

# Curiosity Insists

I charge the phone. I use the outlet
behind my bed, which won't get moved
until tomorrow. Pattyn wasn't home
long after she got out of the hospital,
body recovered from the accident,
psyche not so much. Dad kicked her

to the curb almost immediately, but
she must have had enough time to take
the gun and leave the phone in its place.
I reread the note. Wonder who else
she thought about shooting. I can't
believe that was Pattyn. Insane.

Of course, I've felt more than a little
crazy myself in the last few weeks.
It's not so bad during the day anymore. School has grounded me some,
and it's good to know I've got at least
a few people in my corner. Nighttime

is still bad. I wake up, hyperventilating,
and as I reach that space just before
dreams fade into the reality of darkness,
the flashes come, nightmare leftovers.
I know it's my brain searching for
answers—the ones I'm not sure I want.

# A Thin Scream

Yanks me from my reverie.
*No! Mine!*

It's Georgia.
Now Teddie argues,
*I have to pack it.*

And Georgia repeats,
*No! Mine!*

Invoking Samuel's
You-Woke-Me-from-My-Nap
*mewl.*

Mom yells,
*Someone please get the baby.*
'Lyssa responds,
*On my way.*

This is our house.
Sometimes a madhouse,
even when we're not all whipped
up by the chaos of moving.

I wade straight into the middle
of the maelstrom. Mom is in
the kitchen making peanut butter
sandwiches. 'Lyssa brings her Samuel,

diaper freshly changed. He's hungry,
too. "I'll feed the kids," I tell Mom.

# Nothing New

Except everything, and the tension
is building. Some men from church

will bring their trucks tomorrow after
sacrament meeting. Tomorrow night

we'll sleep in different bedrooms.
Meanwhile, there's still a lot left to

put into boxes. I start pulling pots and
pans from the cupboard. "'Lyssa, Teddie.

Come help me. Mom? Should we pack
all this or do you need it for dinner?"

> She looks away from Samuel, who
> is nursing. *I was thinking we might*
>
> *order pizza for dinner. We've worked*
> *so hard today. What do you think?*

"Pizza? You mean, like from the deli?"
We usually just do the frozen ones.

> *Yes, from the deli. We deserve a treat.*
> Nothing new, except everything.

# Case in Point

Driving to church in the Tahoe,
an eight-seater that we all fit into.
As the oldest, I get to ride shotgun,
in a bucket seat, no one close enough

to elbow me, with an unobstructed
view of the road, which is freshly
plowed. It snowed all night. "Looks
like we'll have a white Christmas."

> *I just hope the storm breaks for*
> *the move,* says Mom. *After that,*
> *let it snow! Wow, this road is slick.*
> *Thank goodness for the four-wheel drive.*

She's managed with two-wheel
drive for years, so whatever.
I'm having a hard time with her
newfound cheerfulness. Saccharine.

Right? I mean, she couldn't have
suddenly discovered happiness,
wrapped up inside Dad's life
insurance policy. Could she?

# I Endure

The usual three hours of song, prayer,
teaching, and testimony, hoping
the weather will hold. It does, and

our cadre of volunteers follows us
to the house we're about to desert.
When we arrive, there's a strange

       truck parked out in front, and who
       should be inside it but Gavin?
       When I step out of the Tahoe,

       he comes over, smiling. *You mentioned*
       *you'd be moving today. I thought*
       *maybe you could use some help?*

"Uh . . ." I might have told him
this was the day, but did I say when?
"How long have you been sitting here?"

       *I'm not sure. An hour? I figured*
       *you'd be back after church. It wasn't*
       *so bad. A little cold, but I've got a heater.*

Mom is gawking, so I introduce Gavin.
"He wants to help and waited all morning.
Is that okay?" How can she say no?

# I'm Very Happy

It's Gavin who moves my mattress
    and finds Pattyn's cell phone.
        He taps me on the shoulder.

    *Here. Don't think you want to leave*
        *this behind.* He can have no idea
            who it belongs to. Not even sure

how much he knows about my sister.
    He and I have talked about many
        things. But not her. Now I say,

"Thanks. Definitely wouldn't want
    to forget my phone." But that reminds
        me. When he carries the mattress to

his truck, I dive under the dresser,
    extract the 10mm carton before
        he can return for the box spring.

If he notices me shoving something
    into my backpack, he doesn't say
        so. And when I choose to stay behind

while the first load moves to the new
    house, ostensibly to babysit Samuel
        as he naps, no one else comments, either.

# With Everyone Gone

I sit on the floor, notice how much
lighter the carpet is where the sofa
and Dad's chair sat. Mom will have
to get Stanley Steemer out here or
something. The rug is seriously dirty.

Pattyn's cell has two numbers
programmed into it—Ethan's and
Aunt J's. There are messages here
from both of them. Ethan's has
the earliest date. I play it first.

> *Hi, baby. I'm running a little late,*
> *and there's a serious storm on*
> *the mountain, but I'm on my way*
> *to get you. Hang tight. I'll be there.*
> *The three of us will be okay. Promise.*

I never had the chance to hear
his voice before. It was a deep,
soft bass, overflowing with love for
her and the baby that would never
be. Oh, Patty, I'm so, so sorry.

I wish I could give them back to you!

# That Message

Came the same day as the accident.
Probably just hours before. Wonder
if she even got to hear it. The next,
from Aunt J, came several days later.

*Just calling to see how*
*you're holding up. I don't*
*know what to say. I can't*
*make things better. Please,*
*listen to me. You've always*
*got a place here. I've told you*
*that, but I want you to believe it.*

*You blame your father for this,*
*and his hand is heavy in it.*
*But some of the burden falls*
*on me. Forgive me for not*
*taking better care of you.*
*Forgive me for not being*
*stronger. Please call. There's*
*a lot of sadness here right now,*
*and more sadness over there.*
*Maybe we can help each*
*other through the sadness.*
*Kevin and I love you.*

# There Are Three More

All from Aunt J.

Message one:

> Want you to know we brought
> Ethan home. The funeral is
> Saturday. We wanted to wait
> for you to get out of the hospital.
> Can you make it? I'll come get you.

Message two:

> I called the house. Your mother
> said Stephen made you leave.
> Why haven't you called?
> You still have a room here.
> And Diego's missing Ethan
> something awful. He's wantin'
> a good run. We all need you.

Message three:

> Goddammit, girl, what have
> you done? What have you done?

The last isn't angry.

More like mystified.

# I Must Admit

To being a little mystified
myself. So many what-ifs.

What if she would have
begged to stay in Caliente,
where people loved her?

But I know the answer. Dad
never would have agreed.
He was not the type to lose
control over something—
someone—he considered his.

What if the road would have
been dry when Ethan picked
her up? Where would they be?

Living large in California, or
even living small but satisfied
because they had each other?

What if Pattyn had listened
to these messages? Did she?
Did she ignore them? What
if she would have listened,
gone back to Aunt J? What if
she never came looking for revenge?

# By Dinnertime

The old house is emptied
except for a few boxes.
"Please stay here," I say out loud.

> *Are you talking to me?*
> Gavin's voice flutters
> over my shoulder.

I turn, to find him very
close behind me. "No.
I'm talking to the ghosts."

> *Ah. And are there a lot of them?*
> He brushes a random strand
> of hair from my face. So gently.

I glance cautiously right and
left, but we seem to be alone.
"Enough of them. Too many."

> *My mom used to say that*
> *a kiss can silence ghosts.*
> *Wanna try?* He tips my chin,

brings his lips very close
to mine. Waits, patient as sunrise.
My answer doesn't require words.

# Gavin's Kiss

Is warm and yielding and so,
so sweet. No grasping. No pushing.

No insisting. Nothing but a gentle
hint of something just beyond friendship.

So why is my first reaction to jerk
away as if a rattlesnake just struck?

His eyes fill with hurt, and that melts
the ice veneer I've frozen around myself.

"Oh, God, I'm so sorry! It's just . . .
I—I've only kissed one guy before. . . ."

    *Caleb McCain,* he says with certainty.

"Yes. And then . . . I mean . . . that's all
I wanted. But he . . . he wouldn't stop.

I begged him to stop, but he was so strong,
and then, and then . . ." I'm not supposed to tell,

but I really need to confess to someone, and
the words escape my lips, "He raped me."

    Gavin rests a hand against my cheek. *I know.*

263

*Pattyn*
# The Word

"Escape"

can be defined as a short
vacation. An "I wanna get
away" for a little while.
A quaint detour that

can

carry you to places
unimagined. But what
often goes unsaid is that
unfamiliar territory can

be

far worse than the status
quo because when you have
no clue what's around
oppositional corners, you

just

can't know which way
to go. It's one thing to crave
a shot of adventure, a taste
of something new, and quite

another

to become immersed in
the extraordinary, where
you're not quite certain
if you're safe or stuck in

limbo.

# Stuck in Limbo

Can't go forward, because I see no
options. Can't turn back, because all
that's left in the past are memories.
The bad eclipse the good, and the horrible
are the ones I find most often, so I do
everything in my power to avoid yesterday.

I can't help but visit there sometimes,
and the driving factor is guilt. If not
for me, Ethan would be heading home
from college to spend Christmas with
Kevin and Aunt J in Caliente. I can see
him pull into the driveway, wave at Aunt

J standing at the door, a "welcome home"
smile stretched across her face. If not for
me, my sisters would be hoping this was
the day Dad would arrive with the Christmas
tree strapped to the roof of the Subaru,
branches grasping needles against the wind.

Why couldn't I have just taken the easy
way out, dropped down off that freeway
overpass in front of a speeding semi, or
put the 10mm in my mouth and pulled
the trigger? Jackie had it wrong. I may not
be afraid, but I definitely am a coward.

# If I Could Just Get Past

A certain flashback—walking into the shed,
seeing Dad pummeling Jackie; the way
he turned toward me, leisurely, like he had

all night, then grinning as if he'd expected
my arrival; his challenge, approaching
demand, that I just go ahead and do it;

Jackie's screaming, *Shoot! Kill him! Hurry!*;
the struggle to take the gun away, and then
the way it went off; watching the surprise

in Dad's eyes replaced by vacancy; the blood,
oh God, the blood. Every time that memory
attacks, it is just as fresh as before, and I

don't think it will ever fade or soften around
the edges. I think it will remain razor-wire
sharp, and every time I try to climb over,

it will slice me far beyond skin and flesh,
organ and bone, through the hollow space
inside, all the way into my soul. Some people

blunt such pain with dope or booze or
a dive into madness, but I don't have such
luxuries available to me. All I have is sleep.

# Even There

Nightmare faces haunt me sometimes.
I never know until they jump out and say

*boo.* On the days I work myself bone
weary, they don't bother me. Lately, I invest

a lot of physical labor in a pretty little
filly named Shoshone. I talked to the mister,

got his permission to work with her.
His initial reaction was surprise that

> she was so green. *That son of a bitch*
> *told me she was well broken. I should*
>
> *kick his ass, get my money back. Last*
> *thing we need around here is a liability.*

"But she's willing," I insisted. "She just
needs a caring hand. With work, I think

she'll be a good horse for Sophie." He wasn't
totally convinced, about the filly, or my ability

> to bring her around. *You can try, I guess.*
> *What have I got to lose, except patience?*

# She's Wary

Of men, that's for sure. Doesn't surprise
me much, the way they bring the wild
horses in off the range—driving them
from their homes with helicopters, running
them full speed across the playa, no worry
about the pregnant mares, or the foals
already born, who can barely keep up
on their spindly legs. The ones who survive
are funneled through shoots into holding

pens, the first fences they've ever known.
Some fight the wire, fail. Others suffer
cracked hooves or splintered shins or
severe dehydration. Maybe a quarter die
from the stampede, or are put down
due to "defects." The lucky ones travel
to adoption centers where more will
succumb, some people say, to broken
hearts, blood born to freedom.

Those with iron temperaments survive
long enough for sorting—the aged ship
straight to slaughter, while the young
and trainable might find strange homes.
Start to finish, it's a terrifying experience
for animals who've never known anything
but liberty. And this is their first taste of man.

# Shoshone's Journey Here

Is largely unknown. Some men broker
sales, and who can say how they manage
the animals left in their care? With much
patience, I've gotten her to accept the halter
and lead fairly easily. But I'm so far from

an expert horseman, I have no idea where
to go from here. I wish I could talk to Aunt J.
She'd know what to do. Guess Shoshone and I
will have to educate each other. But not today,
and not for several more. It's Christmas Eve

and the Jorgensens have gifted their help
with a holiday vacation. It would look strange
if I didn't spend this time with Angel and "our"
family, and so we're going to Vacaville. Truthfully,
I almost feel like a relative. I spend every Sunday

with Angel, or at least at his little "hacienda."
With most of the other workers elsewhere for
the winter, his life is a little lonely, too, and
a friendship has taken seed. I know much more
about him than he does about me, of course,

but he doesn't seem to mind that. *When
you are ready to talk, I will listen,* he says.

# What I Know About Him

He's almost twenty-two.
Never been married.
Twice in love.
But not enough to weather circumstances.

He lived in Mexico two years.
Has lived in California for two decades.
Graduated high school.
Wanted college, but how could that ever be?

He used to follow the crops.
Moving was easier than coping.
But eventually he wanted roots, however shallow.
He is like his father in that.

He is, in his words, a bad Catholic.
Goes to Mass when he should.
Reports to confession regularly.
But sometimes it's just too hard to believe.

In that, we are alike.
It would be good to have faith.
A certainty of something beyond this life.
But for now, this is all we've got.

# What He Knows About Me

I
am
living
a
lie.

And
I
have
sisters.

# One Sunday Afternoon

We were alone in his living room,
sipping tequila. I know I shouldn't.
Drinking anything stronger than water
is a bad idea for me. But that day I felt
a bone-deep need to dull the edges.

I hadn't had more than a shot glass
full, but that's all it took. Outside, rain
spit against the windows. "Wish it
would snow. I love when it snows—
everything goes silent. Not like rain."

> Angel had imbibed quite a bit more,
> and his voice fuzzed. *Snow. No snow
> here.* He paused. Then, *Don' you miss
> home? Don' anyone there miss you?*
> His eyes remind me of marbles.

I looked deep into their black and
pewter swirls, searching for motive.
But there was no sign of deception.
Rather, they held nothing but affection,
which made evasion come harder.

"I miss home, yes, but not what I left
behind. My sisters might miss me a little.
But they're better off with me gone."

# It Stung

To say that out loud. My eyes smarted,
but no way would I let myself cry, so I

changed the subject instead. "Do you ever
miss Mexico? Do you ever want to go back?"

> *How can I miss what I don' remember?*
> *All I know is California. This is my home.*

"But what about your parents? Don't
they have family they want to see again?"

> He was quiet for a few thoughtful moments.
> *When I was little, Mamá and I followed*
>
> *Papá from farm to farm. Mi mamá, she*
> *worked the fields, too—strawberries and*
>
> *artichokes and lettuce. After Adriana came,*
> *Mama, she got very sick in her* . . . He pointed
>
> to his stomach, and just below. *Her next baby*
> *die before it was born, and the next, and the next.*
>
> *Poison, the doctor say. The pesticides they spray.*
> *Mamá can no have more babies, and sus hijos—*

273

*her children—sleep beneath California*
*soil. She has more family here than in Mexico.*

He reached for the tequila, poured
himself a glass, offered another to me,

and for whatever reason I nodded. The buzz
felt good. He had opened a box of painful

memories. So when he pried gently,
*You have sisters? How many?* I rewarded

him with an accurate head count, though
I withheld their names and ages. And now,

as we swing through Sacramento for some
last-minute Christmas Walmart shopping,

Angel asks, *What about your sisters?*

Which yanks me out of my reverie.
"My sisters? What about them, what?"

*Won't they be sad without you there?*

It's nothing but the truth when I answer,
"It may be their happiest Christmas yet."

# He Shakes His Head

Not comprehending. But that's okay.
He already knows more than he should.
He whips into a parking space at the far
end of the Walmart lot. "Looks like a lot
of people procrastinated this year."

*Pro-cras-ti-nated? What is that word?*

"Oh. It means 'waited till the last minute.'
Like us. Hope the store isn't too picked
over. What would your mother and father
like?" We start across the very long stretch
of asphalt. The wind kicks up, nipping.

He reads my mind. *Something warm.*

I've never seen a store so crowded,
but the truth is, I've never gone shopping
the day before Christmas. The truth is,
I've never had disposable money to spend.
And I've never bought presents for anyone

but my family. My real family, although
the Medinas are a good approximation,
closest I'll get to family for a long while.
Maybe the closest I'll ever have again.

# It's Kind of Fun

Shopping for my pseudo-family.
Angel and I take separate carts, head
in opposite directions. For his mom,
I find a big, fluffy robe. On sale, it's only
twelve dollars. For Mr. Medina, a flannel
throw, in handsome blue-and-red plaid.

For María, a basket of soaps and lotions,
already wrapped in cellophane, tied with
a purple ribbon. A girly outfit for Teresa,
large enough for her to grow into, plus a gel
teething ring. She'll need that soon. Adriana
is harder. I want her gift to be special.

It takes some time, but finally I settle
on a leather satchel with plenty of room for
textbooks. Which leaves Angel. I've noticed
how he dresses up for Mass, and also how
worn his nice Sunday clothes have become.
I choose a sweater in forest green and a light

green chamois shirt to go under. They
take a chunk of my savings, but he's
become my lifeline. The wrapping paper
is cheap, at least, this close to Christmas.
I pass the toy aisle, notice a doll Georgia
would love. Turn away. Hurry on by.

276

# I Even Buy

A few things for myself. Two pairs
of jeans. A faux-cashmere sweater in
pale lavender. A heavy sweatshirt, denim
jacket. The roots of my hair are peeking

through, red against black. This time I
pick hair color that is dark coffee brown,
hoping when the auburn lifts it will look
less obvious. When I get to the checkout,

I notice Angel waiting against the wall
on the far side. The line is long, but as I get
close to the checker, I gesture for him to go
on ahead. "Meet you at the truck," I call.

> I don't want him to see his presents.
> I'm paying for my purchases when a small
> commotion begins nearby. *What the fuck
> is wrong with you? Forget your glasses?*

The voice is too familiar. Deirdre is just
over there, yelling at the elderly woman
behind the returns counter. Tears stream
down the lady's cheeks and she trembles.

# Deirdre's Boyfriend

And another, who looks to be his brother,
stand behind her, taunting the woman while
Deirdre spews obscenities in her face.

I want to help the woman, want to stop them.
But I can't draw attention to myself. Not here.
Not back at the ranch. Not anywhere.

It's okay. Here comes a manager. But
before he can reach them, some anonymous
guy steps between Deirdre and the returns lady.

        Almost everyone is staring as the man
        gets in Deirdre's face. *I don't know what
        your problem is, but take it somewhere else.*

Deirdre's boyfriend draws back his fist and
his brother steps forward, but the manager
stops them and I realize I should get out

of here now, before I somehow become a target.
I gather my shopping bags, turn toward
the opposite exit, escape into the December

day, and am halfway across the parking lot
when a police cruiser comes speeding
in my direction. Oh my God. What did I do?

I break out in goose bumps and winter
sweat and the blood rushes from my face.
I can't duck, can't reverse direction too quickly.

All I can do is keep walking toward the truck.
When the cops draw even, I chance a glance.
They don't even look at me as they whoosh

past, lights flashing and giving short siren
bursts to warn wayward Christmas shoppers
of their approach. They park right in front

of the store. Deirdre and friends. They're here
for them. Oh, jeez. The mister will have a heart
attack. But not over me. They're not here for me.

My own heart knocks loudly against
my chest and finding breath is a chore. One
foot in front of the other, I reach the pickup,

toss my packages on the seat, and climb in
after them. "Did you see . . . ?" I wheeze
at Angel. I gulp air. "Did you see who that was?"

> Angel is staring at the front of the store,
> where a bear-size cop has Deirdre against
> the cruiser. He shakes his head. *Muy mal.*

# Very Bad

Seems like an understatement.
But there's nothing we can do except
continue on our way. "What do you
think the mister will do?" I ask.

> Angel shrugs. *The mister, he talks*
> *rough. But inside, I think, he's soft.*
> *The missus is more hard. But she never*
> *gets angry at the girl, no matter what.*

The pale gray of winter mist settles
against the darker gray of the freeway,
a curtain of monotony. "Why does Deirdre
act like that? She seems . . . unstable."

> *Unstable?* Angel snorts. *Does that*
> *mean "crazy"? Some people are made*
> *to go crazy. Others come into the world*
> *that way. A few are born del diablo.*

Of the devil? "You mean born evil?
I'm not sure I believe that." But the mister
is kind enough, and the missus, though harsh,
isn't cruel. So, Deirdre? "Or maybe I do."

# Journal Entry, December 24

We saw on the news tonight that three
juveniles were arrested at a Sacramento
Walmart today. They didn't release
their names, but Angel and I were there.
It was Deirdre, her boyfriend, and his
brother. A search of their vehicle netted
two assault rifles; enough ammunition
to supply a small insurrection; an ounce
of marijuana; and a trace amount
of a substance known as bath salts.

It's called a designer drug, meaning
some mad-scientist chemists developed
the recipe, and from what I've read,
it makes people crazy. They commit
horrific acts while under its influence.
Is that what flips that switch in Deirdre—
the one that makes her do things like go
off on a poor old woman, just trying to
do her job? Or is there something else,
some intrinsic malevolence, embedded
in the deepest part of Deirdre's psyche?

Angel believes in an actual force doing
evil deeds in our world. Satan. And he
thinks some people are born expressly
to work side by side with the devil.

*Can someone be born evil? I never
thought so before, but now the idea
has taken root. Is "evil" really just
another name for some types of insanity?
When I had the luxury of a library
to borrow from, I read a lot. Mostly
fiction. But I went through a nonfiction
phase, and some of those books were
about serial killers. Yes, some of them
were mistreated as children, but others
had uneventful childhoods and no one
knew exactly why they went off the deep end.*

*The Columbine shooters were like that.
Average kids from average families, who
had no clue their sons were plotting mass
murder. The idea belonged solidly to Eric
Harris, and the word that psychologists
attached to him was "psychopath." Could
psychopathy be another name for "evil"?
Is it born completely in brain chemistry,
or could it, in fact, be the spawn of God's
nemesis, el diablo? Questions, questions.*

*Jackie*
# Questions

Life presents us with few enough
absolutes—things that cannot be
doubted. Even science deals in
theories,
which may or may not be proven,
depending on the outcome of
a series of perfectly controlled
experiments.
What's the point of demanding
definitive answers when swimming
a sea in constant flux and your
queries
ebb and flow with the moon-
driven tide? Surely certainties
are less vital to happiness than
beliefs,
which feed the heart, sustain
emotion. And though these may
change, revision-ready
chapters
in a memoir-in-progress,
they are necessary facets
of the overarching story arc
of living.

# Christmas Eve Morning

I wake up in a familiar bed, between
familiar sheets, and a familiar little
sister snoozes beside me. But that is
all that's familiar. This is not the room
I've slept in pretty much all my life.
The walls are dusty rose, not dirty yellow,

and light streams through an eastern
window frosted by overnight snow.
My old bedroom faced north and morning
came shawled in shadow. The brightness
is disorienting, but there is no fear beneath
the covers. This is new, and I think "new"

is good, or will be, once I finally get past
all the baggage associated with what went
before. There are no ghosts in the hallway
here, at least none that belong to me. No
memories hang like smoke in the living
room or kitchen. And we left the shed

back at the old house. It still needs to be
emptied. We ran out of time yesterday.
But here we have a big garage and a pantry
to keep our stores. Mom says that solid
reminder of the worst of times can stay
behind. We see eye to eye on that, anyway.

# Quiet Envelops the House

As far as I can tell, everyone else is still
asleep, so I allow myself the luxury of
lying here, thoughts tumbling against
my pillow. Firmly ensconced in the when

and where of today, I stray back into
yesterday and recollections of a kiss
that frightened me, one I pulled away
from. I remember the sadness in Gavin's eyes,

how my explanation blunted his upset,
how he already knew my reasons. He coaxed
me into his arms, whispered into my hair.
*I know you've been hurt, Jackie. But I want*

*to fix that. I want to make you happy.*
This time when his lips touched mine
in warm invitation, I kissed back, refused
to pull away until we were literally

breathless. My heart stuttered wildly, not
because I was afraid, but rather because
this was what I'd been dreaming of. Yet,
when I opened my mouth, out slipped, "Why?"

# He Didn't Hesitate

*Because I care about you.*

That was hard to understand.
Still is. No one has ever really
cared about me. I mean, yes,
my sisters, to a degree. Pattyn,
especially. But not like this.

Lying here, cozy and safe,
I want to believe him. But trust
is something I'm afraid to give.
And that's what I told him.

> *That's okay. Trust takes time,*
> *I get that. There's no hurry.*

It was so confusing. Still is.
I'm a sophomore; he's a senior.
I have no friends; he has plenty.
I am clueless; he's sophisticated.
And that's what I told him.

> *Don't sell yourself short. There's*
> *something very special about you.*
> *You might not know it, but I do.*

# I Shut My Mouth

Afraid I'd somehow sputter whatever
words would break the spell he was under.
That must be it. Witchcraft or wizardry.

But who would bother to craft a spell
benefiting me? Beside me, Davie snores
softly. We don't usually sleep together,

but last night she was scared to be in
a strange, new room, so she crawled into
bed next to me. I wanted to tell her I am

no match for the boogeyman. But she
has faith in me. I am also teetering on
unfamiliar ground. Can I ever believe

in Gavin the way Davie believes in me?
Am I a fool for even wanting to try?
My body has mostly knitted itself back

together. As for my psyche, I'm not sure
it was ever completely healthy. Dysfunction
defines this family. Can you walk away from that?

I have to stop overthinking, accept the gift
Gavin has offered me, even if it's only
a fleeting taste of something brand-new.

# Joy

And now I've thought the word,
      the carol infiltrates my tentative brain.
            *Joy to the world! The Lord is come.*

At least, that's what we celebrate
      tomorrow. Meanwhile, it's up to me
            to create a little Christmas Eve joy

in the kitchen. I sneak out of bed,
      let Davie enjoy her pastel morning
            dreams, cover my red flannel pajamas

with a threadbare navy-blue robe,
      pad down the hall—longer and better
            carpeted than our old one—to see

what I can find in the not-quite-
      organized-yet cupboards. Everything's
            still pretty much a mess. Mom says

the old "place for everything and
      everything in its place" rule can wait
            a day or two. But as I root around

for pancake mix and a bowl to put it in,
      I see the need for order. An hour later,
            I've created that, if not an abundance of joy.

# Eventually, the House Stirs

The slow build of noise is familiar:

> Samuel cries.
> Mom shushes.
> 'Lyssa moans.
> Roberta whines.
> Teddie giggles.
> Davie yells, *Jackie, where did you go?*

"In the kitchen," I call. "You do want
breakfast, don't you?" Now the usual

morning parade begins. What's different
is we have three bathrooms. The one by

the laundry room is tiny, but that extra
toilet is worship-worthy, especially this

time of day. I've already used it, making way
for whoever waits in the hall. One reason

I've always gotten up early was to pee
before the line began to form. Now it will

be two lines and, in a pinch, someone
can use Mom's. Talk about small miracles.

# This Christmas

Is an abundance of small miracles.

New used house.
    New used car.
       New used furniture.
Bigger kitchen.
    Roomier legroom.
       Extra closet space.

There are bigger miracles, too.

More optimism.
    More cheerfulness.
       More ho-ho-ho spirit.
Less stress.
    Less tension.
       Less fear.

And all because of the biggest miracle of all.

Dad is gone
    and he won't be
       coming back.

# I Have the Girls

Settled at the table, chattering around
mouthfuls of pancakes, when Mom
finally makes an appearance. She puts

Samuel in his infant seat, comes into
the kitchen and, when she reaches for
a glass, notices I've put things right.

> *Did you do this, Jackie, or did Santa*
> *send his elves? No, they must be too busy*
> *this day, of all days. Thank you, honey.*

She hasn't spoken so kindly to me
in weeks. Not since *that* night. I say,
"You're welcome," but search for some

> ulterior motive. I'm sure it will surface
> soon enough. And of course, it does.
> *After breakfast, we need to do a couple*

> *of things. The shed has to be boxed up. I*
> *thought I could leave that to you while*
> *I go to the store and stock up. The fridge*

> *looks pretty pathetic. Can't do Christmas*
> *dinner like that, can we? Oh, I should*
> *mention we're having guests tomorrow.*

# We've Never Had Guests

For Christmas dinner. There's barely
enough room at the table for us. Of course,
the head chair is conspicuously empty.
Still . . . "Guests? Like who?" But I intuit
the answer even before she offers it.

> *Josiah. And Caleb, of course. They were*
> *planning to go out to a restaurant. I told*
> *Josiah that was just silly. He's been so*
> *good to us and all. They'll be here at four.*

I do my best not to yell, but my voice
rises steadily as I respond, "You seriously
expect me to share Christmas dinner with
Caleb McCain? Or any meal, for that matter?
You don't mean it. Tell me you don't mean it!"

> The table quiets, and the girls look at us
> anxiously. Mom forces her voice very low.
> *Caleb made a mistake, Jackie, and so did*
> *you. Let it drop. And grow up, would you?*

"I was forced to grow up a long time ago,
Mother. In fact, I really have to wonder who
the adult is here, not to mention the parent.
A real parent would understand what she has
just asked of her daughter. Obviously, you don't."

# Her Eyes Are Vacant

No understanding. No concern. No affection.
She doesn't even bother to respond. "I'll get
dressed," I tell her. She's not going to change
her mind, so again I'll just have to deal with it.

Outside, snow comes down in gentle flurries.
I choose a heavy sweatshirt. The shed is unheated,
and promises to be cold inside. Mom wants me
to empty those shelves, yet another sign of her

indifference to my feelings. I've avoided
that place completely, detoured widely around
whenever I had to walk by it. I'm certain
ghosts inhabit that space, wisps of smoke

left over from life fires within, I'm just not
sure whose. But what does it matter? Maybe
they'll respect me for being there. Maybe they'll
enjoy sharing time with me. Maybe one of them

is a little piece of my soul that escaped and
stayed behind. Despair claws at me suddenly.
I am not afraid of ghosts—remnants of a past
already waded through. It's the future I fear.

# While I Wait for Mom

I straighten the drawers of my dresser.
Its contents were unpacked hurriedly,
haphazardly. They'll be messy again
soon enough, but for now, everything
in its place. A sudden strange vibration
draws my attention. The cell phone—
once Pattyn's, now mine. I've told no one
about it, except for one person. "Hello?"

     *Hey. How's it going?* Gavin would
     undoubtedly be surprised to know
     I've never talked on a cell before.

"Uh, okay, I guess. . . ." But that's a lie,
isn't it? "Actually, things could be better.
Listen, can I call you back in a little while?"
I want the phone to stay secret, so don't dare
talk long. Guess I'll have to learn how to text.
"Gavin? I'm feeling better now. Thanks."

Feeling better, for no other reason than
because he called just to see how I am
today. Feeling better because I think
that means he really does care. Feeling
better because there might be a chance
someone wonderfully awesome cares.

# Mom Leaves 'Lyssa to Babysit

Straps Samuel into his car seat as I toss
a dozen boxes into the back of the SUV.
On the short, snowy drive to the old house,

> she gives me directions. *Obviously we*
> *can't get it all in one trip, but we definitely*
> *need the canned vegetables, fruit, and soups.*
>
> *Oh, and dig out the boxes of Christmas stuff.*
> *I plan to bring home a tree. Another little*
> *one this year, I'm afraid, but next year . . .*

She prattles on and on, zero comment
about our earlier run-in. It's as if it never
happened, and I'm pretty sure in her mind

it didn't. Finally, I can't take it anymore.
"You know . . . ," I interrupt. "I haven't
been inside the shed since that night."

> *Of course I know. I've been talking*
> *with Bishop Crandall. We decided*
> *you really need to face your demons,*
>
> *and since we're leaving the shed behind,*
> *this would be a good way for you to do it.*
> *It's kind of your last chance, you know?*

# Bishop Crandall, Psychologist

Except, he's not. Not even close.
"Hey, Mom, if you want to have me
psychoanalyzed, you should probably
use a professional psychologist, not
a financial planner." Not even actual

clergy. LDS hierarchy consists of
laypeople, not ministers. "Bishop"
is just a title borrowed from other,
older faiths. "But really, I'm sort
of surprised that you even pretend

to worry about my mental well-being.
I mean, you've obviously got plenty
to stress over without even taking
into consideration the welfare of one
of your many children. Especially me."

> *Jackie, how can you be so cruel?* Yay,
> I've elicited feigned hurt. *Of course
> I worry about you. Why do you think
> I'm asking you to do this? I want you
> to get over what happened that night.*

She turns into the driveway, pulls all
the way back to the shed. "Thanks, Mom.
I'm truly happy to think you might care."

# The Sarcasm Is Totally Lost on Her

She smiles. Looks at her watch. Tells me
  she'll be back around two. And I swear,
  though I've hinted as strongly as I could
that I'm afraid to go inside that shed

without someone strong by my side to help
  me through it, she drives away without so
  much as walking me to the door. I stand
shivering in the gathering storm, blinking

away dime-size snowflakes. The boxes
  start to grow wet at the edges, and I know
  if I don't at least get them out of the damp
they'll be useless for carrying jars. I open

the door. Stand back. One step forward.
  Turn on the light. Look down. Can't help it.
  Right there is where I last saw my father,
motionless in pooling blood. He's not there

now. And the only sign of leaked body
  fluids is the faint hint of a rust-colored
  specter. Someone determined to wipe
the cement clean of him almost succeeded.

# To His Credit, I Guess

Bishop Crandall didn't find it necessary
within his pseudo-psychology philosophy

to give that job to me. That demon I would
have refused to face. I toss the boxes over

the spot, step well across it myself, and
before I start off-loading jars from shelves,

locate two small plastic containers of dollar-
store ornaments and small rainbow-colored

lights. As I reach for them, I hear Dad's
voice, *Who the fuck wants white Christmas*

*lights?* I spin toward the door, but he's not
there. Still not. Never will be again. The air

in here is crypt-cold, but I'm sweating as if
it's summer. "Stop it, Jackie. You're freaking

yourself out." I say it loudly, and the sound
of my own voice seems foreign, quivery, like

an old woman's. It's stupid, but I don't think
I can do this. Still, I dump crumpled newspaper

from the boxes I brought, start wrapping jars,
half wishing the End Times we're stocking

this stuff up for would hurry up already. But
only if they're really the end, and not a pathway

to eternity. Forever is a very long time
to spend this alone. It's freezing in here,

and so quiet. Too quiet. And now a shadow
falls across the light streaming in through

the door. "Who's there?" I yell, but the silence
swallows my words. Footsteps. Are those

footsteps crunching through the snow
outside? I duck down behind the boxes

heaped on the floor. Hold my breath.
But it's nothing. It's nothing, right? "Okay,

Jackie, there's only one way to find out."
I grab a bottle off the top shelf, grasp it by

its skinny neck, stomp to the door, avoiding
the stain. But when I look outside, nothing.

# Stupid, That's What I Am

There's no one here, flesh or fleshless. I'm a raving
idiot. I look down at the bottle. Johnnie Walker
Black Label. Figures. One of Dad's leftovers.
Hmm. Would a quick sip give me a shot of courage?

I've never even considered tasting alcohol before.
The idea is quite un-Mormonly and suddenly very
appealing. I duck back inside the shed, twist the cap,
but it doesn't budge. Over on the workbench, a pair

of pliers gleams, as if it noticed my problem and
wants to help. "Thanks, pliers." Yeah, yeah, I'm
talking to myself. But, hey, someone should talk
to me. With the pliers' aid, I finally open the bottle.

The familiar smell almost knocks me over, and
that night comes rushing back at me, carried in
the cloying perfume of scotch whiskey. I don't
think I want to do this after all. But I recap and

stash the bottle in a canvas bag I find. Just in case.
I go back to packing, forcing myself to ignore
the creak of wind in the rafters and the lean
of shadows. The real danger here isn't ghosts.

# It's Me

Or something inside me, and that thought
        gives me pause. Surely Bishop Crandall's
        poor counseling can't have netted an aha

moment. I keep wrapping jars, putting
        them inside boxes until every carton is full.
        Mom still isn't back, so I call Gavin, who

        picks up on the first ring. When I tell
                him where I am, he says, *Holy shit.*
                *You're not there all by yourself, are you?*

        When I tell him I am, and Mom's reasoning,
                not to mention the conspiracy behind it,
                he says, *You're kidding, right? Uh, Jackie . . .*

"Nope, not kidding." And then when
        I tell him it gets even better, guess who's
        coming to Christmas dinner tomorrow,

        the far side of our conversation grinds
                to a complete halt. *Wait. What? How*
                *could your mother put you through that?*

        When I repeat her advice—to let it drop,
                move on and please just grow up now—
                he asks, *What time did you say dinner was?*

# I'm Pretty Sure He Wouldn't Dare

But it's kind of fun to consider
        as I start stacking the boxes close

to the door. Mom should be here
        any minute. A sudden gust sends

a sheet of snow snapping into my face
        and I jerk back away from the door,

step squarely on the stain I've so
        carefully avoided. I can't help but

notice the vague human outline,
        and unreasonably, I bend to trace

it with one finger. *Snap!* It's almost
        like an electric jolt to my brain. I look

up, the way I did that night when
        Pattyn came through the door. *Snap!*

She yells at Dad, *Get off her!* Dad
        laughs. I scream. Dad laughs louder.

Pattyn backs away. Dad follows.
        And then . . . The memory fades to black.

*Pattyn*

# Memory Holds On

To some holidays more
tenaciously than others. Even
to my poor messed-up family,

                    Christmas

was always special, though
usually in more of a "silent night"
way than "up on the rooftop."
One of my favorite recollections

                    is

sitting cross-legged on the living
room floor, drinking cocoa while
Dad recited "The Night Before
Christmas," something he

                    never

did after the third or fourth
daughter came along, so that
was a very long time ago.
Even then, that was not

                    an ordinary

event. Dad, sober and caring,
caught up in nostalgia and
sharing a remembrance of his
own childhood? No, that was
an amazing, extraordinary

                    day.

# This Christmas Is Extraordinary, Too

For very different reasons. Reasons bound
up in sweet Christmases before. Ones full
of family. I have no family now, except

for the one I don't really belong to, no
matter how hard they try to make me feel
at home. And they are trying. Angel even

> insisted I sleep in his bed last night.
> *I am used to strange beds, or no beds*
> *at all. The sofa is good enough for me.*

His parents celebrate a combination
of American and Mexican traditions.
For instance, dinner will be turkey

tamales. María, Adriana, and Mrs. Medina
worked for hours yesterday, mixing masa
and soaking corn husks to wrap around it.

I watched, fascinated, helped when I could,
but they were much more efficient than I,
who had never even imagined it done.

So many things left to learn, if given
the time and opportunity. Unbelievably,
I'm starting to want both more and more.

304

# I'm Growing Immune

To the pain. Numb to the memories.
And that is both good and terrible.
Good, because each day is easier
to wade through and the nightmares
rarely rouse me from sleep. Terrible,
because I don't deserve the respite.

At midnight Mass last night, the joy
was palpable. Visceral. Overwhelming.
I've never known anything like it, not
on a personal level certainly, nor as part
of something bigger. The unshakable
belief in a savior whose mission is to invite

our evils unto himself, suffer for us, die
so we never have to? I've heard the story
before, of course. But I've never latched on to
the philosophy behind it. Not where I come
from. Not in my home, or at sacrament
meetings. Not in seminary or Mutual.

I'm not sure I latched on to it last night,
either. But I definitely felt closer. If there's
the slimmest chance at some ultimate salvation
for Ethan, for our baby, maybe even for my father,
perhaps one day I can throw off the guilt. And
if there is, is salvation possible for me?

# How Dare I

Think of these things, lying here in
       the bed of a stranger, not so unfamiliar

anymore? It's very early Christmas
       morning, barely enough pewter light

through the window to assure me that
       daybreak has arrived. How many children

have already tiptoed to their trees to peek
       at the bounties Santa has left on his annual

pilgrimage? Who's up at home? Teddie,
       yes, and Georgia and 'Lyssa, and this year

they won't have to wait for Dad to crawl
       out of his Johnnie stupor. Jackie will have

to make breakfast. Mom only cooks when
       she must, and then it's basic stuff—oatmeal

or grilled cheese or hot dogs. But today
       the girls won't care. Something to warm

their tummies will do. It will be cold
       outside, but is there snow on the ground?

We always crossed our fingers, looked
            up at the sky, and asked out loud for a white

Christmas. Oh, how I wish I could be there
            this morning! But I can't, and this stupid

internal monologue is starting to depress me.
            This bed is a quagmire of useless longing.

I toss back the covers, throw on clothes,
            locate the Walmart bags, and begin to

wrap. No small children live in this house,
            and baby Teresa, next door, is still too

little to care about holiday ceremony.
            I don't expect anyone else to wake before

midmorning. How often do they get days
            off and the chance to sleep in late? Too bad

my body clock won't let me do the same,
            but I was cursed with an early-riser gene.

So, when the presents are in a cheerful pile,
            I grab my jacket. Might as well take a walk.

# The Fog-Draped Fields

Are puddled, the recent rain impossible
to absorb. I can't see the Sierra from here,
but it must be beautiful beneath thick mounds
of snow frosting. I walk in that direction,

as if I might get a glimpse, though I know
that's impossible. When I tire from the weight
of homesickness, I turn around, and am surprised
to see Adriana coming toward me. We draw

> even, then she turns on one heel and we
> head back, shoulder to shoulder. *¿Cómo
> estás?* she asks, and it's awkward because
> she suspects the answer I won't articulate.

"I'm okay." I sigh, and that gives something
away. "I mean, I've been better. But I've been
a lot worse, too. Thank you—and your family—
for all you've done. Angel has been so good to me."

> She shrugs. *He likes having someone
> to talk to. That's what he says. I think
> he likes having a girl to talk to. But that
> he would never say. And so, your job is okay?*

# The Change of Subject

Is welcome. Small talk is easiest
when you have very little to say.
I tell her about the big house, and
little Sophie. About the missus, mister,
and my special project, Shoshone.

      Adriana says she's looking forward to
      returning to school after the semester
      break. Oh, and she heard from the Reno
      Fire Department regarding the application
      she turned in the day before we met on

the bus. The day before . . . Refocus.
"I didn't know that's why you were
in Reno." For whatever reason, we never
discussed how she happened to be there.
"What did they say?" I truly want to know,

      and my interest seems to make her happy.
      *They put me on the list for seasonal*
      *work. When school gets out, I'll fight*
      *fires in Nevada. For the summer.*
      *After that, who knows? But it's a start.*

# Aunt J

Used to say, *Life moves forward another*
*notch or two.* When the saying surfaces
inside my head, so do thoughts of Caliente.

I hope Aunt J and Kevin are sharing a warm
Christmas hearth, and a warmer Christmas bed.
Have they managed to creep out of mourning?

Is it possible to cast it completely away?
Adriana and I stop outside the trailer,
which leaks cheerful chatter, much of it

in Spanish. Next door, I hear Teresa cry,
hungry for breakfast. If I were home, that
would be Samuel, and the excited dialogue

would be in English. Otherwise, it's not
so very different. "Later, will you help me
do my hair?" I ask Adriana. We go inside,

tossing around ideas about a different style
to go with the new color. Warmth—mostly
the human kind—enfolds me as I join

the Medinas for coffee and pan dulce—sweet
bread. Fewer people crowd this table than
the one at home. But it holds no less love.

# After Breakfast

We open presents. There is no tree,
but otherwise this, too, feels familiar.

Mr. and Mrs. Medina are surprised
that I've brought them gifts, and now

they insist I call them by their given
names—Julio and Lucinda. I'm glad

I know their story—how they fell in love
as teenagers, married young, and started

a family, then came to this country, hoping
their children might have a better life.

How, once Lucinda became so ill, God
blessed Julio with an employer who offered

year-round work and a semipermanent home.
How Adriana was the last baby Lucinda would

carry to term. I'm not sure if they realize
Angel told me these things, but I'm grateful

that he did because I see how worry,
not time, has etched their faces so deeply.

# The Plaid Throw

Is draped over the sofa, and Lucinda wears
the pink robe like it's a mink coat. The other
presents have all been opened and exclaimed
over. I didn't expect anything, and so when
Angel brings one over to me, I'm stunned.

"Really? You didn't have to . . ."

*I wanted to. I looked all over. Open it.*

He sits beside me and watches as I carefully
pry the wrap. Inside are two DVDs—the Robert
Redford movie called *The Horse Whisperer.*
And a training video with the same name.
"Thank you!" I say, but that doesn't seem

like nearly enough, so I give him a hug.
The intimacy startles me, and in this moment
I realize that, other than a measly baby and
a squirmy three-year-old, I have had no
physical human contact in months.

I pull back and repeat, "Thank you."

His smile is genuine. *De nada.*

## Journal Entry, December 25

*I'm a mess. Totally confused. It's sort of
like my brain is split in two. Half contains
the overriding sadness that defines life
with Ethan excised, Aunt J erased, my father
dead. I always hoped Dad might discover love
for me. Now, even the slenderest chance
of that has been eradicated violently. All
because of me. Oh God, why couldn't I see
how I would condemn myself to an eternity
burning up, inside out, with a fever of guilt?*

*Then there's the other part of my brain.
The one that keeps insisting on grasping
at the tiny tendrils of happiness threatening
me with hope. I am maneuvering this surreal
world, wondering when I'll finally wake up
and accept that this is all an impossible dream.*

*What a Christmas. Turkey tamales. Pineapple
and brown sugar, too. A haircut and color
that make me look different. Older. Not bad,
I guess. Watching* The Horse Whisperer *with
my Mexican family. Talking late into the night
with Adriana and Angel, who asked why I came
to California instead of going back to eastern
Nevada. I told him I wanted to see the ocean
before I died. He nodded, as if he understood.*

*Jackie*
# The Brain

Is complicated circuitry—
a biological computer that gathers,
stores, and processes information
in a number of ways. But if that

gives

the impression that neurons and
glia are divorced from emotion,
it shouldn't. Scientists say the mind
and the brain work together. The more

you

try to understand that symbiosis,
the harder it becomes. Perception
leads to learning, leads to motivation.
Simple. But then you look at sleep,

a place

where the brain, you'd think, might
take a break. Wrong. Activity continues,
in differing waves, resynchronizing
the cortex. But what does that do

to

the psyche? Can slumber help
you work through a childhood trauma?
Do dreams sort out memories,
or are they only closets where monsters

hide?

# Christmas Arrives at Midnight

Sleep fights me tonight, but it has nothing
to do with expectation. I hear no tiny
hooves on the rooftop, no jolly old elf
crashing down the chimney—not that
we actually have one. No, what keeps
me awake is that snippet of time I still

can't grab hold of. It teases. Taunts.
Finally, I slip out of bed and into the cool
obsidian morning. I turn on the Christmas
tree lights, sit watching their muted pulse,
wondering what it is that's missing when
I try to re-create that night. I count the gifts

beneath the tree. Fifteen. The girls and I
each drew one name to shop for, plus we
chose a gift for Mom, another for Samuel.
Those eight we brought out before bed,
with great ceremony. "Santa" has brought
the other seven, one for each of us kids.

This is our tradition, except for two
things. Dad had always played the part
of Saint Nick. This year, it was Mom.
And there are no presents for Pattyn.
"Where are you?" The opaque darkness
swallows my whisper. "Where are you, Patty?"

# But I Hear No Answer

Intuit no intimation of her presence, close
or distant, and in this moment it strikes me
that she might have vanished forever—dead

or hidden or locked away. Forever. I want
to talk to Gavin more than anything right now.
But I don't dare dig the cell phone out of hiding.

I have to do something, though. There's lots
of prep work to be done for dinner. Maybe
I'll work on the pumpkin pie. Mom decreed

there will also be apple—Josiah McCain's
favorite. I think she should bake that one,
and I don't plan to share it. Once the pumpkin

is in the oven, I wash those dishes, put them
away, unload the ones from the dishwasher.
I look for something else to do, find it inside

the pantry—our new house has a pantry!—where
the cartons of jars from the shed are stacked. I start
unwrapping them, wipe them newsprint-free,

place them neatly on the shelves, like contents
together—peaches, pears, and fruit cocktail from
the first; soups, stews, and chili from the second.

The third holds pickles, tomatoes, and spaghetti
sauce. I pick up a jar, peel the paper away, start
to clean the newspaper grime, but it isn't ink

smearing the glass. I hold the jar up to the light,
peer closely at the tiny red spatters. Blood! And
bits of . . . flesh. Specks of Dad. I cough back

my scream, but the jar slips out of my hand,
shattering against the linoleum, spraying
canned tomatoes everywhere. Blended

in them somewhere are bloodstained slivers
of glass, and now there's vomit, too. I heave
and heave, until there's nothing left to heave

but air. Stomach cramping, tears cascading,
I sit, head on my knees, until the rank smell
of burning pie over puke yanks me to my feet.

Smoke puffs from the oven—the pumpkin's pyre.
I spend the next hour scrubbing the pantry
walls and floor, disposing of pie corpse,

and washing myself in the tiny bathroom
next to the laundry room. Merry Christmas,
Jackie, girly-girl. Merry Christmas, everyone.

# That Sets the Tone

For the day. Samuel wakes
up colicky, and no amount
of walking him quiets his
crying until he flat wears
himself out. We take turns
pacing as everyone opens

their presents, the ones from
each other first—Walmart
this year instead of the dollar
store. We're moving up
in the world. Still, we have
budgets. Crayons and coloring

books are quite popular.
Also Play-Doh and puzzles
and basic Barbies, plus one
generic outfit for each.
I get a poster from Georgia,
who drew my name—a fairy

     riding a unicorn. It's a little
     young, but so is Georgia,
     who's almost five. She looks
     up at me expectantly with huge
     doe eyes. *Like it, Jackie?*

"It's so pretty," I tell her.
"And the colors are perfect
to go in my new bedroom.
Thank you, honey." She puffs
me a pouty kiss, and that makes
me happy for the first time today.

Now we're ready for Santa's gifts.
He was a tad more generous
this year. There are legit board
games. A couple of baby dolls,
plus clothes. Generic. A set of
Laura Ingalls Wilders to be shared.

There's an art set for 'Lyssa,
who's always doodling and
wants to be a fashion designer.
Who would have guessed Mom
had an actual clue? My present

almost gets lost in the piles of
wrapping paper. It's an envelope,
and inside is a gift certificate
for a driver's training course.
This can't be real. It's too amazing.

# I Look Over at Mom

She smiles at the disbelief—shock, even—
that must register clearly in my eyes.

> *Santa reminded me you've been old enough
> to get your permit for months. You should
> learn to drive.* She leaves it stalled there.

I perceive an unspoken ulterior motive,
but hardly care. A driver's license is freedom,
and I turn sixteen in February. This is the best
gift, ever. "Thanks, Mom. Uh, I mean, please
thank Santa for me." Anticipation buzzes,

but the haze of euphoria dissipates almost
immediately as Samuel fires up his wailing
again, and Roberta and Davie start arguing
over who has whose Barbie. Rather than
officiate, I volunteer to work on dinner.

'Lyssa joins me and together we manage
all the cooking, including the apple pie.
I owe Mom. No one has even noticed
I lost one pumpkin pie. I replace it with
End Times supplies. If it all comes down
as they say it will, who'll care about pie?

# With Dinner Planned for Four O'Clock

The McCains arrive at three forty-five.
Mom invites them in, tells them to make
themselves comfortable, then pretends
the kitchen is all under her supervision.

She's done nothing for two hours but
"make herself presentable." I have to admit
a little makeup and some time with a curling
iron have done wonders for eliminating frump.

To her credit, she does set the table, while
Mr. McCain attempts small talk. I keep
my attention on the vegetables, but notice
how Caleb settles into Dad's chair, focuses

> on his cell phone without so much as a glance
> at a single one of us here. Suddenly, he says,
> *Bitch!* The girls giggle, Mom gasps, and when

> his father asks what's up with his language,
> he replies, *Tiffany says she's too busy to talk,*
> as if that's a perfectly fine excuse. He's a lout.

I call him that under my breath and 'Lyssa
asks, loudly enough to be heard, *What's a lout?*
And I can't help but burst out laughing,
all the while thinking how very much I hate him.

# Embarrassment Blossoms Red

In Mom's cheeks.
Mr. McCain ignores that,
and all the rest. Completely.
The kids go wash up for dinner.

But now I've drawn
Caleb's attention. He brings
his gaze level with mine, challenge
in his eyes. I force myself to not look away.

"Hope you're hungry. I made
something special for you."

I actually did make
an apple pie, and it's extra
special, so that wasn't a lie.

But I'm hoping
he takes it the wrong
way, finds the implied threat
that's, in fact, nothing more than that.

But Caleb is
the master of poise.
If he's worried, he doesn't let on.

*I'm starving. In fact,*
*could you move a little quicker?*
*It's past four, you know.*

Now my face
erupts a flush of heat,
matching Mom's exact
shade of scarlet, I'm sure.

Respond. Come on,
Jackie, say something.
Not sure how to. Or what.

Instead, 'Lyssa
and I start ferrying
food to the table and Mom
calls everyone to dinner.

She actually leaves
Josiah McCain sitting
as head of the table and that
bothers me on a visceral level.

I think I hate him
almost as much as
I hate his son.

# Still, We Manage

To make it through prayer and passing
plates before everything blows sky-high.
I watch how Caleb observes everyone
else taking bites of turkey, stuffing, and
potatoes before scarfing down his. That
gives me a minuscule sense of satisfaction.

Every time he finally puts food in his mouth,
I smile and wink, and I think that might
actually be working until I notice a subtle
exchange between him and 'Lyssa, who's
sitting beside me and across from him.
Oh my God. The jerkoff (did I just think

that?) is actually flirting with her in that
faux-suave way of his—the exact same moves
he used on me to make me feel like I was
someone special. He looks at her as if
she's the only person at the table, grinning
his handsome grin when she says anything

at all, as if he really cares what she has to say.
I might even be able to handle that, except
now she smiles back at him. She's thirteen,
and even more ignorant about his attention
than I was. I give her a solid sideways kick.
When she complains, he turns his smile on me.

I flash back to that night: *He comes to me,*
*tells me how pretty I am, how he can't help*
*but want to kiss me. I'm scared because*
*I've never kissed anyone before, but not scared*
*enough to say no. We're kissing. Kissing.*
*I like it a lot, and I'm growing warm in places*

*not talked about except in sex education.*
*But they don't tell you how just kissing can*
*make you want to do those things, even though*
*you know you can't—you're not ready yet.*
*And they don't tell you what to do when*
*you say no but he keeps saying it's okay,*

*that he only wants to make you feel good,*
*but you find out real fast he doesn't care*
*about you at all, only about himself. And*
*then . . . and then . . . it's pain and disgust*
*and that's all before what happens when*
*your father finds you. . . .* I pull back into

the moment, the turkey and dressing and
mashed potatoes, and I see my little sister,
only thirteen years old, flirting back with
the monster who would do the same thing
to her, and I yell, "Leave her alone, pervert!"
And just as the table reacts, the doorbell rings.

*Pattyn*
# This Moment

Defies expectation. You can
watch movies, documentaries,
study photos, and cobble together

                                dreams

of such things, but until you stand
on the brink, all doubt tossed aside,
wondering if you can trust your eyes,

                                visions

such as these seem impossible,
improbable at best. Is there, in
fact, an Everest? Until you

                                take

a trip to Nepal, look directly into
the face of the mountain, how can
you be sure? And if you

                                hold

fast to doubt, your passion
for truth will falter. Sparks of time
such as these might occur once

                                in

a lifetime. Blink, you miss
them. Close your eyes, the flame
dies down into an ash of

                                imagination.

# I'm Standing on the Fringe

Of the Pacific Ocean, just north of the Golden
        Gate Bridge. I expected it to be blue. But all
        I see, as far as my eyes can travel, is gray.
        Salt mist hangs heavily in the air, and seabirds

dive toward the breaks below the cliffs. Except
        for their squawks and the occasional bellow
        of a semi's horn above the almost imperceptible
        growl of traffic, the morning is quiet. Sleepy.

"Can we get closer?" I ask Angel. "I want to hear
        waves break." He nods, and we climb down
        the rocks to the beach. My shoes loosen stone
        as I walk, every foothold as tenuous as my life.

This is Adriana's gift to me, though it took
        Angel to make it happen. So it comes from
        him, too. It didn't take us long to get here
        from Vacaville, but it means so much to me.

I'd thank him again, but he pretty much told
        me to stop already. If he didn't want to be
        here with me, he would have turned east
        on the freeway. Instead, he brought me west.

# The Wind off the Water

Scratches my jacket. It's cold, but I'm not.
My feet dig into the sand, which is different
from the desert cushion at home. This is firmer.

Damper. Dirtier—too much evidence of human
disregard. But the ocean had nothing to do
with that. *Shhhhhh. Shhhhhh.* It whispers again

and again toward the shore, curling its soft
tongue against the beach, licking sand out,
and spitting it back as it has done for eons.

Time is encapsulated in these waves, and in
every drop of spray, a billion yesterdays misting
my hair. I find an odd comfort in that.

But there is also deception here, beneath the gentle
coaxing—a power beyond any earthly control.
This is not a place I would choose to swim.

Angel must feel it, too. He stands well back
from the water's edge, mostly watching me,
I think. I wave to let him know I'm going to walk

a little. He follows at a respectful distance,
but close enough to make me feel safe, and when
I finally turn around, he waits for me to reach him.

# We Find a Big Piece of Driftwood

Sit and say nothing for a while, but something
I've been thinking about finally spills out.

"If it wasn't for Adriana and you, I don't know
where I'd be. Maybe in a shelter, or sleeping

on the street somewhere, or . . . worse. I . . .
I'm just so grateful." I don't know why, but

I reach for his hand, slide my fingers between
his. "Without you I would be alone."

His fingers close gently over mine. His skin
is textured from work, softened with lotion,

and warm. So warm. *You don't have to be
alone. All men are not like your boyfriend.*

"My boyfriend?" Oh, the fictional one.
The truth is on the tip of my tongue, but I

don't dare confess, and it skitters off, a spider.
"I know." I squeeze his hand, then pull away.

"Thank you again, for showing me
the ocean. I'm ready to go if you are."

## Journal Entry, December 28

Back "home," if I can think of the ranch
that way. Back to work, which is welcome
enough, except for the atmosphere, which
is even more muted than usual because of
Deirdre's arrest. Mr. Jorgensen claims
he would have left her stewing behind
bars for a few days, but the missus insisted
they bail her out before Christmas Day.
She's confined to the house, and her usual
surliness has become borderline viciousness.
Everyone, even her father, goes out of their
way to stay out of her way. That includes me.

Sophie is majorly hyped up over her new toys—
a giant dollhouse, plus to-scale furniture
and a family of dolls—and her new "pony."
She says she has to wait until Sho'ne gets
"all broke," but that's okay 'cuz she loves
her so much. That makes me smile, and so
does the training video Angel gave me. I
really think I can do it. The method makes
perfect sense. I'll start back in tomorrow,
after Mass. I can hardly wait to work with
Shoshone. And to spend time with Angel.

*Jackie*
# Time

Is fickle, and rarely kind. When
you really don't want swift progression—
say, toward an appointment for a root
canal—you can't force today

to

postpone its relentless pursuit
of tomorrow. It simply won't slow
down. But in those tedious sections
of time you're anxious to

move

closer to—a party or a prom
or maybe just seeing someone
special again—time is determined
to tarry, teasing, and trying to push it

forward

faster is a losing proposition.
No use staring at the clock,
willing its cooperation. The second
hand spins at its own pace.

# What I'm Looking Forward To

Right now is New Year's Eve. Unbelievably,
        I've got an actual date. Not only that, but Mom
        sanctioned it. She thinks Gavin is a nice boy,

even if he isn't LDS. At this point, I think,
        she'll do just about anything to get her crazy
        daughter back on track. I came very close to

totally losing it at Christmas dinner, and
        I swear if Caleb McCain so much as glances
        in the direction of any of my sisters again,

I will go ballistic. I definitely might
        have, if Gavin hadn't rung the doorbell
        right then. The word "pervert" was barely

out of my mouth when the fortuitous
        interruption occurred. Fortuitous, because
        poor Mom was about to have a heart attack,

and I'm pretty sure apoplexy had already
        struck Josiah McCain. His face was ripe
        plum purple, and he was literally sputtering.

        It all rolled right off Caleb, though.
                *Takes a perv to know one,* he said. But
                it was swallowed up by the commotion.

# Teddie Ran to Answer the Door

*It's that boy,* she yelled. *The one from before.* Meaning the one who helped us move. *Jackie's friend.* Meaning she wondered if he was my boyfriend. And

so do I. It just seems so unreasonable. Why does he like me? In my limited experience, anything that seems too good to be true most definitely is.

I left Caleb with a scathing glare, went to the door. Gavin stood there in a very nice suit, holding two Christmasy bouquets. "What are you doing here?"

He winked and offered a conspiratorial grin. *I was hoping you might invite me to dinner. My mom* (meaning the one of his two who is still alive—that has not,

as yet, been discussed around here) *is a horrible cook. I figured you have to be better.* Just like that, everyone's mood improved. Well, except for Caleb's.

# Except for His

Because not only did I suddenly have
a staunch ally, but as it turned out, Gavin
was a real crowd-pleaser. Witty. Intelligent.
Charming. The last was lost on the totally
not charming McCains, but it impressed
the rest of us, especially Mom. I invited

Gavin in, and he handed me a dozen
red and white roses. *Merry Christmas.*
The tulips and lilies were for Mom.
*Hope you like Stargazers. They were
my mom's favorites.* The past tense
reference went unnoticed and without

comment. Mom never gets flowers, and
I think the gesture kind of overwhelmed
her. She blushed and sputtered about how
pretty they were and happily allowed Gavin
to share our table. When we brought out the pies,
the girls all picked pumpkin with whipped

cream, as I knew they would. As Mom cut
the apple, I nudged Gavin. "If I were you,
I'd go for the pumpkin. The apples were
a little, uh . . . sour." I winked at Caleb,
who skipped dessert. Wonder if he noticed
that the apple agreed just fine with his dad.

# The Upshot

Is I apparently have an official boyfriend.
Maybe. I hope so. I need something
positive in my life, and Gavin is that.

He's amazing in so many ways. I'm not
sure if what I feel for him is a whisper of love,
or a shout of like. But I think love should

grow from like. I fell too hard, too fast,
in what I thought was love for Caleb.
Looking back, that overwhelming rush

was complete infatuation, at least
for me. And for Caleb, it was nothing
but selfish lust. I know it isn't that for

Gavin, who is patient and a giver.
That he's willing to give his affection
to me is borderline overwhelming.

For New Year's Eve, he's taking me
out to dinner, then to a small get-together
at his house. Mom talked to Gavin's mother,

who let her know I'd be safely chaperoned.
Gavin spent Christmas with my family.
Only fair I spend New Year's Eve with his.

*Pattyn*
# A New Year

Is traditionally the time
you decide to alter
yourself, as if heartfelt

           desire

for transformation
arrives in the afterbirth
of January. Or

           is

it the death of another
year that makes us
reconsider

           the

future as we are?
Do we find within
December's folding an

           impetus

to grow? Or is it merely
impatience with the status
quo that creates a need

           for change?

# Another Year Succumbs

I think New Year's Eve, for most
people, is about looking forward.

What's ahead?
What's new?
What's better?

I want that, really I do, but all I can
see is what's happened just behind.

Who lived?
Who changed?
Who died?

The last question keeps pelting
me like baseball-size hail.

Who died?

Who died?

Who died?

And chasing right behind, the three-
letter word that I just can't escape from.

Why?

# As Per Our Agreement

Missus Jorgensen has called me to her
office to discuss my staying on here.
My trial period officially ends at midnight.

> *Sit down.* She points to the chair across
> the desk from her. *We've had a few hiccups,*
> *but for the most part, I think you've done*
> *very well. Sophie, of course, adores you.*

I nod. Remain quiet. Don't speak until
spoken to. Don't hiccup. So she straight-

> out says, *Craig and I have discussed it,*
> *and we'd like to keep you on, same terms,*
> *until June. Then we can renegotiate. Is that*
> *agreeable? I like your hair, by the way.*

The compliment comes out of left field, and
I blink. "Thank you. Yes, I'd like to stay."

> *Craig says you've been working with*
> *the little filly. I didn't realize your résumé*
> *included "horse trainer." How's she coming*
> *along? Javier says she's a handful.*

"She is." I can't help but smile. "But
she's very sweet, and she's learning."

*She's a knot head.* It's Deirdre, who stands
leaning against the door frame. *Might as
well put a bullet in her brain right now.*
She sneers, daring contradiction. I know

better, but the missus has plenty to say.
*This is a private conversation, Deirdre.
I'd be grateful if you could please find
something to do besides eavesdrop.*

Like what, Mother? You've got me
on house arrest. Besides, what can you
possibly have to say to the maid that
can't be said in front of me? Huh?

What an obnoxious twerp. Doesn't
she realize her mom is her only real ally?

At least, she was. She stands, walks
around the desk, and Deirdre shrinks
noticeably. *That's enough,* the missus
says. *I'm tired of your bullshit.*

Deirdre fades away into the other room,
a shadow beneath a thunderhead.

# When She's Gone, However

The missus's bravado falters and as
she passes, I notice the delicate trembling
of her hands. She's afraid of Deirdre, too.

> *I apologize. My daughter is going through*
> *a phase. I hear it's not uncommon.*

"It's okay," I say, though it isn't at all.
That girl is a stick of dynamite. With
a very short fuse. God help us all when

> she blows. *Okay, well, I take it you and*
> *Angel have plans for the evening?*

I nod, and it's weird, because it's true
that we do, something I would not
have anticipated before Christmas.

> *Leave dinner ready to heat, and take*
> *tomorrow off. Happy New Year, Patty.*

"Happy New Year to you and the family,"
I say. But what I mean is, I really hope
this isn't the year the TNT detonates.

# As Instructed

I prepare dinner—corned beef and cabbage—
leave it on very low heat in the Crock-Pot.
Mr. Jorgensen says they always have cabbage
on New Year's Eve because it signifies wealth
to come in the next twelve months. Some sort
of a family superstition, or at least a tradition.

Now I change into old jeans and a sweatshirt.
They're pretty beat up, but Shoshone won't care.
I only had an hour to work with her last Sunday.
Today, I've got three. As Monty Roberts—
the original Horse Whisperer—counsels,
patience is key to building the human-horse

relationship because that connection can't be
forced. It evolves out of mutual respect. I'm
really excited to try. The afternoon is brilliant
blue, just a few small puffs of white in the sky.
Otto and Milo follow me, hoping for a treat,
and I don't disappoint them. Shoshone hears

us coming, nickers a welcome—to me,
the dogs, or the grain she expects. She trusts
me enough to come willingly to the circular
training pen. This session is about true
respect building, and that must come from
both horse and trainer. Monty Roberts calls

it "joining up." It starts by sending her away
from me—facing her square and encouraging
her to canter around the pen, with the gentle slap
of a light line against the dirt behind her heels.
She loves to move, and she's beautiful doing it.
I turn her, canter her the opposite direction.

In theory, by telling her to go away from me,
eventually she'll want to know why, and ask
for my attention instead. I watch for the telltale
signs—turning an ear in my direction, listening
to my constant patter of praise; lowering her head,
a sign of submission; opening and closing her mouth.

After a while, I see those things. That Monty's
a genius. Maybe. I stop, turn my shoulders
forty-five degrees away. She halts too, studying
me. I turn toward her, eyes lowered (no challenge),
inviting her in. Unbelievably, she reaches her nose
toward me, asking for attention. I stroke her face

in reward, turn away again, and take three steps
forward. She follows. I stop. She stops, near.
"What a good girl you are, Shoshone. What a good,
good girl." Now I walk her around the ring, no rope
attached, no grain bucket to track, just her desire
for my approval. Shoshone and I are joined up.

# In His Videos

Monty Roberts has done this and progressed
to putting a saddle and rider on an unbroken
horse. But he's the expert. I'm new to this,
afraid to push Shoshone too hard, too fast.

Before the session is over, however, I do
have her standing, untethered, while I run
my hands all over her body—neck, legs,
rump, belly, even her flanks, which are

a horse's tender spot. I've even got her
picking up her feet for me, an important
motion because you must inspect equine
hooves for stones, not to mention shoeing

them. It can be dangerous with a skittish
horse, and Shoshone's willingness makes
me believe we've accomplished actual
bonding. "Next time, we try the saddle."

> *Next time, I think you will go to*
> *the hospital.* Angel, it seems, has been
> watching, camouflaged by the mottled
> shade of the barn. *But what I see is good.*

"It's all about building trust," I say, but
now he's got me thinking. "Come here.
I want to see something." He hesitates, and I
cajole, "What's the matter? Don't you trust me?"

He comes through the gate and I instruct
him to move slowly. The filly's ears cock
backward. "Wait." He stops and I soothe,
"It's okay, Shoshone." Her right ear flicks

back toward me. "Okay, again, only talk
to her. Tell her she's a good, good girl."
He does, and I keep chanting the mantra,
too. Her ears move independently, one in

his direction, the other in mine. I hold the lead
rope, prepared to drop it quickly if I must.
This can't become a fight, or we'll lose
what we've gained. I run my hand down

her nose, along her neck, and even though
Angel is very close now, she relaxes. "Keep
talking to her, but now I want you to touch
her, gently, like the scared baby she is."

# He Speaks Equus

I suspected he did. Shoshone drops her head,
the bow of submission, and now both of us
are telling her what a very good girl she is.

       *Maybe there will be no hospital.* He smiles,
       and as his own tension dissolves, we have
       become a threesome. *But this is fast, no?*

"Not as fast as the Horse Whisperer,
but he's had a lot more practice. Give me
time. Give me time." Shoshone stands

calmly between us, and I feel more hopeful
than ever that I can help her become a good
horse for Sophie. Or someone, anyway. "Let's

see how she goes back to her stall." I keep
the lead slack, and Shoshone cooperates
completely, walking with her face planted

between our shoulders, nostrils blowing
warm steam into the failing afternoon light.
Angel opens the gate to her stall, and she follows

me inside. "It's going to be a good year,
isn't it, girl? For you, and for me." It's the first
time I've dared think it. And why should I?

## Journal Entry, January 1

*Is it even possible to live out your life*
*pretending to be someone you're not?*
*You always get caught in the end, don't*
*you? Seems so to me. So how do I look*
*forward, always expecting the past to*
*tackle me from behind? How do I hope?*
*How do I dream? And how could I ever*
*consider sharing a dream with someone?*

*Last night might have been magical,*
*an escape into some fantasy land where*
*love might again be possible one day.*
*Angel and I were a bit heady over our*
*success with the filly. We shared a simple*
*supper and, since it was New Year's Eve,*
*a little tequila. This lovely warmth began*
*to creep from my stomach, through my*
*body. Angel was his usual sweet, gentle*
*self. His question, I know, came from*
*a pure place, and his desire to help me.*
Tell me about your boyfriend, *he said.*

*And I started to talk about Ethan, how*
*I fell for him the first time I saw him and*
*how he changed my life. I almost said for*
*the better, then realized Angel wanted to*
*know about the one I'm supposed to be*

*hiding from. The one who beat me, made me
run, forced me to consider life away from
my family, because that was the only way
I could be safe. And the sudden need to quit
living this lie—one of the lies—almost
overcame all caution. I shut my mouth,
but he understood that I conceal secrets
inside, things that I wanted to tell him,
struggled to hold on to instead. Angel knows
too much, and suspects a whole lot more.*

*Because if I tell him about Ethan, admit
he was my only boyfriend ever, spill the story
about how he died, I'd have to tell the rest.
Otherwise, why am I here? And to get to
the heart of that, I'd have to confess about
Dad, how I'm running away, not from some
crazy mean boyfriend, but from prison. I
don't want to go there anymore. Not ever.
Not even if I deserve it. I've found a shard
of light shimmering in the darkness and I
don't want that tiny glimmer to snuff out.*

*But if I admit any facet of the truth, the rest
will beg disclosure, too, one card falling
against the rest until the house of lies tumbles,
leaving me helpless at the bottom of the pile.*

*Jackie*
# The Truth

Some people say confession
is a balm for the hurting soul. But
if the offending information takes
cover within the soul, extricating it

can

get tricky. Do you start with
a scalpel, carve thin slices into
your consciousness, hope for a slow
leak of psyche? Would a quick

rip

be more efficient, or would snippets
of reality then slip away into forever?
And once your very essence lies
opened and exposed, how do

you

protect it from those who would
do you harm? Self-preservation
is the heart of deception, and once
you crack the carapace, pry it

apart,

the truth you've allowed to escape
becomes uncontainable. Unstoppable.
You'd better be good with that.

# Stroke of Midnight

The New Year arrives with a kiss.
Gavin holds my face in his cupped
palms, covers my mouth gently with
his soft, warm lips. It's luscious, and
it lasts a long time, though we know
others can see us. Finally, he draws

back. *Happy New Year, Jackie.* All
around us, others are kissing, and lifting
their glasses, toasting the future. This—
everything about this—is totally new,
completely foreign. I've never even
stayed up this late, except maybe covertly,

hidden by blankets, before. "Happy New
Year, Gavin." To be invited into this
gathering, merge with the love so evident
in this room, is unbelievable, and I am
grateful. Gavin and I are the youngest
people here, though there are a few

not so much older. Mostly, though,
they're Beatrice's friends. Gavin's mom
is in her late forties, and I guess if I were
to describe her, I'd say she's handsome,
though her eyes wear sorrow in their creased
corners, and the silver tipping her spiked

hair betrays her age. Still, she is outgoing,
warm, and laughs easily at the jokes being
passed around as freely as the champagne,
which doesn't smell nearly as bad as scotch.
It's been offered, but I've declined. There's
at least a little Mormon left inside, although

that piece of me isn't any more bothered
by the openly gay couples here than
the openly heterosexual. They intermingle
effortlessly, everyone friends here, and
I love the energy. One pair definitely stands
out, mostly because the woman is probably

in her early twenties and statuesque, with
striking red hair against flawless white
skin. The man whose arm she clings to
is about three times her age, eight inches
shorter and totally bald. Curiosity gnaws,
and I nudge Gavin. "Who are they?"

>    *That's Barnard Willoughby. He produces*
>    *casino shows. I'm not sure who she is, but*
>    *my guess is she stars in one of his revues.*
>    *She has star quality, don't you think?* He
>    delivers the last sentence with a fair amount
>    of sarcasm. Then adds, *My mom is his boss.*

# His Mom Is General Manager

At one of the big downtown Reno casinos.
His other mom—the one whose photos
pretty the hallway walls—wrote for
the local newspaper. They met, Gavin
explained, when Annette covered a story

about Beatrice being the casino's first
female exec. "So it was love at first sight?"
I asked, sure that's how every such story goes.

> He laughed. *Not even close. Mom Bea*
> *was kind of condescending toward*
> *femmes at the time. Mom Ann thought*
> *Bea was a stuck-up dyke. Wisely,*
> *didn't include that in the story.*

I knew what a dyke was, vaguely,
anyway. But femmes? I figured it was
important, so I went ahead and asked.

> *You know, femme, as in "feminine." Mom*
> *Ann was girly, you know? Mom Bea, not*
> *so much. Eventually, they ran into each*
> *other again. That time, for whatever reason,*
> *something clicked. Love can take you by surprise.*

# Love Surprised Them

For twenty-three years. Then, death
    did. Though Beatrice seems content
    enough—happy, even—among friends,

her eyes are haunted, her laughter
    hollow. I don't know if everyone
    notices. Maybe only a stranger would.

A stranger like me. A little after
    twelve, Beatrice makes her way over
    to Gavin and me. She takes my hand

    with cool marble fingers. *I gave
        your mother my word that Gavin
        would have you home by twelve thirty.*

    *It was wonderful to meet you, and
        I do hope we'll be seeing more of you.
        If Gavin has his way, I think we might.*

I see Gavin blush, feel myself do
    the same. But for once it's a good
    blush. "I hope so, too." And I really do.

# The Roads Are Plowed

But icy. Gavin navigates them
carefully, and I feel safe with him
in the driver's seat. I feel safe with
him, period, and that's a good thing.

> *So how did you like the party?*

"It was great. I probably shouldn't
tell you this because you'll know what
a total loser I am, but I've never been
to a real party. Only the church kind."

> *Wow, that's kind of weird. But it
> doesn't make you a loser, only . . .
> overprotected, maybe?* He reaches
> for my hand, which makes me feel

vaguely better about being a loser.
"Good thing you're so charming,
or I probably wouldn't have gotten
to a real party for another fifteen years."

> He laughs. *I practiced my charming
> especially for your mom. And speaking
> of moms, what did you think of mine?*

"Are you kidding? She's amazing."

*Glad you think so. Some people
are a little put off by her, uh, edge.*

"You mean because she's a strong
woman? But she has to be, doesn't
she? No, I like that. And her."

*Good. I was kind of worried, since
your church is so staunchly antigay.*

I could tell him it's not, but that
would be a lie. "Aren't all churches?"

*Some hold stronger views than others.*

"Look. I don't like some things about
my church. That's one of them. In fact,
I have a half brother I don't even know,
because he's gay and Dad disowned him."

*That's awful. But now . . . I mean,
it's not too late to build a relationship.*

"I know. I've been thinking about
it since I saw Douglas at Dad's funeral.
I'm not sure how Mom would react.
But I'm definitely considering it."

# We Pull into the Driveway

At twelve twenty-nine, approximately,
depending on the clock. Close enough.

Gavin held my hand almost the whole
way home and now I don't want him

to let go. I love the suede texture
of his skin, the comfort of his fingers

interlocked with mine. "I'm supposed to
finish boxing up the shed on Friday.

Don't suppose you'd agree to come over
and help?" Mom wants it finished before

school starts again next week. Despite
everything—Christmas Eve, tonight—I

>               expect him to find some excuse to say no.
>               What he says instead is, *Do you think*
>
>               *I'd let you do that alone? Of course I'll*
>               *help. What time should I pick you up?*

"Mom will drop me off on her way to
take Samuel in for his checkup. Meet me

there around noon, okay?" Why tell Mom
he's coming to help? Less information

is probably prudent. "Thank you for tonight."
I hope for one final kiss, and Gavin does not

disappoint me. This one is even better than
the ring-in-the-New-Year kiss earlier, doubtless

because there are no eyes to pry here, and it
doesn't end with a gentle amen, but rather

it keeps building beyond breathless, and
when I have to pull back to draw in air,

his lips move like a whisper down, down
to the pulse in my neck. They stop there,

> rest against the steady tempo. *I've never
> said this to anyone before, and I'm scared*
>
> *right now, afraid you'll bolt, but I can't not
> say it, so here goes. I think I love you, Jackie.*

# It's a Lifetime Movie Moment

Except it's real, and I need to know
it's really real, and it doesn't feel
that way because this is insane. Who
in their right mind could love me?

I know the right response is something
close to reciprocal, but "insane" is
the word that has stuck in my head,
so instead I reply, "Are you crazy?"

> He brings his lips up against my chin,
> stares me straight in the eye. *I've been
> called worse things, so if you're trying
> to insult me, you've got a long way to go.*

His words wash sensuously against
my skin. I wish I could find the perfect
return sentiment, but giving voice
to my feelings is not something I know

how to do. "I . . ." He waits. Patiently.
He's a spectacular waiter. Silence
bloats the minuscule space between us,
until there's really only one thing to say.

"Oh, Gavin, I think I love you, too."

# In a Bodice Ripper

(Yeah, yeah, I've read a few, "sexy" being
preferable to "sappy"), this is where the cute
(no, hunky . . . yeah, hunky) leading man

literally sweeps the innocent (or *is* she?) heroine
off her feet, carries her into the bedroom
(or barn, or IHOP, and c'mon, what if she's

allergic to artificial maple-flavored corn syrup?),
and has his way (or maybe, if you read between
the lines, *her* way) with her. But this is neither

Lifetime nor Harlequin. This is some strange
unnamed reality show starring (impossibly)
Gavin and me. Which means our clothes stay

on and he makes no move to have his way
with me. Instead, he gives me one more lovely
kiss, walks me to the door, gifts me with yet

> one more. *I'll see you at noon. If anything*
> *changes, you've got my number. Love you.*
> *Sweet dreams.* He walks back to his car,

and I watch him go, wondering what I
could have possibly done to deserve him,
or the way I feel right now—like I have wings.

# I Fly

Through the deep space of velvet
black morning, toward the rising sun,
knowing I dare not travel too closely
to the burgeoning light. Morning looms,
infusing my dreams with warnings.

You
are
infected.

You
are
quarantined.

You
are
banished.

You
are
exiled.

You
are
damned.

I wake, sweating dread, as if the thing
that has been chasing me is nipping
at my heels. Yet it still denies revelation
unless I accept confrontation. And I know
what I fear is meeting the devil's eyes.

*Pattyn*

# The Devil's Eyes

Are deceptive. Just more
of his lies. They appear as
shallow pools. But succumb
to temptation and dive in,

                              you

discover they're bottomless,
shoreless seas. No way
to escape, your only choice
is swim or float, and if you

                              lose

all hope of rescue, down
you sink, inhaling brimstone
water. That's what he's waiting
for—the quick shed of

                              faith

as your lungs fill and you see
that theories about eternity
do not include guarantees.
And if eternal life exists,

                              in

which direction do you go
to find it? Perhaps forever
is only there in that ocean,
and not in some mythical

                              heaven.

# I Try Not to Think About Heaven

Or cheerful things like everlasting
damnation. It's all way too confusing,
not to mention depressing. I gave up
believing in the three-kingdom Mormon
fantasy way back when I decided my fate
should lie in my own hands, and not be up
to some possible future LDS husband.

Any contract for eternal life should be
strictly between the good Lord and me.
If it doesn't work that way, I opt out.

I'm not sure about the Catholic version,
either, or Methodist or Baptist or any
other. The basic concept seems simple
enough. Believe, ask for forgiveness
for your sins, and ye shall enter. I know
Ethan believed. He told me so, that night
we spent beneath the stars, on the cattle drive.

He said he saw God everywhere,
heard him sighing through the junipers,
smelled him raining life down on the desert.
He asked if I could feel God in the way
he kissed me the very first time. That memory

will haunt me the rest of my days,
and maybe for eternity, too, if there
is such a thing. Do I have a chance
at it? Did Ethan? Yes, he believed, but
did he ask forgiveness for his sins before . . .
Is that, in fact, a prerequisite? And was
what we were together, what happened

between us, and what that created, sin?
Is love that deep and true and perfect
ever really sinful? Too many questions
without any answers until my earthly
experience ends. As for me, I've asked
for forgiveness more times than I can
remember. Do some sins—murder, for

instance—require more entreaties than
others? Are some sins unforgivable?
Do one or two simply disqualify you?
Harder even to get to is belief. I'd given
up on it until Ethan mostly convinced
me otherwise. But I'm not sure again.

Where is God in my life now?
Where is his hand in what I've done?
Where is his hand in what I've become?

# Who Knows?

Maybe he is here somewhere.
      Maybe he led me here for a purpose
      I haven't yet recognized. Maybe this
      was always meant to be my mission.

And maybe that's all just a crock.
      At this point, all that matters is making
      it through another day. Right now
      that means changing sheets. I've

finished the master bedroom bed,
      replacing red satin with lavender
      flannel, at the missus's request. Sophie
      will sleep with Cinderella for the next

few days. Now it's Deirdre's room.
      She isn't in here at the moment.
      She and her parents are meeting with
      her attorney. I'm a little uncomfortable

changing her sheets, which could
      have just about anything on them.
      I've seen her disgusting boyfriend.
      I strip them carefully, touching only

the very edges, toss them in the laundry
basket, make the bed with crisp, red
percale, bend to pick up the dirties
to take to the washer. I straighten,

accidentally bump into Deirdre's
computer desk. The jolt wakes
her sleeping iMac, and the giant
screen lights up. I can't help but

notice what's there, and a chill
slithers up my spine. Why would
anyone offer step-by-step directions
for making a pipe bomb? And why

would someone want to know
how? And the biggest question
of all—what do I do with this
information? Do I mention it to

her parents, risk putting myself
squarely in her sights? She couldn't
actually be planning to build one.
But then again, what if she is?

# I Go About My Day

Laundry.
Dusting.
Vacuuming.
Mindless activities.

Good thing, because my mind
is pretty busy elsewhere. I wish
I hadn't seen that stupid article.

But I did. And now dizzying
possibilities are spinning in my head.

By the time the Jorgensens return,
I still have no clue what to do, but now
with the missus home to watch Sophie,

I have a couple of free hours until
I have to make dinner. I'll go crazy

in my room, so I think I'll work with
Shoshone. In the tack room, I find
a small English saddle and pad. I take

them to the training ring first, then
go for the filly, who seems happy
enough to see me and comes along
eagerly. Hope she feels the same way

when we're finished. Before I try
anything new, we repeat the things
we did last time. No problem at all.
Now I let her see the pad, and rub it

gently over her body. She snorts and
chews and twitches away as I slip it
up over her back. "No worries, girl,

it won't hurt you," I soothe. I slide it
off, go through the exercise again and

again, until she trusts the thing won't
hurt her and stands quietly. Now for
the real test. The saddle is light, but

it's the most weight the filly has ever
had on her back. "Easy. Easy." I keep

talking as we play this new game, and
though her ears go back at the strange
leather beast, she doesn't move until

I bring the girth up under her belly
and start to buckle it. She tells me
she doesn't care for the pressure
with a solid crow-hop or two.

# As Monty Roberts Would Say

"That's okay. It's your first time
and all. You're allowed to worry."

I calm her long enough to make sure
the saddle is buckled snugly. Don't

want it to slip sideways. Then I let her
loose for a canter around the ring,

using the same "join up" technique
that worked last time. When I send

her away, she bucks a few times, but
not too hard, and not in a way that

threatens me. Before long, she slows
to a trot and signals her willingness

to let the saddle stay. When I turn
away, she comes into me quickly.

A low whistle on the far side of
the fence draws our attention. Today,

                    it's not Angel who's observing
                    us. It's the mister. *I'm impressed.*

I take hold of the lead rope, and
Shoshone politely comes along

with me to where Mr. Jorgensen
is standing. "She's going to be fine,"

I tell him honestly. "She's learning
to trust." He peers at me curiously.

> *Seems she's got a fine teacher.*
> *But who taught you to do that?*

I smile. "The Horse Whisperer.
It's a game, and patience is the key."

> Now he looks at me incredulously.
> *I don't think it's a game just anyone*

> *can win, patience or no patience.*
> *You've got a gift.* He reaches tentatively

toward Shoshone, expecting her to show
teeth. But she lets him rub between

her eyes, like the good girl she is. "Enough
for today. Tomorrow, the bridle. And then . . ."

Now the mister grins. *Rider up?*
*That, I have to see. Let me know*

*before you try. I'll have my camera*
*ready.* He tromps off toward the near

orchard, where Angel is tossing hay
to the cattle. Not much grazing in winter.

I lead Shoshone back to her stall, take
off the saddle, and brush her the way

she likes, beaming at Mr. Jorgensen's
praise. As I finish up, Angel comes into

the barn. *The mister said you saddled*
*the filly. You will need help to do more.*

*Come find me first, okay?* Concern pulls
his face into a frown. It's totally cute.

"I will. I promise." I need to wash up
before dinner, but before I head for

the shower, "I need your advice." I tell
Angel what I saw on Deirdre's computer.

# His Initial Reaction

Is masculine dismissal. *No.*
*This is not a thing girls do.*
His surety makes me bristle.
If only he knew the things

women are capable of. "Girls
do lots of things, Angel. Some
even blow stuff up, especially
if their boyfriends encourage
them to. But maybe with
the arrest and all . . ."

He thinks a minute, shakes
his head. *I don't see worry*
*in the girl's eyes. All I see*
*there is anger. And that boy—*
*Jason Heckle—in him, I see hate.*
*But until there is more than*
*a picture on the computer . . .*

"There really is nothing to tell,
is there?" Still, there's an itch
inside me, something I can't quite
scratch. "I'll stay quiet for now.
The mister might believe me,
but the missus would probably
tell me to mind my own business."

# As I Turn Away

Angel stops me, laying a strong
hand on my arm and tugging
gently. Our eyes meet, and in

> his I find affection. It's at once
> comforting and disconcerting.
> *Be careful. I'm worried for you.*

I nod. I'm worried for me, too,
on several levels. "I'll stay out
of her way as much as I can."

It isn't until I'm turning the knob
on the back door that it hits. Why
is Angel worried about me?

I didn't even mention the way
Deirdre went off on Thanksgiving,
or how she and that Heckle boy

left with their guns one afternoon and
came back without any game I could
see, yet I had to clean a fair amount

of blood off Deirdre's jeans. That scared
me, but I said nothing. What does Angel
know? How frightened should I be?

# Whatever It Is

Staying away from Deirdre
is impossible. She accosts me
almost as soon as I walk through
the door, and since she hardly ever
appears on this side of the house,

no doubt it's me she's looking
for. *Were you in my room today?*

I choke back dread. "I changed
your sheets this morning."
I try not to look her in the eye,
because vileness is all too apparent
there. It's a losing battle, though.

*You messed with my computer.*
It's a straight-out accusation.

I doubt my explanation—which
happens to be completely true—
will satisfy her, but here goes.
"I didn't touch it. I bumped into
your desk accidentally, and—"

*What the fuck did you see?*
She suspects exactly what I saw.

But admitting it would be crazy.
"Nothing. I was carrying a big
basket of laundry." Let her worry.
Her expression tells me she can't
quite believe it. For some reason,

> she backs off. Sort of. *You'd better
> have more respect for my stuff.*

The implied "or else" gives me
the creeps, but I don't let her
see any reaction. She stomps off,
confrontation over, at least for now.
Maybe somewhere in her warped

little brain she thinks I'd have
busted her, had I actually seen
what was there. Maybe she's just
warning me not to. I don't know.
I am careful to lock my bedroom

door before I shed my horse-
dirtied clothes. There's something
comforting about the equine
smell clinging to my jeans. Good.
I need a little comfort right now.

## Journal Entry, January 3

Just when I start to feel a little
comfortable, and maybe even
a tiny bit hopeful—BAM! Reality
slams into me full speed ahead.
At the core of my current unease
is Trouble, with a capital D.

Today there are two little voices
inside my head. One is certain
I should inform the Jorgensens
their daughter is quite likely plotting
mayhem. The other keeps playing
devil's advocate. "The article
said many pipe bombs are built
strictly for amusement." Some fun.

One thing the two voices seem
to agree on is that I should pack
my stuff immediately and get out
of here ASAP. No, actually, what
they're saying is, "Before it's too
late." But they don't tell me what
that means, or offer ideas about
where I could possibly go. Anyway,
when you've survived straight-on
artillery fire, it's hard to be afraid
of scattered potshots in the distance.

*Jackie*
# Abuse Survivors

Stash the damage deep inside
their psyches. Problem is, sooner
or later, it eats its way out, acid.
Whatever the individual
experience,

eventually common symptoms
tend to appear. Anxiety.
The need for control.
Irrational, all-encompassing fear.
A slow

creep of anger snaking
their veins, filling their hearts
with venom. And unless
the poison can find safe
release,

premature death may be
preferable to the alternative—
brain cell by brain cell deterioration
fueled by a bottomless well
of pain.

# I Think I'm Losing It

Yesterday I was hanging
clothes in the closet. 'Lyssa
came up behind me and reached
for a jacket, bumping me from
behind and pushing me into
the dark space in front of me,

and all those sleeves seemed
to grab at me and I totally freaked.
It was like one of those dreams
where you're sure you're going
to die and your heart goes crazy
and you hyperventilate until
maybe you really are dying a little.

And you're just so scared for no
real reason at all except you just are.

Then this morning I went off on
Teddie for spilling her milk. I mean,
the floor was a mess and was a pain
to clean up, but it wasn't the major
catastrophe I made it out to be.

It isn't the first time some huge
swell of anger has burst out of me.

What's weird is, I don't always feel
it building up before the big blast.
I hate when the emotional shrapnel
blows toward one of the girls,
especially over something as stupid
as butterfingering a glass of milk.

But sometimes, to be perfectly
honest, I like how it feels to go off.

Some people have earned my rage.
Caleb, of course, and his father,
plus Bishop Crandall and everyone
else at church who encouraged
the cover-up. Problem is, they deserve
worse hurt than I could ever inflict
on them, which only makes me angrier.

I still haven't figured out how to chill
my taste for revenge and serve it up
later. But I will. Oh yes, I definitely will.

# When I Really Consider

The person who makes me
the absolute angriest, though,
it isn't any of them. It's Mom.

In fact, when I think about things,
I hate her single-mindedly.

I hate her for agreeing to
keep quiet about my rape.

I hate her for daring to say
it was partially my fault.

I hate her for never lifting a hand
to defend me against Dad's beatings.

I hate her for taking them herself,
and absolving him of blame.

I hate her for loving him in
spite of everything he did.

I hate her for loving him so much
more than she ever loved me.

# I Display

Other disturbing behaviors.
        I'm anxious, and more than
                a little OCD, another reason

I flare so easily when someone
        leaves clothes on the bathroom
                floor or a dirty dish on the counter.

That stuff never used to bother
        me, at least not so much that
                I'd yell about it. Sometimes, for no

discernable reason, big fists of fear
        grab hold and shake me to the core.
                I want to crawl into bed, put a pillow

over my head, and sleep for a long
        time. Except sleep brings terror-
                laced dreams, and dread of those

often keeps me churning the covers
        until exhaustion finally wins. Once
                in a while I duck imagined movement

at the corners of my eyes, some
        forever damaged part of me certain
                Dad's alive, and that he's come for me.

# Officially Messed Up

That's what I am, and there's something
else growing inside me, some new desire.

They say addictive tendencies are genetic.
If that's true, I'm pretty sure I inherited

a desire for escape through self-medication
from my father. I didn't realize it was part

of me until I ran out of my pain meds.
I liked the way both fear and anger melted

in the haze provided by a little pill. I loved
how the past dissolved in a muddied puddle

of the present. I adored how every tiny
hint of pain vanished into the ether,

cushioning my brain. But eventually,
every tablet was gone and I crashed

back down onto solid ground. It was
a tough landing. And now the only time

I feel close to okay is when I'm with
Gavin. But we can't always be together.

## We Will See Each Other

Later today, and that's good.
The waiting is killing me.
And I've got nothing to blunt
that. Thus, my current irritability.

What I keep thinking about
is that bottle of Johnnie Walker
I stashed. Granted, last time I
considered it, the smell alone

made me change my mind. If
I could just get past that, though,
could it make me feel even close
to the lovely way Percocet did?

The question whirls around inside
my head, along with words like "sin,"
"brainwashing," "strength of will,"
"alcoholism," and "programming."

I'm starting to get dizzy, so am
grateful for the distraction of
a vibration in my pocket—a text
message, and it has to be from Gavin.

It is. *RUNNING A LITTLE LATE.*
*HOPE THAT'S OKAY. PROMISE*
*YOU'LL WAIT? LOVE YOU.*
The last two words are almost

as good as Percocet. I answer,
I'LL WAIT. BUT PLEASE GET
THERE ASAP. LOVE YOU.
I still can't believe we're using

those two little words. I get this
crazy rush in my stomach. I wish
I had someone to tell! Oh, Patty.
I wish you were here. I wish things

were like they used to be, before
everything went all to hell. But no.
Because that would mean living
in the old house with Dad riding

roughshod over our lives, no
Ethan, no Gavin, no love possible
for either of us. I've actually found it.
Will you ever be able to find it again?

# Mom Drops Me Off

At our old house around
eleven fifteen. She doesn't
have to leave for a couple
of minutes, so we take a quick
look inside. It's so empty it
feels hollow. And it's cold.

>*Looks like they've shown
>the place quite a few times.
>That's encouraging, anyway.*
>She roots through the dozen
>or so real estate cards that

decorate the kitchen counter.
"I thought nothing is selling."

>Mom shrugs. *If the price
>is right, people are buying.
>Anyway, things turn around.
>They've sure one-eightied
>for us, don't you think?*

She's talking about for her,
but certain things have circled
toward the positive for me, too.
"Yes, actually, I do." That's
all I'm saying, at least for now.

# No Jinxing

And no making her wise to how
serious my relationship with Gavin
is becoming. Double fingers crossed.

We circle around back, to the shed.
*You'll be okay, right? You did fine
last time.* Nice of her to ask, even

though she's more worried about
me "facing my demons" than if I'll
freeze to death out here. "No problem."

She takes Samuel for his appointment,
leaves me with the same dozen cartons
I had last time. Same newspaper, too.

I open the door and a slant of morning
spotlights the silhouette on the floor.
The stain is only a few days older

than the last time it confronted me, so why
am I surprised that it hasn't faded more?
It should be gone by now. Vanished,

like the man it outlines. But maybe
it can't. Because, like him, it is stamped
so firmly into the cement of memory.

# It's Hard to Ignore

I toss the cartons over it, toward
the back of the shed. Circle
the offensive spot as widely

as I'm able to. At least all
the jars that were closest

to the scene of the crime—
those bearing telltale traces
of murder—are already gone.

    *Murder. Murder.*

The word repeats itself in Poe-
like fashion. I can picture a huge
black raven with morgue-slab eyes.

    *Murder. Murder.*

Jeez, man, quit. I try to focus
on Gavin's arrival while I reach
for a jar. There's something on it. . . .

    *Blood and bits of flesh.*

I jerk my hand back, but it's only
some speck of dirt. Okay! Enough!

# I Zip My Jacket

Up my neck, trying to fight
the shivering that has more
to do with the chill emanating
from me than with the frozen air
inside the shed. Why didn't I
remember to bring gloves?

My stiff hands are threaded
blue as I pack the few jars
and cans left on the shelves
into a single carton and move
on to the workbench. Dad
wasn't a big tinkerer, but his
tools will fill three large boxes.

At least I don't have to wrap
them. I'm not very careful
as I toss them from their pegs
and drawers into the cardboard
containers. A pair of pliers
slips from my hand, goes
sliding across the floor. When

I go to retrieve it, my eyes settle
on a canvas bag, the one I stashed
the Johnnie in. Should I take a sip,
if only to warm me up a little?

But I think about the smell
and no, maybe not. I put
the bag on the workbench. I'll
have to do something with it
eventually. Meanwhile, I finish
with the tools. In the bottom
drawer, way in the back, is
a single small key. I know
what it must go to immediately.

Dad's gun cabinet. It's about
the only thing left here. Our
orders were never to open it,
and I never have. Until now.
There are two big rifles Dad
used for hunting, and a smaller
one I used to see Pattyn carry
sometimes—her impossible
effort to impress Dad enough
to earn his praise. The most
she ever got from him was,

*Not bad. Pretty good,*
*in fact. For a girl.*

# I Didn't Hear Him Say It Then

Pattyn relayed the story.
　　　But I can imagine him

saying it now, as easily
　　　as I can remember him

saying to her that night, *What
　　　are you going to do, little*

*girl? Shoot me? You*
　　　*haven't got the balls.*

　　　　　　*Snap!*

　　　Now Dad laughs, and oh
　　　　　God, beyond all the fear,

　　　anger explodes. I hate
　　　　　his laughter, hate him, and . . .

It's gone again. I carry
　　　the rifles to the door, stand

them beside it. Return
　　　to the cabinet to pack up

the ammunition and there,
      next to the bullets, in a pretty

wooden box, is a handgun.
      It is unfamiliar and looks

nothing like Pattyn's pistol.
      It's smaller and the metal

is darker. So why, when I
      touch the box, does the back

of my neck start to tingle?
      And why do I get the urge

to feel the gun, to lift it
      from the box, and caress it?

            *Snap!*

      I can barely see through
            my swelling eyes, but I watch

      Dad stand and move toward
            Pattyn. *Go ahead, bitch. Shoot.*

# Here, Real Time

I start to sway.

Like I did that night . . .
Was I on my feet?

>Snap!

>Pattyn lifts the gun, points
>it at Dad's chest. *Back off.*
>There's so much confusion
>in her eyes. He sees it. Stops.

Yes, that's right. I'm sure
that's right. So what . . . ?

>Snap!

>Pattyn starts to cry. *Why,*
>*Dad? Why couldn't you love*
>*me? That's all I wanted.* Her
>hand begins to shake. . . .

Like mine is quaking now,
the gun swinging slightly.

>Snap!

Dad has practiced cruelty.
He's already demonstrated
it to me tonight. Now he
heaps it on her. *Love you?*

*Who could love you? That
boy? He didn't love you.
All he wanted was an easy
screw, you stupid little thing.*

*Shut up! He did. We did. We
loved each other, and you took
that away from me. You had no
right, and you deserve to die.*

He did, he did. But . . . what?
Come on. I'm almost there.

*Snap!*

Suddenly, everything is in
motion. Dad starts toward her,
and she backs away, and I
start to crawl, get to my feet,

"Shoot!" And now . . . and now . . .

Oh my God. I remember!

# No

That can't be right.
It's impossible. But . . .
It is. I start to pace.
Oh my God. Oh my God.
I can't . . . What do I do?

I go past the workbench,
see the bag sitting on it.
That's what I need. It will
relax me, help me think.
Despite the smell—

> the same smell that fell
> all around me that night—

I take a long swallow. It
burns going down, and I
fight not to gag it back up.
But it warms my gut and
makes me flush. I take
another and another and

before long I think I must
be a little drunk. It's not bad.
Kind of weird and woozy,
and my head is too thick
to let my brain worry.

I peruse the big bottle—peruse,
good word. Close to a quarter gone.
How much does it take to get drunk?
Am I mostly there already? I swig
again. It doesn't taste nearly
as bad as the first swallow did.
Huh. Does it keep getting better?

Footsteps. Footsteps outside.
Mom? Can't be. Dad? No way—

                remember the weight of his
                walk in the gravel?—

and, oh yeah. He's dead. Duh.
I laugh out loud at that thought.
Except now, I remember again.

    *Murder. Murder. Bits of death.*

             Footsteps. Right outside, and
             now a voice, *Hey, you in there?*

"Gavin? Yesh." My voice
is molasses. I clear my throat.

             Gavin takes one look at me.
             *Hey. Have you been drinking?*

# He Sounds Disappointed

I hold out the bottle. "Shorry.
I shoulda offered you some."
He comes closer, much closer,
but he doesn't take the Johnnie.

> *What are you doing, Jackie?*
> *Getting drunk is so not you.*

"No. Not me. But you don' know.
I didn' know, either. I'm shorry.
Sorry." Sharp tears carve into my eyes.
"I don' think I feel too good."

> *I bet you don't. You don't look*
> *so good, either. But . . . why?*

"It's jush-just being here, seeing . . ."
I point to the handgun sitting next
to the canvas bag. "I . . . something
came back to me. Something awful . . .
important . . . and I dunno what to do."

> He comes to me, takes me into
> his arms. *What is it, Jackie?*

And I love him so much. But still,
I have to say, "I can't tell you."

*Pattyn*
# Memory

In a book I once read,
one of the main characters
tells readers she thinks

                memory

is like a rainbow's end.
Something you can't quite catch
up to. I think the real problem

                is

when *it* catches up to *you*.
Regardless of your head start,
eventually you'll fall prey to

                the stab

of its claws. You might
wrestle away, escape for
a short while, but then all

                of a

sudden, you'll feel its hot
breath on your neck, and
to be perfectly

                blunt,

it's about as sensuous as
a barefoot walk along
the blade of a serrated

                knife.

# January Drags

Closer to February, and the omnipresent
gray mornings are starting to get old.

At home winter is either white or brilliant
blue. Snow? Yes, we get that, maybe even

for several days in a row, but then the clouds
clear and the sky becomes the most amazing

azure you could possibly imagine. A tsunami
of homesickness swamps me. But if I really

dissect it, it isn't neighborhoods filled
with cubicle homes sporting two requisite

front yard trees I miss. It's Caliente's playa
and mountains and verdant ranchland.

It's Paprika and Diego and cats and geese
and herding dogs. It's Aunt J and Kevin.

Ethan. For about the thousandth time,
I reach for the gold locket he gave me,

only to find it missing. I lost it in the scuffle
that night. Is it still there in the shed

somewhere or did somebody find it?
I want it back. It's my one photo

of Ethan and I need to remember him.
It's only been three months, but his face

is fading, my mind's eye going blind.
I stare out the window into the gray,

try to reconstruct him. Tall, yes, with
a body built by ranch work. His eyes

were green and clear, like emeralds,
and his dark wavy hair hung long.

I picture him hefting big grain sacks
over his shoulder. I conjure him astride

his big black horse, Diego. And now
I'm behind him, hugging his waist

as we cross a meadow at a full gallop.
I rest my cheek against his sun-warmed

shirt, inhale his favored Irish Spring.
Stay with me, Ethan. Don't fade away.

# A Tiny Voice

Interrupts my reverie.
*What's a matter, Patty?*
*Why you cryin'?*

I didn't even realize
I was. "Oh, I'm not crying.
I got something in my eye."

*Daddy says maybe I can*
*ride Sho'ne soon. He says*
*I have to ask you 'cause*

*you the boss. How come*
*you the boss?* She stands
there, hands on hips, and

the pure consternation on
her face makes me laugh.
"Oh, honey, I'm not really

the boss. It's just, Shoshone
knows me best right now.
But she's very smart and

soon she'll get to know you,
too. And when she does,
you two will be a great team."

Now she crosses her arms.
*You mean like a football*
*team?* Her frown deepens.

I bend down and give
her a hug. "No. Just a
Sophie and Shoshone team."

She puts one hand on each
of my cheeks, studies my
eyes. *Is the thing gone now?*

Her concern is so sincere
it almost makes my cry
again. I push back the tears.

"Yes. It's gone. Don't worry.
Everything's just fine.
Now you go play, okay?"

*Can I watch TV? Is it time*
*for SpongeBob?* Her favorite
show. How could anyone say

no to that cute expectant
face? "Almost time. Let's
go turn on the television."

# Sophie Settles

In front of the TV in the family
room. I start back toward the kitchen,
and can't help but catch one side
of a heated telephone conversation
leaking out of the mister's study.

> *Susanville? What the hell*
> *are you doing in Susanville?*

Pause.

> *I know it's a three-day weekend. . . .*

Martin Luther King weekend,
not that it means much to me.

> *But who told you it was okay*
> *to go running off with those*
> *so-called friends of yours?*

Pause.

I shouldn't listen in, but curiosity
wins out. What's Deirdre up to now?

> *You do realize I've got a crew*
> *coming in for the spring pruning,*
> *right? I can't just drop everything.*
> *What the hell is wrong with you?*

Pause.

The missus has heard the yelling,
too. She clomps down the hall,
into the office as the mister continues,

> *Okay. Put him on. But you owe*
> *me big-time. We'll continue*
> *this discussion when you get home.*
> *And that better be damn soon.*

I hear the missus ask what's
going on, but the mister shushes
her, lowers his voice, addressing

> someone new. *You're sure?*

Pause.

> *How long will it take to fix it?*

Pause.

> *What's the bottom line?*

Pause.

> *Fine. I'll get my credit card.*

Ooh. Sounds expensive. I quit
the shameless eavesdropping,
check on Sophie, who sits, neck
craned toward the TV on the wall,
immersed in undersea adventure.

# That Might Be That

Except now the conversation
in the other room heats up.

*Did you say she could go?*

*Yes, I did. Why not?*

*With those Heckle boys?*

*They're her friends, Craig.*

*They're delinquents, Diane.*

They hiss and spit the first
names at each other. Sophie

sighs heavily—she's heard it
before—and turns up the TV

to cover the sound. And now
all I hear are snippets.

*. . . broken axle*

*. . . end of the world*

*. . . kissing her ass.*

# They'll Iron It Out

They always seem to, although
the arguments come more often
since Deirdre got arrested. Missus
Jorgensen may not exactly kiss
her ass, but she's awfully lenient.
A pushover, actually. It's weird.

Looks like this three-day weekend
has been extended at least an extra
day for Deirdre. I doubt the Heckles
go to school and even if they do,
their parents probably won't give
a darn, either. Turned out the guns

they were arrested with belonged
to their father. All three had charges
reduced to misdemeanors, and got
off with written (and heartfelt, I'm
sure) apologies to the Walmart
employee, plus a little community

service. When Deirdre came home
after court that day, I kind of wanted
to smack the smug look off her face.
I think her dad did, too. But the missus?
She asked me to make Deirdre's favorite
fried chicken dinner to celebrate.

# Speaking of Dinner

It's time to get it started.
        No Deirdre tonight, so I won't
        need to bake as many potatoes.

I go to the pantry, take them
        from the bin, scrub the skins,
        and as I start to wrap them in

foil, out the window I see
        a pickup pull up to the crew
        housing. Four young men—

all dark skinned and darker
        haired—spill out. They grab
        their meager possessions,

and without any directions,
        three head to one house; another
        goes to the one Angel lives in

with Javier. Obviously,
        they've worked here in the past.
        Must be a good sign they're back.

# I Don't Meet Them

For a couple of days, until I have
time to escape to the barn again.

The filly is coming along pretty
well. She'll take a light snaffle,

and she allows me on her back.
I'm working on her reining when

two of the new guys walk by
the training corral. I wave and say,

"Hola. ¿Cómo están?" Asking how
they are only seems polite. The duo

swing toward the fence and
the taller one says, in almost

> perfect English, *You are Patty,*
> *yes? I am Mateo. This is Pablo.*
>
> *Angel says this horse was loca*
> *until you talk to her. My mama*
>
> *is loca. Will you talk to her, too?*
> The men laugh and I smile.

"I think horses are easier
than people. Especially some

people." I tilt my head in the direction
of Deirdre's truck, now fixed and

barreling up the driveway. Mateo
and Pablo look toward the spectacle.

> Pablo nods. *That one is la hija
> del diablo.* The devil's daughter

punches the gas, kicking up
a big cloud of dust. It rolls

toward us, stealing our smiles.
"I'd better finish up here and get

back to the house. I'll see you on
Sunday, if not before then." I take

Shoshone back to her stall, remove
the saddle and bridle, give her

a quick brush and a handful of grain.
Then I go to shower and change.

# This Time

The argument I am unfortunate
enough to overhear is happening
in the kitchen, and it is between
the mister and his daughter.

> Mister: . . . *know why you were
> in Susanville. I did a little research.
> You'd better sever ties with them
> immediately. Do you understand?*

> Deirdre: *Whatever.*

> Mister: *What are you doing, Dee?
> Are you really so hell-bent on tossing
> your life into the trash heap? Consider
> what you'll be giving up if* . . .

> Deirdre: *If what?*

> Mister: *If you go to prison. If some
> trigger-happy cop or FBI agent
> decides to take you out. If one of
> your asshole friends is a bad shot.*

> Deirdre: *That would make it easy,
> wouldn't it?* Flat. Chilling.

# I Run the Shower

Very hot.
I feel soiled,
and not just
from equine
dust, but from
the conflicting
words that
punctuated
their quarrel.

*Those boys are nothing but thugs,*
*and they're turning you into one, too.*

*What do you know about them?*
*Hell, what do you know about me?*

*I know I didn't teach you to use drugs*
*or run around with assault weapons.*

*Have you ever heard of the Second*
*Amendment? We're constitutionalists.*

*First of all, there is no "we." I forbid*
*you to see that Heckle boy again.*

*And second, the Constitution does not*
*give your friends the right to be anarchists.*

> *First of all,* she mimicked, *they aren't*
> *anarchists. They're survivalists.*

> *And second, just try to stop me from*
> *seeing Jason. Forbid me? You wish.*

*Dee, he's part of a movement that*
*wants to overthrow the government.*

*Homegrown terrorists. He's probably on*
*a watch list. And so, I'm afraid, are you.*

> *Like I care! Fuck the watch list, and*
> *fuck you. Terrorists? We're patriots!*

I shampoo. Wash.
Scrub every inch.
But I'm becoming
more and more sure
something I can't
put my finger on
is about to stain me.

# Or Maybe It Already Has

The thing about stains
is you're not always aware
of them until you actually
see them, often when you
really want a crisp, white,
unblemished appearance.

As I towel my hair, I turn
on my TV, flip through
the early evening programs.
Passing one of the omnipresent
news channels, a stock photo

of galloping, teeth-snapping
wild horses catches my eyes,
mostly because of the headline
superimposed across their heads.

CALIFORNIA MUSTANG MASSACRE

I stop the toweling, turn up
the volume, though I know
what I hear will devastate me.
It does a lot more than that.

410

# It Spins My World

Off its axis and out of control,
with the newswoman's opening

> sentence. *In the hills northeast*
> *of Susanville, California, today,*
> *a pair of ATV riders happened*
> *upon a gruesome scene—a dozen*
> *wild horses, including several*
> *pregnant mares, massacred.*

She goes on to describe what
they found, with a warning about
graphic footage to follow. I can't
pull myself away, but one word
keeps repeating itself in my head:

Susanville. Susanville. Susanville.
No. It couldn't have been. But every
vestige of doubt is erased with
the final nauseating information.

> *Investigators are still combing*
> *the area for evidence, but tell*
> *us the horses have been dead*
> *for three or four days. In addition*
> *to bullet casings, there are remnants*
> *of what appear to be pipe bombs.*

# The Story Wraps Up

With a plea for information
and an 800 number to call.
I don't bother to write it down.
I won't call. I have no proof
it was Deirdre and her friends.
And if the authorities come

looking for her here, she'll know
it was me who turned them in.
But maybe the mister will call.
He'll hear the news, and he'll
know who slaughtered those poor
defenseless horses. Okay, against

a mountain lion, hooves and teeth
might serve as a decent defense. But
against semiautomatic weapons
(at least three, the reporter said),
they didn't stand a chance. The video
was awful, though it couldn't show

the true carnage. Much of it had
already soaked into the ground,
or been picked clean by carrion
eaters. I know firsthand the damage
a single bullet can do. A hailstorm
of bullets . . . unimaginable.

## Journal Entry, January 26

It's been a few days since the news
about the wild horse killings. I keep
an eye out and my ears open for any
sort of updates from the authorities.
So far, they seem to be completely
in the dark, and so do the Jorgensens.

When I rode to Mass with Angel today,
I told him everything I know. He agreed
that I need to keep quiet. "The police
will learn the truth," he said. "And we
must be very careful when they come."

He has no idea. The problem is, I'm
torn. Shredded by the desire to bring
justice for those poor mustangs, not
to mention eliminating a fair amount
of pipe bomb paranoia. I've almost
called Secret Witness several times.

What trumps that is hoping everything
might be able to stay like it is, a tentative
status quo, despite knowing in my heart
the protective walls I've built around
myself are destined to crumble, and
I will be clawing my way out of the ruins.

*Jackie*
## Justice

Isn't

    one size fits all. Some do
    deserve eye-for-an-eye,
    tit for tat, I'll get you back
    same way you gave it to me.
    The problem with that is it's

always

    possible to go a little too far
    over the now-we're-even-steven
    line. And what if the infraction
    was misunderstood or, worse,
    in some small way deserved? Not

so

    easy to read the retribution
    meter when it's clouded. Things
    become even more muddied
    when the revenge seeker

just

    can't take satisfaction in apology,
    not even when a heartfelt
    "I'm sorry" is, in fact, adequate
    punishment for the crime.

# An Eye for an Eye

Has always seemed totally fair to me.
But in the wake of new understanding,

I'm starting to waver. When it comes
to payback, where do you draw the line?

I suppose it boils down to living with
yourself and your actions post-revenge.

And I guess being okay with what
you've done, no matter how terrible,

might have everything to do with
your mental stability. Do crazy people

ever suffer remorse for things like serial
raping or mass murder or cannibalism?

*Jeez, I'm really sorry now for munching
that guy's brains. They were so yummy,*

*and I was starving for gray matter.
But it made me feel so awful, I could*

*never, ever do anything like that again.
Besides, the indigestion almost killed me.*

# Almost a Month

Since memory rammed
into me, altering the way
I look at everything,
especially myself.

I am thin
on morals

obese with rolls of guilt
over something I dare
not confess because that
was Pattyn's plan and I
promised I'd never tell.

That's what I keep
repeating to myself.
Pattyn's plan.
Pattyn's plan.
Pattyn's plan.

And if I say it
enough times,
maybe I'll start
to believe that's
why I haven't
said a word.

## Not One Word

Not even to Gavin.
Especially not to him.
He's hurt because he
knows I'm keeping it

from him. He's a no-
secrets-from-each-other
kind of guy. But this?
This would destroy us.

Maybe it will anyway,
or maybe it will just
annihilate me. I wanted
to know. Kept seeking

the truth. And when I
found it, all I wanted to
do was hide it away
again, so nobody else

could see. Hide from it
again, so I wouldn't have
to face it. I can't. I won't.
No matter how close

it follows me.

# It Stays Right on My Heels

And it's distracting. I'm trying
my best in school, but I can't
concentrate. Gavin is still tutoring

> me, but he's starting to get annoyed.
> *Pay attention,* he tells me now. And
> I know his irritation is rooted in

the knowledge that my mind
is wandering away from the truth
in this textbook, toward whatever

truth I'm concealing from him.
"Sorry," I say, settling my hand
on his knee, beneath the table.

> *I know. You're sorry about a lot*
> *of things lately.* He softens. *I wish*
> *you trusted me enough to let me help.*

"I know you won't believe this,
but I trust you more than I've ever
trusted anyone. That is the truth."

> *Then why . . . ? Never mind.* He slides
> his hand under mine, knots our fingers
> together. *This isn't the place to tell me.*

# Not the Place

Not the time, and it never
will be, although he seems
to believe I'll give in at some
point. Not going to happen.
I just wish that I could forget.

In the larger sense, it doesn't
matter. It wouldn't change
anything, really. I mean, maybe
Pattyn could come home. But
how would she even know it

was okay? And even if she knew,
would she want to come home,
and would Mom let her? Would
Mom believe me? Would anyone?
Because the more I think about

what the truth is, the more it seems
like a lie. Maybe what I remembered
isn't real after all. Maybe it's just
more of my psyche tumbling end
over end, wrestling with the part

I played in Dad's death. If I hadn't . . .
If I would have . . . If only God
had whispered a warning . . .

# The Last Bell Rings

End of the day. Time to go
home. Our hands unlock and
I hate how it feels, like I just shed
a very big piece of me. Outside

the library, the corridors swell
with movement and odors and
noise. Gavin slides his arm around
my shoulder, which makes me feel

marginally better about the buzz
growing inside my head. When it
starts, a headache usually follows—
one of those big thumps right above

    my eyes. As we turn past the library
    window, Gavin stops. *Check it out.*
    *Wanna go?* The red poster he points
    to advertises: Valentine's Day Dance.

The only dances I've ever been to
were at church, and there wasn't
much actual dancing going on.
More like kinda moving around.

I'm embarrassed to admit that, but
at least it might divert his attention
away from the big secret. "I, uh,
don't really know how to dance. . . ."

Someone bumps us from behind.
*Yeah, but you know how to do
other things, don't you? Fun things,
too. Sort of, anyway,* Caleb snickers.

Gavin rotates on one heel, steps
protectively in front of me. *What
the hell is your problem, McCain?
Why don't you keep on moving?*

Caleb steps forward, reaches
around Gavin, brushes my face.
*I think your boyfriend is jealous.
But I don't mind sharing if he doesn't.*

Up comes Gavin's arm, knocking
Caleb's hand away. *Don't touch her.
Never touch her again, or I swear
everyone will know what you did.*

# Caleb Just Smiles

What did I do, faggot? Or should
I say son of a faggot? Are lezzies
fags or just regular queer?

Gavin's face colors, but he stands
his ground. *You are a cretin. That
means "moron," by the way.* The energy

exchange is electric, and it's building
into something ugly. Gavin presses me
backward, away from all-but-certain

violence. I am sandwiched between
him and the window, and the pressure
makes it hard to draw breath. It reverse

transports me to a dark cold night
in a dimly lit shed, and the sound
of Caleb's voice keeps me there,

beneath him as he grips my hands,
holds them above my head and lifts
my skirt as I beg, "No, please, no."

And I'm begging now and Caleb
laughs, just like he did that night,
and I'm there, and I'm here, and . . .

## I Scream

Stop.

Don't.

Please.

You're hurting me.

Stop.

Don't.

Please.

Oh, God, no.

Leave me alone!

No. No. Not my fault.

Don't hurt me.

Please.

Stop.

Please.

No, Dad, no.

Die.

# I Sink to the Cold Cement

Gavin shoves forward, gives me
the space I need to stay cognizant.

I'm barely here, but I see Caleb
swing at Gavin's face and connect.

> The gathering crowd hoots and cheers
> as, blood dripping from his nose, Gavin

> punches back. *Come on, asshole. I'll
> show you how a faggot fights.* Except

>> Ms. Rose appears, like an angel. *That's
>> enough! Both of you! Can't you see*

>> *she needs help?* Suddenly, there is
>> space around me as everyone moves

away. Gavin maintains a safe zone
while Ms. Rose bends to talk to me.

>> *Are you okay? What happened?*
>> She listens as I tell her how Caleb

started the altercation, and as the story
spills, he tries to escape the scene.

Unfortunately—for him, anyway—
he bumps straight into Mr. Barrett,

the football coach and boys' PE teacher,
who has been drawn by the commotion.

> *I think these young men should
> straighten things out in the office,*

> says Ms. Rose. *Will you escort them,
> Paul? I'll take care of Ms. Von Stratten.*

> *We'll be down to talk to Mr. Scoffield
> in a few minutes.* She helps me to my feet

and we watch Mr. Barrett follow
Gavin and Caleb to the office.

> *Come with me for a minute,* she says,
> taking my hand and leading me into

the library, which is mostly empty
now. She takes me back into her own

> little cubicle behind the desk. Sits me
> in a comfortable chair. *Talk to me.*

# I Have No Idea Why

But I do. I totally spew.
"It was the night Dad died,"
I start. And as the words
tumble out of my mouth,
her eyes go wider and wider,
though the rest of her body
moves not at all until I start
to cry. "He r-r-raped me."

It's a stupid stutter and I hate
that I can't just come out
and say it without tripping
over the word. "And then
my dad came in, and Caleb
ran, and Dad didn't believe
me when I told him what
happened. And that's why
he beat me, and that's why . . ."

Go ahead. Tell her. You've
told her everything else.
But I can't, not the whole
hideous confession, so I
finish, "That's why he died,
and it's all my fault."

She shakes her head. *No.*
But she's wrong. "Yes, it is."

## That Makes Her Squirm

But she doesn't address it.

> Instead, she asks, *Does anyone
> else know you were raped?*

It's so embarrassing, but I
go ahead and admit, "Yes.
My m-mom knows, and Caleb's
dad, and our b-bishop. Maybe
other men in our church."
I don't mention Gavin.

> *But you didn't press charges?*

Anger stops the stutter.
"Mom didn't want me to.
She had enough on her mind
with Dad dying, she said.
And, besides, our bishop
told her Caleb and I were
equally guilty. But I just . . ."

> *Just what, Jackie?* Her voice
> is honey, and her eyes are caring.

"I just wanted him to love me."

She comes around the front
of her desk, perches her narrow
hips on its leading edge.

> *Jackie, are you seriously
> telling me your mother talked
> you out of pressing charges?*

When I nod, she continues,

> *That was wrong, in all kinds
> of ways. I truly can't understand it.
> And as for you being equally guilty,
> well, that is just so much bullshit.
> "No" means "no." End of story.*

"But I invited him over. Let him
kiss me. And when he touched
me the first time, I let him. I . . .
think I am partially to blame."

> *Stop it, Jackie. Lots of people make
> out without one of them forcing
> himself on the other. If you don't
> come clean about it, he'll probably
> do it again. You have to report him.*

# I Want To

I really do. But what
would be the point?

No one will back me.
No one will believe me.

The evidence, such as it
was, is long since gone.

I understand that he'll do
it again, and I feel bad

about that. But girls need
to be smarter. Girls must

consider possible outcomes
before they invite boys inside

their sheds. Caleb is in
the driver's seat. Eventually,

he'll head-on into a wall.
But it isn't one I'm willing

to build. Now what I want is to
disappear. "I'm sorry. I can't."

# That's What I'm Thinking

As Ms. Rose and I head
to the office.
        D
         i
          s
           a
            p
             p
              e
               a
                r

We deal with Mr. Scoffield,
who wants to know

> *why on earth would Caleb*
> *McCain pick a fight with you?*

"I have no idea. Did you ask
him? I think he's certifiable."

Lucky for Gavin and me, there
were plenty of witnesses, including
poor Ms. Rose, who's dying
to say a whole lot more than,

> *They were minding their own*
> *business, Chuck. I saw it all.*

# Maybe It's What Happened

With Dad, or maybe it's what
happened last year with Pattyn,
or maybe it's the combination,
but I notice the way Mr. Scoffield

winces when he lets Gavin and me
walk away punishment-free.
He has no choice but to suspend
Caleb, and gives him three days

at home. Whoopee. Caleb's self-
satisfied, better-than-thou expression
almost makes me blurt the truth after all.
But then I study Mr. Scoffield's face.

I think he feels sorry for Caleb. "Boys
will be boys," and more than that,
"Josiah McCain won't like this."
Okay, I might be making the last bit

up in my head. Or maybe I'm spot-
on and it's because of Caleb's
suspension last year. I bet his lawyer
father was looking for loopholes

to keep his academic record
scraped squeegee clean. All
the best colleges, most certainly
including BYU, tend to frown

on applicants with felony assaults
under their belts. The thought makes
me snort, not that it's really so funny.
After all, I was on the receiving end

      of one of his under-the-belt
      assaults. *Something amusing,*
      *Ms. Von Stratten?* Mr. Scoffield
      shoots me a scathing scowl.

Impatience with this ridiculous
situation balloons into sudden
irritation. "Amusing? No, sir.
I was just wondering how far

a person would have to go—I
mean, since punching someone
in the face didn't qualify—to face
actual assault charges. Any idea?"

## My Question

Is not much appreciated,
but Mr. Scoffield lets it
go. Gavin offers a ride
home. Good thing, since
the bus is long gone. He
leaves me standing here
while he runs for a book.

Caleb exits the office and,
unbelievably, approaches
me. *Thanks for the vacation,
bitch.* He flips me off and
walks away, snickering.

I whirl at the sound of soft
footsteps behind me. But
it's only Ms. Rose, who
watches Caleb until he's out
of sight. Then she says, *If
you don't report him, how
will you ever begin to heal?*

*Pattyn*

# How Far

Are you willing to watch
someone go before

you have

no choice but to jump up
off the sidelines and into
the game? Do you let him
gain advantage until there
are too few minutes left

to play

to renegotiate the win?
What if you wait, expecting
the defense to step it up
any second now, and

by

the time that happens, all has
been lost, no turning back,
and the outcome would have
been different if you'd only
insisted on governance by

the rules?

# Deirdre's Game

Has no rules. And that is marrow-
deep frightening because she has
no real filters, either. If she'd kill

wild horses in the California hills,
mow them down, blow them up,
she wouldn't think twice about

taking out Shoshone. I remember
her words. *Might as well put a bullet
in her brain right now.* I'm terrified

she'll do exactly that, and not need
a reason to pull the trigger other than
Sophie makes her angry. Or I do.

Over the last couple of weeks,
I've learned way too much about
what she was doing in Susanville.

Between the things I've overheard,
and what I've discovered through
research, I am more than vaguely

uncomfortable about what's in store
for any of us here. I just hope, in
the end, sanity wins the day.

# What I've Learned

The Heckle family subscribes
to an ideology known as sovereignty.
Sovereign citizens don't believe in

> taxes
> licenses
> authority
> government

or anything that wrests any form
of power away from themselves.
They claim to adhere to God's laws
only, but you wouldn't know it to
look at some of the things they do.

The large majority are nonviolent.
They shoot at their perceived enemies
with paper ammunition—filing false
liens and fake 1099s, disrupting
the lives of their targets, utilizing

the very system they claim to disdain,
and believing themselves quite clever.
But a few sovereigns have moved
beyond nuisance into the realm
of mayhem. Law enforcement

from coast to coast is increasingly
worried about this segment of
the movement. This is where militias
form. This is where hatred brews.
How immersed in hate the Heckles—

and Deirdre—have become is a matter
of debate around here. The missus
glosses things over, says her daughter
is no better nor worse than any girl
her age. That adolescence is exactly

the time you're supposed to look
for answers in all the wrong places,
so that by the time you become an adult,
the foolishness is out of your system.
The mister insists on digging deeper,

and that has led to more than a few
"discussions" lately. Which is why
I'm privy to as much as I am. Which
is why I work dawn to dark every
day and fall into bed exhausted, but

still can't manage to sleep without
diving into blood-caked nightmares.

# Granted

A lot of that blood
isn't invented in some
demented corner of
my brain. Most of it

is filed away in a deep
pocket of memory. I
have witnessed things
I dare not call up into

the scrutiny of daylight.
They are not safer to
conjure beneath wings
of sleep. But there, I have

no control over what
monsters appear in
my dreams. Mostly
it's zombies who stalk

me there—faces chewed
by death, but recognizable.
I can run faster, but they're
relentless. Starved for revenge.

# I Take Haven

In two places. The barn, of course.
Lately, I've stolen a couple
of hours every day to work
with Shoshone, who has come
so far in so little time, it's hard
to fathom. She's wonderful,

especially out of the ring, on
the trail. I often ride her into
the orchards, where the crew
busily prunes and fertilizes
and regards the health of each
tree. Most people who buy

those June peaches have no clue
what it takes to get them, fresh
and unblemished, to the market.
I definitely didn't. But I do now,
or at least I have a much better idea.
I have yet to witness a harvest.

Shoshone seems to enjoy our
tours through the trees, which
are still just branches, although if
you look real hard, you can see
hints of the buds to come. In a few
weeks, Angel says, the orchard

will wear crowns of flowers.
One thing I've learned about Angel:
he's an incurable romantic, and if
he put his mind to it, he could be
a poet. Sometimes, without even
meaning to, he talks in poetry.

My second refuge is his house.
It's busier now, with the crew here.
They often stop by just to hang out.
Maybe they like poetry, too, I don't
know. No matter who's there, I feel
safe in their company, but it's best

when it's just Angel and me. Like
tonight. Friday night, and the rest
of the guys are in town, blowing
off a little steam, as Aunt J might
say. Aunt J. Thinking about her
makes me a little sad, and Angel

notices. *What happened? Where
did your smile run away to?*

# We're Sitting Very Close

On his couch, not that we have
much of a choice. It isn't very big.
We often sit this way, watching
sitcoms or cop shows or other
mindless network television.

Tonight, for some reason, I take
advantage of the strong shoulder
beside me and lean my cheek against
it. "Every now and then, I think about
home and feel a little sad. That's all."

> In a most unexpected move, Angel
> kisses my forehead. Tenderly, his lips
> barely there. *Maybe you should go
> back. Maybe everything is different
> now. You don't know unless you see.*

"No." I feel the ghostly impression
of his mouth, inhale the soap scent
I first smelled on his pillow back in
Vacaville. I should pull away, move
off the sofa, leave this house, and

hurry to my room. But I don't want
to be alone. And if I'm truthful
with myself, I want to be right here.

# Right Here

Beside a living, breathing human
being who cares for me. I can see
it in the cool lagoons of his eyes,
hear it in the timbre of his voice
when he speaks my name.

Right here.

Where the warmth of his skin
tempers the February cold and
the thinnest beam of his inner
light overcomes winter's pall.
He is a candle in the wilderness.

Right here.

Where the omnipresent specter
of death takes flight, awed
by the power of the two of us,
hearts beating in unison, as we
stumble through the darkness

toward one another.

# And So

When he lifts his arm, inviting
me beneath it, I draw into the refuge

waiting there. And when his hand
laces into my hair, lifts it gently,

I tilt my head in offering. The sultry
wind of his breath falls against my neck,

circles left, and his kiss drifts down
upon the pulse quickening behind

my ear. He leaves his lips settled there,
where the beat can speak to them.

>     His reply is a whisper. *I have
>     no right to love you, but I do.*

I should pull away, run away, fast
and faster without looking back.

Love is pain in disguise, a scorpion
lying in wait for just the right moment

to strike and inject you with its poison
before scuttling off into the shadows.

So why, when his lips brush up over
my jaw, soft and urgent as hummingbird

wings, do I turn my face toward them,
open my mouth and meet their approach?

Gnawing need upwells inside me, releases
in this amazing kiss, melted butter hot

and rich. There are unspoken words here.
We kiss poems. Stories. We kiss books.

Volumes of things left unsaid, emotions
untapped. We kiss loneliness. Heartbreak.

Rejection, confusion, resentment, rage.
We kiss, scribbling hope onto pages left

blank too long, and when they're filled,
we kiss joy. Elation. Longing. A spark

of desire fanning quickly toward flame . . .
And there we stop. Close the covers.

# I Draw Back

Look into his eyes—those black
pools, brimming love. I'm speechless,
really, don't know what to say
except, "Thank you. I thought
I'd never do that again."

> He smiles. *I hope it isn't the only*
> *time. Oh. Wait a minute. . . .*

He gets up, goes into his room, and
when he returns, he is holding a small
box wrapped in red paper. He offers it
to me. "What's that? It isn't my birthday."

> *No. Today is El Día de San Valentin.*
> *Uh, Valentine's Day. Please.*

"Oh! I forgot all about Valentine's Day."
Other than the usual elementary school
card exchanges, no one has ever
remembered me on this occasion.
"But I didn't get anything for you."

> He bends down, kisses a reminder.
> *You gave me that. Anyway, you don't*
> *give a present expecting to get one.*

# I Accept the Box

And he sits at my feet, waits
for me to open it, and I do,
slowly unpeeling the paper.
Relishing the mystery.
What will I find inside?

"Oh, Angel." It's a bracelet
of interlocking silver hearts,
with three dangling charms:
> A *P* for Patty.
>> A horse with a long wavy
>> mane, reminiscent of Shoshone.
>>> And a question mark.

> *You like it?*

"It's beautiful. Help me?"
I hold out my arm and he

> clasps it around my wrist.
> *So now you will think of me*
> *with love every day.*

"I already do." And it's true.
"More than once or twice."
I kiss a thank-you. But I can't
quite bring myself to actually
say the words, "I love you."

## Journal Entry, February 14

*Valentine's Day has never in my entire
life meant anything even close to love
before. Here I am, teetering on the brink
of love, toes right up against the edge.
The only thing that's holding me back
is you, Ethan. I swore I would never
love again. How can I even consider
letting go, dropping over the cornice,
if you're not below to catch me?*

*Angel is wonderful. I think you'd like
him. And I know you'd appreciate how
kind he is to me, the way he gathered
me in, sort of like Aunt J did. I wish
I could talk to her about everything.
She's the wisest woman I've ever met,
except maybe for Ms. Rose. Pretty sure
my favorite librarian learned most
of what she knows from books, though.
What taught Aunt J was stumbling
through life, absorbing the blows
until she figured out how to make them
bounce off her. She defines "survivor."
I want so much to be like her.*

*Oh, Ethan. Why can't you reach out
from wherever you are now and
let me know how you feel about Angel
and me? Do you care? Is there a way
to communicate your blessing?*

*Angel gave me a bracelet. Three charms.
Two are easy enough to understand
the logic behind. One symbolizes me.
The second, the animal who first gave
me a reason to keep moving forward.
But the third. In some way, I think
it represents you. The big question
I can't yet give him the answer to.*

*But here's the thing. I can't give
him my heart with you beating so
loudly inside it. I can't give him
my heart with it snared
in this net of lies.*

*Jackie*
# Hearts and Flowers

Hallmark, some say, invented
Valentine's Day, or at least
promoted it heavily, in its quest
to corner the greeting card market.
In fact, its history is much older,
and more than a little convoluted. There

are

stories of martyred saints named Valentine,
two whose heads remain preserved
in Italian basilicas. Ah, romance.
Another Valentine is said to have cured
the girl he loved of her blindness, a not

insignificant

undertaking, from behind prison bars.
Before his execution—convicted of
illegally performing marriages—he sent
his love a note signed, "From Your
Valentine." That *is* romantic, and similar

tokens

of affection, made of heart-shaped
paper, decorated with lace, began
to appear after English poets created
a day to celebrate love. Hallmark,
it seems, took its cue from Chaucer.

# The Valentine's Day Dance

Is a regular spectacle of red paper
hearts and pink crepe flowers. It must
have taken hours to decorate the commons.

I can't believe I'm actually here.
As I predicted, Mom was very unhappy
about "the role I played" in Caleb's

> suspension. *How could you get him*
> *in trouble like that? Josiah is upset.*

"Uh, hello, Mom? If it was in any way
my fault, I would have been suspended,
too. Nope. This is completely on Caleb."
I gave it a day before I asked about

> the dance. She was hesitant. *You two*
> *are getting kind of serious, aren't you?*

"Define 'serious.' We're not discussing
marriage, and we're not even close
to having sex. But he makes me happy,
and he keeps me safe from jerks like Caleb."

> *Watch your language. And be careful*
> *of what you say about other people.*

# I Wasn't Certain

Which word she found offensive—
"sex" or "jerks." Personally, the only one
that offended me was "Caleb." But
I kept quiet and after several gentle
nudges, she let me go to the dance.

So, here I am with Gavin, pretending
I know how to move to the DJ's
decent mix of dance hits and classic
rockers. Gavin is totally adorable
in khaki pants, a mint button-up shirt,

and forest-green bow tie. So handsome,
especially when wayward strands
of his hair fall haphazardly down
over his forehead, giving him that
quirky professor look. I don't know

if every girl would think so, but I
definitely do, and for some stupid
reason, I feel the need to tell him.
I move into him, push up on my toes
so I can get close to his ear. Hopefully

he'll be able to hear me over the music.
"Did I ever tell you how cute you are?"

He grins, leans down to say into *my* ear,
*I was wondering when you were going*
*to get around to that. What took so long?*

The music fades out, segues into
something quieter. Gavin wraps me
in his arms, holds me very close and
starts to sway. I've never slow danced
before and feel awkward at first, but

soon absorb his confidence. Now he
bends, brushes his lips up along my jawline.
*Did I ever tell you how amazing you are?*

This giant rush of pleasure mushrooms
inside, and it's his words, and it's the love
in his eyes and it's the way he caresses
me, all rolled up into one big exhale
of magic. How can this be me, pressed

tightly against this amazing guy,
anticipating the electricity his hands
generate as they travel up my spine?
I thought I'd never let a guy touch me
again. Now I'm praying he never stops.

# But the Music Stops

So he does, too. All good things
must skid to a halt eventually,
I guess. He pulls me off into
a darkish corner and kisses me

out of the chaperones' view.
*Thanks for being my Valentine,*
he whispers. *I love you, Jackie.*

The critically romantic moment
is interrupted by a screeching
sound across the quad. *Hey!*
Everyone's attention is drawn

to a girl—a freshman, I think—
standing with Caleb, whose arm
is draped over her shoulder, hand
dangling toward the low cut

of her very tight dress. She teeters
on heels she's obviously not used
to, and he takes full advantage of it,
pretending to steady her when all he wants

is to grope her. A low growl of anger
begins in my head, and Gavin must
hear it. He squeezes my hand. *Wait.*

# The Girl's Squealing

Has caught the attention
    of our chaperones. Ms. Rose
    and Mr. Barrett swoop to the rescue.

Both understand that Caleb
    is more than capable of causing
    trouble. Mr. Barrett might only

know about the fights, but
    Ms. Rose knows about other
    treacheries. She glances at me

before moving between Caleb
    and his date, who may dress like
    she's going out for drinks in a bar,

but whose face betrays not
    only her age, but her inexperience
    with anything quite like Caleb.

I want to tell her to sprint, very
    fast and very far, in the opposite
    direction of the barbarian who

she doubtless sees as her knight
    in shining armor. But what kind
    of knight gropes his maiden fair?

# The Music Resumes

Gavin pulls me away from the scene
across the room and back onto

the dance floor. We lose ourselves
in the smoking beat. (Me, saying

"smoking"! This guy is improving
my vocabulary, as well as my math

skills.) The DJ plays a forty-minute
set and we keep moving the whole

time. Rocking out is fun, but the slow
ones are the best, and the night melts

away. When we finally have to stop,
I notice Caleb and the freshman are gone.

I have no clue if they left together,
or if Ms. Rose convinced the girl

to peel herself off the philistine
and find another ride home. I hope

it's the latter, but the acid churning
in my gut stems from the overriding

fear that they are right now in some
too-dark, too-private place and he is

on top of her and she's saying please,
no, and he's saying come on, you want

this, a hellish déjà vu, and I'm not even
in the vicinity. I keep replaying two

scenes—that one, and the one I star
in with Caleb—over and over, until

Gavin has driven me halfway home.
Finally, I say, "Do you think she's

okay? The girl with Caleb, I mean."
Gavin glances at me sideways,

eyes filled with "duh." *I know
who you mean, Jackie. I was there,*

*remember? Ask me, I'd say the real
question is, do you think she's okay?*

456

## No

It's the short, simple,
not-so-sweet but totally
accurate answer. Five very

long silent seconds swell
with certainty. "I should
have said something to her."

> He shrugs. *Unless someone
> steps up and says something,
> Caleb won't stop, and if he doesn't,*

> *his behavior will probably
> escalate. I tried to stop him
> last year. I really d—*

He brakes his monologue
suddenly, and some inner
turmoil creases his face,

making him look much older.
He has his secrets, too, and
they're serious. "What happened?"

# He Tosses Something

Around in his head, slows
the car. Guess it's a long story.

*Look. I didn't want to tell you
this because I wanted you to
come to the right decision on
your own. Besides, I could get*

*in a lot of trouble. But I really
think you need to know. Remember
last year when Caleb was suspended?
Well, that "little incident" wasn't*

*so little. I know because I witnessed
it, and I'll never forget what I saw.
There was a kid at school, Shawn.
He was openly gay, and for whatever*

*reason, that got to Caleb. He and
his jerkoff buddy, Tyler Bronson,
cornered Shawn in the locker room
shower. He was naked and sitting,*

*back against the tile, water pouring
down over his head. Caleb stood
over him with a baseball bat while
Bronson stood there, laughing.*

I walked in just as Caleb put the head
of the bat against Shawn's mouth. "You
want to suck on something big and hard?"
he yelled. "Suck on this." He rammed

that thing into Shawn's mouth with
enough force to chip teeth and bruise
his throat, and who knows what might
have happened next if I hadn't interfered?

I walked straight up to Caleb, tapped
his shoulder. "Did you know that ninety
percent of homophobic men are, in fact,
questioning their own masculinity?"

He spun around, swinging the bat for
a home run against my head. I ducked
and it connected with Bronson instead.
Then it became a two-against-one

free-for-all. Shawn managed to crawl
past us. He ran and got Mr. Barrett
from his office in time to prevent
internal injuries or broken bones.

# The Upshot

Of that, in addition to a five-day
    suspension, was a court appearance

on a hate-crime-enhanced assault-
    and-battery charge. The upshot

of that was a slap-on-the-wrist
    suspended sentence and a gag

order for all parties involved.
    Josiah McCain represented

his son. The man has friends
    in high places. Still, Mr. Barrett

knows, and so does the school
    administration. Surely they must

understand this is a pathology.
    So why would Mr. Scoffield

question motive when Caleb
    went after Gavin last time?

Did he give poor Shawn the third
    degree about why he was assaulted?

# The Thought

Is out of left field and I know it.
Still, "It's crazy that none of this
got around. How is that possible?"

> Caleb's father asked for the gag
> order right away, so it never made
> the news. I probably would have
> said something, regardless, but
> Shawn's parents asked me not to.

"But, why? I don't get it. Didn't
they want justice for their son?"
My own words slap me in the face.
But Gavin doesn't mention my mother.

> They said they didn't want him
> to become a public spectacle.
> I can't blame them in a way.
> They withdrew him from Carson
> and now he's up at Sage Meadow.

It's an über-exclusive college
prep school. Über-expensive, too.
"Wow. Pricey alternative."

*I imagine Mr. McCain helped
out more than a little. Plus,
the casino earmarks some charity
funds for education. Mom Bea
put in a good word for Shawn.*

*He and I keep in touch, by the way.
The Sage Meadow curriculum
is off the charts, so I tutor him
when he needs it. I also helped him
start up a Gay-Straight Alliance there.*

You always hear about money
and how large amounts of it
can buy things like influence.
Or silence. As an abstract idea,
that doesn't always mean much.

But once you see it in action,
you understand its raw power,
and it's totally awe-inspiring.

Something new nibbles at me.
"What did you mean when you
said you couldn't blame Shawn's
parents for wanting to stay quiet?"

# We Are Almost Home

So he circles the block, finds
an unobtrusive spot to park
for a couple of minutes. He idles
the engine so the heater can work
against the frosty February night.

> *To avoid carbon monoxide*
> *poisoning, I'll try to keep this*
> *story brief. We live in northern*
> *Nevada, and while attitudes*
> *are softening here, it's still*
> *not what you'd call overly*
> *accepting of homosexuality.*
>
> *Caleb is a case in point, and*
> *the fact is, he was only one*
> *of many bullies in elementary*
> *school. I'd see them use antigay*
> *slurs against anyone who dared*
> *cross them. Most of their victims*
> *were straight, but that was beside*
>
> *the point. So, imagine me, with*
> *two moms. For too many years,*
> *I did everything I could to hide*
> *that fact from my classmates.*
> *I knew it hurt Mom Bea when*

*I begged her to let Mom Ann go
to parent-teacher conferences and
school plays solo. But protecting
my secret meant more to me.
Then in fifth grade I got the lead
in our Christmas pageant. Don't
laugh. I made an amazing Santa.*

*You know Mom Bea is a strong
woman, and she looks it. Okay,
she's pretty, but she's never
tried to hide the butch in her.
The night before the play, I was
so excited, and kept repeating
my lines over and over. Mom*

*Bea watched for a while, then
went outside, into the snow.
Mom Ann followed, and when
she opened the door, I could hear
Mom Bea crying. That was
something foreign, and I went
closer to listen. "I love him so
much. Why can't he be proud
of me? I'd give anything for that.
Hell, maybe I'd even go straight."*

*I knew that was a joke, and so
was Mom Ann's answer. "You could
always try. But I'd change you back.
Seriously, though, Gavin is only ten.
Peer pressure is starting to build,
and he isn't strong enough to stand
his ground. Give him some time.
Maybe one day he will be. Anyway,
I'm proud enough for both of us."*

*And then, through the window,
I watched them kiss. It was tender.
Sweet. Filled with love and it
struck me, even at ten, how rare
love like theirs must be. So many
kids I knew lived in single-parent
households, with their grandparents,
or in foster care. My family was solid.*

*I didn't feel any stronger. But I
wanted to be and vowed to get
that way, starting with the next
day's Christmas pageant. I took
some heat following my Santa
debut, and it only got hotter in
middle school, where the bullies
descended like starving buzzards.*

*But after that, Mom Bea came to
every event she could weasel her
way out of work to attend—every
band performance, every track meet.
No matter how well I did, or how
poorly, the pride in her eyes made
me hold up my head. And you know
what? It also made me stronger.*

*The crude comments didn't stop, but
after a while I learned how to deal
with them. Sometimes all it takes
is a well-rehearsed comeback. Other
times it requires physicality. I'm not
by nature a violent person, but I will
defend myself if necessary. And I
watch out for people I love, too.*

He winks. And now he reaches
for me, coaxes me close, and even
though this space is confined, I'm
sharing it with Gavin, and I realize
how much I've come to trust him.
So when our kiss moves beyond
sweet, edging toward passionate,
I give myself up to the waterfall
rush of love-infused desire.

*Pattyn*
# Ascension

Slow rise, warm
air into cool,
like proofing yeast
in a winter kitchen.

Acquiescence.

Gravity relinquishes
control of this voyage
into cloudless cobalt,
blue spring dawning.

Abstraction.

Hurry carries no meaning,
adrift on the whim
of indifferent air current
and capricious breeze.

Awakening.

This is why the eagle flies
here, where neither man nor
bullet dares define his freedom.
I wonder if this is where you are.

Awe.

# Somewhere in the Distant Hills

There is a golden eagle aerie.
I often see the huge birds on
the wing when I take Shoshone
for a spin. They bodysurf waves
of wind expertly, scouting meals.
Sometimes when I watch them,

I wonder what it would be like to
perch atop the food chain, unafraid
of what roams below, certainty
inherent in their predation. But
Angel says in winter when prey
is scarce, even these masterful

killers will settle for carrion.
It's hard to picture them picking
the bones of roadkill. Yet survival
is the ultimate goal, isn't it? And
with the spring, rabbits will run
and mice will scurry and smaller

birds will fly and the carcasses
will be left for less noble raptors.
Some days I feel like a hare,
preparing to flee, not at all sure
what shadow might chase after
me as winter melts into spring.

# Morning Light

Comes a little earlier every day.
It is a subtle change, but one I notice,
mid-February. Spring is still a month

away, but I feel its approach. Maybe
it's because I've lately discovered
a tiny vein of happiness, although

the truth is, that scares me. Happiness
is a bull's-eye, awaiting arrows of pain.
Still, those unexpected moments of joy

are appreciated. I experience them
working with Shoshone, who I think
Sophie will ride one day, not so far in

the future. That child also elicits short
bursts of delight. It springs from her
questions, and from her bottomless well

of curiosity. She is a daily reminder
of home and my family, at least
the snapshots I want to remember.

Pictures like helping with homework
or lighting birthday cake candles.
Jackie turns sixteen next week.

The ones I really want to forget
are all still right there in a drawer
inside my head. If I push hard

enough, I can keep it shut, but in
moments of weakness, some invisible
hand flings it open and out they fly,

nightmares on the wing, except
they are memories, not dreams.
Which is not to say they don't escape

into my sleep as well. They do.
Oh yes, they do, and when I wake
up, drenched in sweat, I don't have

to recall the details to know why
my heart punches my chest, stealing
my breath away. It happens less often

now. And part of the reason is lying
here next to me. His even breathing
is soothing because it tells me he dreams

unafraid. *Innnn-ouuuut. Innnn-ouuuut.*
In that gentle inhale-exhale, I find
a steady give-and-take of love.

# Do I Love Him?

I am in his bed beside him,
totally dressed, because I'm
not yet ready to commit to more
than weaving myself into his arms
and kissing him with immense desire
born of a cavernous need for connection.

Do I love Angel?
Yes, very much.

It isn't a difficult question; the answer
comes easily, and why not? Angel
is patient. Gentle. Understanding.
Oh, and he can make me laugh.
God knows, I believed I was
wrung dry of laughter.

But what about . . . ?
Once-only forever love.

That is the bigger question.
Ethan lingers, an aura, but he
will never return, and I'll never
share his bed. The closest we ever
came was drifting together in meadow
grass, cattle lowing in the near distance.

As the light grows stronger,
I turn slightly so as not to disturb
the man adjacent to me on this narrow
mattress. I study his handsome face, so
peaceful and unworried in sleep. He looks
nothing like Ethan, yet he reminds me of him.

Can he take Ethan's place?
No one can ever do that.

He can never be my first love. Ethan will
always live in that particular room in
my heart. The door to that place has
been sealed, and only I know the
secret way back inside, where I
can visit first love forever.

Can you accept new love?
I wish I knew the answer.

The fact is, I spent so much
of my life lacking love, seeking
it in the wrong places, that when it
finally found me, it seemed impossible
I could ever experience it again. Now, I'm
not so sure. But I'm terrified of the outcome.

# Still, When Angel Wakes

And sees me next to him,
his eyes fill with something
that looks very much like joy.

> *You are still here,* he says.
> *I thought you might disappear*
> *in the night, like a dream.*

I reach out, touch his cheek,
and three pretty silver charms
glitter in soft rays of sunlight

and jingle a bittersweet melody.
"I'm still here. Your bed is
much warmer than mine."

> He smiles. *Only when you are*
> *in it, I think. I like having you*
> *here.* His mouth invites mine,

and after all that internal dialogue,
I find amazing possibilities
in the way our lips speak to each

> other with this kiss. And when
> he whispers, *Te amo* onto my
> tongue, I tell him I love him, too.

# Surprise

Ascends from the dark depths
of his eyes, floats on the surface.

He sits up, leans back against
the wall, studies me earnestly.

>        *There is so much I want to say
>        to you. So much I want to know*
>
>        *about you* . . . I squirm at that, but
>        he rests a gentle hand on my arm.
>
>        *Shh. No tienes que decir nada.*
>        He tells me I don't have to say

anything. But I know it must
hurt for me to grasp my secrets

so tightly when he has confided
his. I hear a voice—oh my God,

Ethan's voice—*We are nothing
if we can't tell each other our secrets.*

It's my choice, I see now—to be
something with Angel. Or nothing,

>                                   alone.

# I Pop Up

Ready to tell him everything,
but just as I open my mouth,
someone knocks on the bedroom
door and I jump as if it must

> be a certain ghost. But no, it's only
> Javier. *¿Estás despierto, amigos?*
> *El padre no le gusta cuando la gente*
> *llega a masa tarde.* Loosely translated:

The priest doesn't like people to
be late. But Javier said "amigos,"
plural. He knows I'm here? What
must he think? "I'll hurry and change."

I run out the door, past Javier,
offering only, "Be right back."
Angel can set things straight
or Javier can believe what he will.

As I approach the main house,
I see Deirdre watching me out
the kitchen window. Her scowl
is evident from here, but what

else is new? Just a few short steps
to my room and by the time I reach
it, Deirdre is almost there, too.
She checks out my wrinkled

> clothes. *Sleeping with one of*
> *the crew, huh? Figures. Hope*
> *he used a rubber. Last thing*
> *we need is more anchor babies*

> *sponging welfare. Goddamn slut.*
> She waits for a reaction, but all
> she gets is a blink, which makes
> her mad. *Say something, bitch.*

"I'm sorry your friends are
teaching you hate. Excuse me,
please. I have to get ready for
Mass." I expect some violent

> reaction. Instead, she moves
> out of my way. As the door closes
> behind me, I hear her say, *You think*
> *you're sorry now. Just wait.*

# I Don't Like the Sound

Of that, but I don't know what
        she means, and I really don't have
        time to worry about it. I slip out

of my dirty clothes into clean.
        On the far side of the window,
        Deirdre is taking off in her truck.

Her father would be angry
        to see her leave. He's kept
        a vigilant eye on her activities

for the past couple of weeks.
        But he's in Chico for some
        growers' conference, and it seems

the missus is still asleep, not
        that she's near the watchdog
        her husband is, even when

wide awake. Total silence
        chokeholds the house, so
        Sophie must be snoozing, too.

Maybe later I'll put her on
        Shoshone and lead her around
        the paddock. She'd like that.

I run a brush through my hair,
>notice the auburn lifting again
>at the roots. Time for a touch-up.

But not now. Angel and Javier
>are outside in the pickup, waiting
>for me. I, quick, do my teeth.

Wouldn't want my breath
>to scare the priest, let alone
>the guys who will be sitting in

close proximity. Good enough.
>As I hurry toward them, the hairs
>on the back of my neck prickle.

Odd. What's bothering me?
>Maybe it's just the way Angel
>is staring, as if hungering for

the confession I almost made.
>The confession I promise to make
>the next time we're alone together.

# But Right Now

I am stuffed between Javier and Angel,
who is driving a little too fast on this

fog-slicked narrow road. Thank goodness,
early Sunday morning it's pretty much

deserted. "Hey. Slow down. We want to
arrive in one pie—" The truck fishtails

suddenly, flashing me back to another
morning not so long ago. Only, Ethan

was at the wheel and snow draped
the hills on either side of us and . . .

*Oh shit!*
"Don't stop!"
*Hold on!*

And that was it. No more Ethan.
No more Pattyn. *Thunk-thunk-thunk.*

Angel pulls to the side of the road,
yanking me back to present time.

> *Flat tire,* he says, then notices the ice
> white of my face. *Hey. You okay?*

# I Grab a Deep Breath

Warmth lifts again in my cheeks.
"I'm fine. Except looks like
we're going to miss Mass."

>Angel tips his head, smiles.
>*Sí, pero Dios va a entender.*
>God will understand. We have

a good excuse. We all get out and,
sure enough, the rear passenger rim
sits on the ground. Must have been

a blowout. The guys start digging
for the jack and spare, and just
about the time they get the lug nuts

loosened, another truck—Deirdre's
truck—zips by. Jason Heckle drives,
and Deirdre is sandwiched between

him and his brother. I watch as, up
the road, the brake lights come on.
Then he makes a three-point turnabout,

approaches slowly. Surely he's not
planning to help? No, they'd never.
That familiar neck prickle again.

Jason creeps toward us, and
there is movement behind
the windshield. I don't like

how this feels—menacing,
but I can't say why. "Hey,
you guys." I reach into the cab,

open the glove box, hoping
for a pen. I find a pencil and
a receipt of some kind.

Quickly, I write on the back:

February 16
        The people who did this
        are Deirdre Jorgensen,
        Jason and Matthew Heckle.

Angel and Javier crawl out
of the dirt and stand. I stuff
the paper in my pocket. Wait.

*Jackie*
# Waiting

It is a journey of impatience,
creeping from then till now.
Time is a worm chewing
its way through the dirt

inside

our skulls, the fertile soil
we call a brain. Moving seeds
of intuition. Clipping roots
of memory. And to a one,

each of us

must allow the permeation,
because even if our choice
is to end the wait with death,
we then stare into the face of

infinity.

# Yesterday

Was a very long day.
I faked sick, stayed
in bed, listening to
the sounds of my family
beyond the bedroom walls.

It snowed, so they were
all sequestered inside.
Without my supervision,
keeping them occupied
became 'Lyssa's job.

As always, Mom had
better things to do than
to settle the little ones
with crayons in front
of Saturday cartoons.

Better things like playing
with Samuel and messing
around on the computer
she bought used. Mom,
online. Totally ridiculous.

She claims she's keeping
abreast of current events—
our governor's affair with
a runway model; a mustang
killing in California; gay

marriage legislation in
several states, and isn't it
disgusting how some straight
people actually support it?
I'm not about to argue, or

try to discuss my reasons
for changing my opinion
on the subject recently. She
still has no clue about Gavin's
two moms, and for now it's fine

that all she knows about Bea
is her profession. I know a whole
lot more now, and everything
I learn only serves to deepen
the respect I already had for her.

# The Things Gavin Told Me

On Friday night struck hard.
The truth simply is.
Embellishments can't change
core facts, and hiding
from what is real won't make
it as if it never was.

*You have to embrace the truth,*
he said, *or it will*
*sneak up from behind and nail*
*you. Sometimes*
*that takes courage, maybe more*
*than you believe*

*you could possibly hold inside.*
*But it's there, Jackie.*
*And if you can't find enough,*
*I'll share mine*
*with you. Together, we can face*
*anything. I love you.*

I thought about courage all day
yesterday. I think
bravery takes time to gather.
I've tried, and so far,
I've failed. If I only believed
Gavin would stay.

# Because Without Him

What do I have?
                    Nothing.
Okay, not totally
true. I also have

                    sisters.
With Pattyn gone,
'Lyssa and I've grown
a little closer. I do have

                    her.
Like it or not,
I also have a

                    baby brother
who is more work
than fun. Diapers.
Bottles. Drool and puke.

I don't really have
a mother. Can't put her
on my list. She's too tied
up "reconstructing her life,"
as she puts it, though she
hasn't managed to build much.

No friends. I've lost the few
I had. Who wants to hang
out with someone whose
sister is a murderer?

## School and Church

I've got those. The former would
be impossible without Gavin there.

As for church, I hate it more each time
I go. I didn't love it when we went with

Dad, but at least it didn't feel like a place
where I didn't belong. Now it seems

so artificial, and the people are superficial.
Big words, but accurate. I can't stand

the way everyone comes up to Mom
asking how she's doing. Like they care.

Hypocrites and users. That's all I see
there. Which is why I'm procrastinating

     now. 'Lyssa comes into the bedroom
     we share. *The kids are all in the car.*

     *Mom said to hurry up.* She watches
     me put on my shoes. *Feel better?*

"I'm okay. Thanks for asking. Be
right there." She turns and as she walks

away, I can't help but notice she has
gained a few pounds. The weight looks

good on her. She's always been rail-
thin. Her hair is darker, too, more auburn

than red. She reminds me of Pattyn
now. Wow. That's twice I've thought

about my big sister in just a few minutes,
and I choke on a heavy helping of guilt.

"I'm sorry, Patty." She is on my mind
all the way to church, despite the usual

cacophony of fussing and arguing and
giggling reverberating off the windows.

I am thinking about her face, creased
with fear that night, the way she turned

away from confrontation, only to be
forced into the fray. I flash on the chaos,

her confusion, denial, and finally
acceptance of the burden, pooling.

# Embrace the Truth

The phrase repeats over and over
as 'Lyssa and I help the girls down
from the Tahoe. As Mom takes Samuel
out of his car seat, carries him over
to a group of brethren waiting

for the sacrament meeting to begin.
No surprise the one she stands
closest to is Josiah McCain. I hate
his smirk. I hate his balding head
and now, as I look at Caleb, I can

see his hairline is already receding
ever so slightly. All he needs is to
grow a big gut and when he does,
he'll be his father. Hmm. Wonder
if Josiah is a degenerate, too.

Is that why his wife walked out
on him? Did he, perhaps, force
himself on the babysitter? Even
if it was something that perverted,
no one would have heard about it.

It would have been buried. Like
what Caleb did. Like Dad was.

# We Go Inside

Sit elbow to elbow in uncomfortable
chairs. Squirm on the metal seats
through hymns and prayers. And now

it's time to hear testimonies. Familiar
phrases permeate them:

> *I know this church is true.*
> *I love each and every one of you.*
> *Something happened this week.*
> *I wasn't going to get up here today.*
> *I know I'm not given more than I can bear.*

I barely listen. This stuff is always
the same. My attention wanders,
and unfortunately it keeps returning

> to Pattyn. Dad. Caleb. Caleb who,
> just now, stands up to give his own
> witness. *I'd like to bear testimony.*
>
> *The Holy Ghost came to me and said*
> *I need to apologize. . . .* He clears his
> throat, looks at me. Oh God, he isn't.

He wouldn't. Apology is a poor
fit on Caleb. It's impossible that
he'd aim one at me. He doesn't.

> *I apologize for my humanness. . . .*

He lists several unsavory human
traits—greed, jealousy, deceit.
Uh, yeah. My face flushes. Hot.

> *I apologize for wavering faith. . . .*

Psh. He has single-minded belief
in Caleb McCain. And who knew
"wavering" was in his vocabulary?

> *I apologize for impure thoughts. . . .*

Impure thoughts? How about vile,
dirty actions? I can feel his hands,
the weight of his body. The tight

space around me closes in like
a vise. Squeezes. Squeezes.
The storm inside me billows.

> *This is how I know the church is true.*

# Testimony Over

Everyone murmurs agreement.
The whispered noise is deafening.
Embrace the truth. That bastard
is a liar. I close my eyes and when
I do I see the freshman tottering,
Caleb dipping into her neckline.

> Mom leans forward toward Sister
> Crandall. *Wasn't that wonderful?*
> she whispers. *Such a fine boy.*

The truth is behind me, claws
digging into the back of my skull,
and that storm has swollen into
a hurricane. "No!" I jump to my feet.
"That wasn't wonderful at all, Mom.
How can you say he's a fine boy,
when you know what he did to me?"

Everyone is staring, and that's good,
because Josiah McCain stands, fists
clenching and unclenching. I think
he would gleefully use them on me,
except there are too many witnesses.
And no one will ever do that again.
"I want to give my testimony. . . ."

*Pattyn*
# I've Heard

People say you can
feel it coming, an omen
on the wind or the whistle
of some otherworldly
train, when

                    death

is headed your way.
Not for me, at least not
the first time. I was
clueless. One careless
overcorrection, everything
worth living for was gone.
I guess it's

                    always

a surprise when you're
stuck in the absurdity
of believing in some
ridiculous hereafter—
a place where only
the hand of the devil

                    wins.

# Death Approaches

I don't know why I feel it
this time round, but as Deirdre's
Dodge rolls this way, Jason
Heckle at the wheel, I know it
as surely as I'm standing here.

"I'm scared, Angel." The truck's
determined approach reeks
of foreboding. Some force
of evil is heading our way.

    He takes my hand. *Don't worry.*
    *I'll keep you safe.* I've heard
    those words before, and the end
    result was overwhelming heartache.

        Javier doesn't understand.
        *¿Por qué tiene miedo. They*
        *come to help us, no?*

He steps forward, to the edge
of the blacktop. Waves a greeting
as the truck draws even. I reach
into my pocket, find the pencil
and paper. For some indefinable
reason, I sign it, *Pattyn Von Stratten.*

# This Is Ridiculous

There is no concrete
reason for my certainty
that this will not end well.

> Javier smiles. *Hola, amigos.*
> Hello, friends. But do friends
> point rifles out their windows?

> > *Hola, you fucking spic,* says
> > Matthew Heckle, right before
> > he pulls the trigger. *¿Qué pasa?*

Down goes Javier, and I hear Deirdre
laugh. Angel pushes in front of me,
in time to take the round intended

for someone else. Me. The impact slams
both of us back against Angel's truck,
spattering the white paint scarlet.

Two more reports shatter the brittle
cold morning. "No! No, no, no!"
The word falls out of my mouth

in mindless repetition. Not again,
dear God, no. Not because of me.
But before they speed away, sure

the three of us are all buzzard
bait, Deirdre's face appears in
the open window. *Told you*

*you'd be sorry, bitch. Don't have*
*much to say now, do you, puta?*
*Rot in hell.* Tires spin, raising

dust and superheated rubber smoke.
Angel slumps, and we fall into the dirt.
My butt bumps hard beneath his slack

weight. "Angel!" I can see two wounds
puffing blood, and at least one bullet
went all the way through. My shoulder

is hot and my arm screams pain
when I try to move it. But I have to
try and stop Angel's bleeding. I scoot

gently out from underneath him,
scramble for something to stuff
in his wounds. Javier lies motionless,

two feet away, vacant eyes staring
skyward in obvious awe. He won't
mind if I use what's left of his shirt.

# Unreasonably, Birds

Start to sing again into the silence.
Before I try to rip fabric strips off
a dead man, I reach into Angel's
front pocket, find his cell phone,
dial 9-1-1. "Help. We've been shot.
I don't know where we are, but
hurry. People are . . . hurt badly."

Angel can't know I think he's dying.

Javier is wearing his favorite Sunday shirt.

There's a giant hole where his heart was.

I turn away and heave uselessly.
Get it together, Pattyn, or Angel
*will* die. I go back to Javier, try
not to look at that gaping wound
or the lake of blood he's floating in.

Who knew people held so much blood?

No scrap of shirt there, only the tails.

How will I rip it with one arm?

Angel makes a mewling noise,
like a kitten. I shove the cell into
my own pocket, maneuver my bad
arm to serve as an anchor, and throw
a minuscule prayer toward heaven.
"Please." And whether it's God,

or just my stubbornness, Javier's
shirt yields and I've got bandages.
I crawl over to Angel, stuff them
into his wounds, which are ugly
but have maybe missed vital organs.

His heart is still beating.

His chest still pants a shallow rise and fall.

And when he sees me, he smiles.

But now I think that must be
his goodbye. No! "Don't you dare
leave me! There's something you
need to know. I was going to tell
you earlier, but never got the chance."

# His Slight Nod

Disturbs the dirt.
Why doesn't he talk?
A word comes to mind: shock.
I take off my jacket.
It's all I have to cover him with.

Where's the ambulance?
I know they'll come.
They can find us via his phone.
But what about his family?
They should know.
Adriana's number is in his favorites.
I hit speed dial.
No answer.
Leave a message.
"Angel is hurt. Help."

I lift his head.
Slip back beneath it.
Cradle it in my lap.
I glance down at him.
His face is white. So white.
"Angel? Please don't go.
Have I told you I love you?"

His eyes flutter open.
And he smiles.

# All I Can Do Now

Is wait. And in that long,
blank space of time, I tell
Angel about Ethan. About
Caliente and Aunt J and Kevin.

I tell him about my family.
My sisters. Brother. Father.
Cold envelops me, and it
is born not only of February,

but also of a night in October.
I tell him about that, too.
My teeth begin to chatter, but
still I talk to him, alternating

sentences with blue-lipped
kisses all over his face. When
I finally hear the sirens approach,
I understand that my time

on the run has ended. And so
has my freedom. Strangely,
I'm okay with that. Except . . .
I don't know if I'll ever see

Angel again. The weight
of new loss is crushing.

*Jackie*
# Liberating

That's how it feels to confess
something that you've stuffed
into a closet inside you.
After a while,

truth

denied begins to go bad,
like an overripe peach, rotting
flesh frothing around the pit
at its heart. Slicing into it early

is integral

to savoring its sweetness.
But even if you have to cut
away bruises, you'll be hard-
pressed to find sweeter

satisfaction

than a perfect piece of truth.

# Perfect or Not

Here comes the truth. This truth
is in serious need of escape, and
I can't think of a better crowd
to catch it. "I want to give my
testimony. No, that's wrong. I have

to give it, and every word I'm
about to say is true, or may God
strike me down right here. . . ."
Everyone stares, slack-jawed and
wide-eyed. Everyone except Caleb,

who leans back in his chair
unconcernedly, a slight smile
dismissing the importance of
my confession. Well, we'll see.
"Caleb McCain is not a nice boy.

He is a monster. He raped me
the night my father died. Yes, I
invited him over. And yes, I led
him out into the shed. And yes, I
wanted to kiss him. But that is all

I'm guilty of. That, and being stupid
enough to think he might love me. . . ."

People are stirring now. Some
women have started to gather
their little ones and coax them
toward the door. "Wait. There's
more, and I want you all to hear

it, to bear witness. Caleb forced
himself on me. I told him no,
begged him no, but he wouldn't
stop. When Dad heard me crying,
he came to see what was going on.

Caleb ran, and Dad blew up, at me.
You all know he used his fists on
Mom. You can't say you didn't see
the bruises or notice how she wore
sunglasses inside sometimes. Well,

he also beat Pattyn and me, and
that night he was going to kill me. . . ."
The words keep coming faster
and I let them, because if I don't
I will lose the steam of courage

I've built. "Please listen. I need
you to know what really happened."

## Something in My Voice

Roots everyone in place.
Good. I repeat the part
of the story everyone has
already heard—

> how Pattyn came in
> yelled at Dad to stop
>
> how he laughed
> told her to shoot
>
> how she backed away
> and he came at her . . .

"I swear I didn't remember
what happened next. Not
for a while. It was stuck
somewhere inside my head.
But then it started coming
back in little pieces.

When Dad went after Pattyn,
I knew he'd take the gun.
I screamed for her to shoot,
but she didn't. I could barely
move, but then adrenaline
kicked in and I got to my feet. . . ."

I glance down at Mom, who can't
meet my eyes. But that's okay.
Probably better. "I yelled at Dad,
'Look what you've done to me.'
Not that he cared, but it stopped
his forward motion. I edged past
him, to Pattyn's side, begged her

to shoot, but she shook her head.
'I can't. He's my father, and . . .
I love him.' That made him laugh,
and it was the laugh of a crazy
man and I knew he was going
to kill both of us so I grabbed
the gun. I pulled the trigger,
not Pattyn. I killed my father.

The noise was insanely loud.
My ears were ringing, my head
started spinning, and I went down,
right next to my dad. The last
thing I heard before everything
went black was the stutter of his
breath and Pattyn saying, 'I did
this, not you. Without Ethan I
have no life. I did this. Understand?'"

# Everyone Is Frozen

Everyone except Mom, who finally
stands, measuring me with her eyes.

> *You're saying you really didn't*
> *remember this? How is that possible?*

She hasn't truly acknowledged
my presence since that night and

now I'm scared she never will again.
"I don't know. It's like I blanked it out.

It kept wanting to come back, but it
didn't until one day when I was packing

up the shed. You said I needed to face
my ghosts, and I did, and this is what

they showed me. And then I was too
afraid to tell you. I'm sorry. So sorry."

> From up in front, Bishop Crandall
> calls, *Let's break for Sunday school.*

Like what I just said meant nothing.
Like everything is totally normal.

# At Least It Thaws

The deep freeze. People hustle
out and the church empties except
for my family and the men up
front, including the McCains.

My sisters gawk at me with huge
eyes. The youngest, I'm sure, don't
understand what I just said. Mom
never discussed the details of Dad's

death with them. But Teddie gets it,
and 'Lyssa, who drips tears. I hand
her the baby. "Take the little ones to
Sunday school. They don't need

to hear the rest of this." I watch
them go, then turn to Mom. "Come
with me, please. I need you." I'm
a little surprised when she complies.

She follows me to where the church
hierarchy stands, mostly quiet for
a change. I walk straight up to Caleb,
lock his eyes with mine. "When I talk

to the cops, I'm telling everything.
You are despicable, but I hope you
get the help you need. And I really
hope the rest of you make sure he does."

All purple-faced and blowing
steam, Mr. McCain pulls up close.
*I sincerely hope you rethink this.*
*No one will believe a word you say.*

I shrug. "What have I got to lose?
Anyway, you know it's the truth,
and so does Caleb, and most everyone
here. Not to mention at least a couple

of girls at school, a gay kid, and
the guy who stopped his assault.
What kind of a person whitewashes
that stuff, even if it's his kid doing it?"

Now he turns on my mother.
*You'd better have a serious talk*
*with your daughter, Janice. She's in*
*a fair amount of trouble here and—*

# Mom Actually Interrupts Him

*I imagine she is, Josiah. But she's*
*right about your son. I'm grateful*

*for all your help, but I'm sorry I let*
*you talk me into staying quiet.*

Oh my God. Is she actually
supporting me? No way.

*But you and I had a deal, Janice.*
*Renege now, I'll call in my loan and—*

*Surely you're not threatening*
*me in front of witnesses? Tell*

*you what. Call it in. We're closing*
*on the old house later this week.*

*You'll have your money by Friday.*
*Come on, Jackie. Let's get out of here.*

My turn to follow. We head
outside, and I take big breaths

of snow-chilled air. We are alone,
but it's the first time in a very long

time I haven't felt lonely beside her.
I reach out to hug her, and it's weird

when she lets me. "Thank you.
I never thought you'd take my side."

She pushes back—that feels right—
holds me at arm's length. *Jackie,*

*I've got years of things to be sorry*
*for, but mostly it's these last few*

*months. I didn't know what you did,*
*but I blamed you anyway, when*

*the fault was always your father's.*
*I hope you can forgive me for refusing*

*to see how much you've been hurt.*
*I guess I was punishing you in some*

*way. And I was scared to be alone,*
*thought I could never handle things*

*on my own. When Josiah stepped*
*in, I became so dependent on him*

*that his threats carried too much
weight, and then I was scared of*

*him, too. But you were so brave,
standing in front of everyone,*

*telling the truth, that I felt ashamed.
I could barely look at you. Not*

*because of what you said. Because
of what I have been afraid to say.*

I absorb every word. Consider
what they mean. "Do you hate me?"

*No. There were times I could
have done the same thing.*

"So, what do we do now?"

*We get the kids, go home,
and call Detective Crow.*

"Can I call Gavin first?
I want him to hear it from me."

*I think it can wait that long.*

# When We Get Home

The message light on the answering
machine is blinking. Did someone
at church already call the authorities?

Mom hands off Samuel to Teddie,
punches the button. The soft voice
on the other end belongs to Aunt J.

> *Did you hear? Pattyn's been*
> *shot. She's going to be okay,*
> *but she's in the hospital. . . .*

Aunt J doesn't know the whole
story, but it's some sort of a hate
crime and she's on her way to

California now. Does Mom want
to ride over with her? She's already
called an attorney. Pattyn will need

one. And so will I, though Aunt J
doesn't know that part yet. While
Mom tries to get hold of her, I go

into my room. My nice, safe room.
Dig out the cell phone and call Gavin.
I don't want him to hear it on the news.

*Pattyn*
# Déjà vu

Of the worst kind. Swim
up into a flat, white
universe, backlit by
fluorescent suns.
                    You

breathe antiseptic,
count the beeps
of the monitor attached
to the arm you
                    don't

feel. The numbness
is an eerie reminder
that part of you is missing
and you don't
                    want to

go looking because
you're afraid of what
you might find in that
place you dare not
                    remember.

# That Place Is Hell

I've visited twice now and I wonder
if next time I'll stay there, where
the brimstone stench is gunpowder.

Funny how your brain plays tricks
on you when you're light on blood.
I was so worried about Angel that

I didn't realize the size of the hole
in my own arm. I remember the sirens.
The purpling of the red-blue-red lights.

A blur of faces, voices, hands. Not
much about that except I kept telling
them to take care of Angel first,

and the chorus assured me he was okay.
I was sure that was wrong, but when I fought
to see, I felt a small sting and gravity lost

its pull on me. The next thing I knew,
I woke up here, clean and bandaged
and warm. "Ethan" was the name I called.

No one knew who Ethan was, but a terse
male nurse assured me Angel was holding
his own. That's all they'll say. We're not kin.

# They Found the Note

In my pocket when they went
looking for some sort of ID.
As soon as I was conscious
and asking questions, a young
detective was asking his own of me.

> Was I, in fact, Pattyn Scarlet
> Von Stratten, who is wanted for
> questioning in Carson City?

Affirmative.

> Did I, in fact, witness what
> happened on Sunday morning,
> February sixteenth?

Affirmative.

> Could I, in fact, identify beyond
> all doubt the shooter and his
> accomplices?

Affirmative.

> Would I, in fact, be willing to
> testify in court about the events
> that occurred on that day?

Absolutely.

# That Was Yesterday

I think. Time passes so strangely
here, adrift on this morphine drip.
One minute you're awake, the next
some indefinable amount of time

has passed and they bring you dinner
or take your blood pressure. That's
what I'm expecting when I hear
footsteps and open my eyes. Instead . . .

> Oh my God. It's Dad! Except, no,
> he's dead, and this guy is younger.
> *Hello, Pattyn. Sorry if I frightened*
> *you. I'm your brother Douglas.*

Turns out he's a lawyer. Aunt
J sent him to me. She and Mom
are on their way, but got caught
in a blizzard on Donner Pass.

> *Pretty slow going up there right*
> *now. I don't expect to see them*
> *for several hours. Let's talk about*
> *you. Where have you been these weeks?*

# I Have Nothing to Lose

I already decided to come clean,
and anyway, he's supposed to be
on my side. I tell him everything,

from the time I ran off into the night,
and got on a bus out of Reno. But
when I finish, he's shaking his head.

> *I want to help, Pattyn, and I'm*
> *happy to represent you. But only if*
> *you're completely honest with me.*

"I don't know what you mean.
I told you everything." Well, except
one thing, but he can't mean that?

> *Jackie confessed. In fact, she got*
> *up in church and told everyone*
> *that she pulled the trigger, not you.*

"I—I . . ." I put my good hand over
my eyes. "I wanted to. I did. But
I couldn't. I'm such a coward."

> Douglas rests his hand lightly
> on my arm. *She said you couldn't*
> *because you loved him too much.*

# Unloading Everything

Is so freeing. Douglas and I talk
for a very long time. He tells me
Deirdre surrendered voluntarily,
but the Heckles decided to put up
a fight. Jason shot a cop, who's in
stable condition. It took a dozen
more to bring the boys in, but
they're behind bars, without bail.

Javier died instantly. I close my
eyes, remembering. *Hola, spic.*
*¿Qué pasa?* One second he was
here, changing a tire. The next,
he was gone. I hope he's dancing
with his saints in heaven. "What about
Angel? They won't tell me a thing."

> *He's critical, I'm afraid, but*
> *they're hopeful he'll pull through.*
> *He lost a huge amount of blood.*
> *If it wasn't for you . . .* He shakes
> his head. *He may lose the use of*
> *one arm. His sister has asked to*
> *see you, by the way. If you want.*

# I Do and I Don't

I feel responsible
and I want her to
know I'm sorry.
But I'm afraid
she despises me now.

Still, she deserves
the right to tell me
off. So I nod. "Okay."
I steel myself for
a hailstorm of anger.

> Instead, she blows
> in warm as a June
> breeze. *Hola, hermana.*
> She calls me sister.
> *¿Cómo se siente?*

I smile. "I've felt better.
But how are you? How
are your parents? Lo
siento, Adriana."

> *Why are you sorry?*
> Her voice is cross.
> *Did you teach those
> people to hate?*

I hang my head. "No,
but if not for me . . .
Those bullets were
meant for me. Angel
stepped between us."

> And he would again.
> Don't you know the things
> love will do? Sometimes
> it brings the lost ones
> home. Call him back.
> He will come to you.

"I hope so. Let me
know if there's any
change, okay? And,
Adriana? Thank you."

I watch her slink
away. Remember
how we first met,
and the facade
she displayed.
She's not so tough.
Unless she has to be.

## Journal Entry, February 18

Writing this, grateful that it was
my left shoulder that took the bullet.
Grateful that it is healing, and so
is Angel. They've upgraded his
condition to fair. I might even
get to visit him for a few minutes.

Aunt J brought Mom over the Sierra
in the biggest snowstorm of the year.
She said it took them six hours to
drive from Reno to Auburn. The trip
usually takes two. But they arrived
safely. I was overjoyed to see Aunt
J, who promises both she and Kevin
want me to come back to Caliente.

At first, I didn't want to see Mom.
Everyone thought I was worried
she hated me for what happened
with Dad. Truth is, I blame her.
She could have made him stop.
When I asked why she didn't, she
put on a pretty good show. Cried
for the nurses and Aunt J. Asked
me to forgive her. Maybe I can one
day. Maybe it will just take time.

*Jackie*
## Time

Heals all wounds, the saying
goes. I think physical wounds
heal more quickly than the kind
that scar your mind.

To

know for sure, all you can
do is keep moving forward,
one day a downhill flow
into the next, until you

build

speed, one week into the next,
into a month into the next,
into a year after year, faster and
faster, reaching maximum

momentum.

My birthday came and went.
Still not driving yet, but at least
when I turned Sweet Sixteen I had
been kissed. By someone I love.

# Winter Flows into Spring

And this year that blessed
     awakening takes on deeper

meaning. New life. Renewed
     optimism. Resurrection. A burst

of green across the valley,
     and in short order, an eruption

of bulbs—lemon-yellow crocuses,
     tangerine daffodils, scarlet tulips,

lavender allium, all planted
     by those who lived here before us.

And all we have to do to take
     pleasure in their beauty is open

our eyes. The girls and I have
     built a garden from old tires left

to molder behind the shed. We
     arranged them on the ground like

a big flower, filled them with
     potting soil, and in the promise

of seeds, set adrift in dark,
        thawed earth, now sprouting

tender shoots, I find hope
        for my own personal rebirth.

Pattyn and I went before
        the judge together, Douglas

at our side. We told sad, but
        true, tales of our upbringing, of

events leading up to that night.
        We told of our father, whose own

demons created the ghosts who
        will live on to haunt our memories.

Our mother gave her word
        that all we said was true, and

in the end we were acquitted
        of wrongdoing. Two people in

the courtroom cheered loudest
        of everyone. Gavin and Mom Bea.

# It Was So Good

Having Pattyn home, sharing
    a room, sleeping in the same
    double bed, whispering into

the deepest part of the night,
    filling in the blanks for each
    other. So hard to picture her

living like she did. So hard
    to hear the guilt in her voice
    when she talked about not coming

    forward sooner. *My heart told*
        *me something terrible would*
        *happen. If I only would have said*

    *something, Javier might still*
        *be alive. If I only . . .* She broke
        then. I don't think I've ever seen

her cry before. Not like that.
    I had no words to console her.
    I didn't even try. But she talked

about happy stuff, too. Angel
    and his family. The little girl.
    And the impossible Shoshone.

# But She Didn't Stay Long

She said this house could never
feel like home. That Caliente

>was calling. *Aunt J and Kevin
>have invited me to move back*

>*to the ranch. That's where I belong.
>Not here. You can come visit anytime.*

>*Bring your boyfriend, too. I like him.
>And I really like how much he loves you.*

I really like that, too. I was amazed,
really, that he stood by me through

everything. Pattyn says guys like
Gavin are rare, and I believe that.

He's graduating in a few months,
and I'm scared I might lose him then.

He promises that won't happen,
and when he kisses me, doubt melts

away in a huge rush of love, and
that gives me a bucketful of courage.

# Courage Creates Courage

That's what I've found.
I promised Caleb I was
going to tell everything.
I kept my word, though
I was very sure nothing

would come of it. Was
I wrong! I stepped up,
stepped forward, went
public. And when I did,
four other girls joined me.

Not the freshman. One tiny
piece of guilt absolved. But
among them was Tiffany
Grant, and the weirdest part
of that is, now we're friends.

As for our church brethren,
they're divided. Those loyal
to Josiah McCain will forever
ban us from their circles. But
others are champions of justice.

# At School

I am half freako killer, half feminist
heroine. Hanging out with Tiffany
once in a while doesn't exactly hurt.

But I spend most every spare minute
with Gavin. He's been awesome
all along, my hero and champion.

> Not to mention, my goofball tutor.
> *Would you please pay attention?*
> He pulls my wandering brain
>
> back into the library. *You are
> so going to flunk this test.*

"Probably. But you will love me
anyway. And that's why I love you."

> *Quit. You're making me blush.
> Hey. You still want to go to Caliente
> over spring break? Mom Bea says*
>
> *it's okay, since Aunt J promised
> her we'll sleep in separate rooms.*

"She doesn't know everything."
I wink. "There's always the barn."

*Pattyn*

# If You've Never

Been in a barn, you have
missed awesomeness.
Doesn't matter how low
the temperature tumbles

        outside,

snuggle up to a horse,
twelve hundred pounds
of body heat, no cold
can touch you. If you
think it's the height of

        madness,

to cuddle with an equine,
still you can indulge
your senses with the rich
perfume of rotting hay,
molasses-sweetened oats

        inside

the grain box; the feel
of well-oiled leather;
the song of creaking
rafters and wind against
the door. This, friend, is

        heaven.

# Heaven on Earth

That's how Caliente looks to me,
throwing off winter and showing
off late spring. The high desert air
is scented with rain-washed sage.
Oh, yes, this is heaven, and it is home.

And I am free.

After all those months of worry and
heartache and living a lie, to walk,
unchained, on any ground I choose
is almost more than I can fathom.
And this ground, this familiar soil,

is soaked with joy.

This happiness comes wrapped in
memories. If I stare across the yard
long enough, I can see Ethan walking
in the shadow of the barn. His big
gelding, Diego, nickers at his approach.

Ethan is here.

And though I can't touch him,
it's enough to feel him, to know
with certainty a part of him lives
on here, on the land he loved, and
that while I'm here, a part of him

lives on with me.

I was so happy that Aunt J brought
me home to the ranch. I stayed
in Mom's new home long enough
to understand I could never return
to those circumstances again.

Resentment is a bitter brew.

Aunt J says time will lessen the bite.
Time, and love, and she's got plenty
of both to invest in me. Kevin's game,
too. And, as if that isn't enough,
they've inched out on a narrow limb.

They're helping Angel, too.

# He's Healing Slowly

One of the bullets went
straight through muscle,
exiting the other side and
drilling into me. I was lucky,
the doctor said. Angel's
shoulder saved mine.

The second bullet hit bone,
bounced around, did a lot
of damage. Unfortunately,
that was his right arm and
it will never be quite okay.

Pruning trees and digging
ditches are doubtful, and
anyway, his position with
the Jorgensens has been
terminated. At his request.
They agreed to a decent
settlement. Which will just
about pay his hospital bills.

He was fortunate to qualify
for temporary legal status
under a two-year deferral
program. By the time that
expires, Adriana will be old

enough to sponsor him
for a green card. Except
he'll need cosponsors
who qualify financially,
not to mention a job.

> And that's where Aunt J
> and Kevin have stepped
> in. *This is a big place,*
> Kevin said. *You'll need*
> *help running it when*
> *Jeanette and I run off*
> *to Tahiti.* The Tahiti
> part was probably a joke.

> But Aunt J says the ranch
> belongs to me. *Who else*
> *do I have to leave it to?*
> *Who else would want it,*
> *except maybe some money-*
> *grubbing developer? No,*
> *I can't see anyone else*
> *here but you, Pattyn girl.*

This will be home forever.

# If All Goes Well

Angel will be here next week.
Douglas's partner (both at his firm
and in his personal life) handles
immigration law and is helping
Angel with the "paper blizzard,"
as Gerard calls it. He and Douglas

are amazing. I'm so happy to have
connected, and not just because
they're great lawyers. They're great
people. And Douglas is my brother.
Despite all he did for Jackie and me,
Mom can't quite acknowledge that.

> Douglas says deeply programmed
> prejudices take time (that word
> again!) to break down. *She'll come
> around eventually. I mean, she can't
> resist my charm forever.* I hope not.
> This family has never been whole.

Not sure we can find a way to put
together pieces that were never
attached in the first place, but I'm
determined to try. After we all heal
up a little on our own. After we all
know for sure who we are as pieces.

# Today

I'm helping Aunt J move the cattle
to the high meadow for summer
pasture. Kevin's coming along, riding

Old Poncho. Aunt J is on Paprika,
and I've got Diego under me. Last time
I rode him out this way, I was double

behind Ethan, face against his back.
The memory swallows me for a minute.
But then Diego demands my attention.

> The black is tall, strong, and in need
> of a good run. Aunt J was right about
> that. *Give him his head,* she urges.

Diego is powerful, but I am in control.
I let him go, and we run. And I know
this is my destiny—to have a brilliant

horse beneath me and run. We go until
he tires and, both of us winded, we turn
back to Aunt J, who is loping Paprika

while Kevin brings up the rear, dealing
with Poncho's uneven trot. The dogs
move the cattle, with us pushing strays.

It's a long ride, hours up into the hills.
"Remember the last time we did this?
I was on Poncho, and barely hanging on."

> *I remember it well*, says Aunt J.
> *You have become quite the horsewoman.*
> *I think you'll make a fine trainer.*

"A year ago, I didn't even know
I liked horses, let alone that I wanted
to train them. So much has happened."

> *It's been some kind of year, hasn't it?*
> She sobers. *My grandmother used*
> *to say God gives us drought years—*

> *years drained of happiness—to*
> *prepare us for bounteous times.*
> *I'm more than ready for bounty.*

A cow bawls for her calf, who
has stopped to nibble at the new
shoots of grass. I'm grateful for

the distraction of shooing the baby
back to its mama. I didn't want to tell
Aunt J how afraid I am of happiness.

# Most People

Would say that's an irrational
fear. How could any sane person

believe they weren't destined
for happiness? Most of the time

I feel balanced enough. Most
of the time I think my brain

is functioning properly. But
somewhere in that gray matter,

profound damage has occurred.
Maybe you can't live through all

I have and come out unscathed.
I'm in need of healing myself,

and I am on a pilgrimage of sorts.
I'm not alone on this journey,

and for that, I'm grateful. But until
I reach that end destination, I will

not search for happiness. Perhaps
it will come looking for me.

# In the Meantime

We coax the cattle through a narrow
gate, onto public land, start climbing.
We ride for hours, over the same
route we took last summer, only,

"We're moving them up earlier
this year." Last time, with Ethan,
it was late June, and sweltering.

> Aunt J nods. *April gave us a little*
> *heat wave. The snow melted off*
> *and it's been mostly dry 'cept for*
> *that humdinger rain that came through*
>
> *a couple of days ago. Might as well*
> *save the lower pasture some wear*
> *and tear. Anyway, I thought you might*
> *want to see where we laid Ethan to rest.*

"Ethan?" Sadness swoops down,
perches on my shoulders. "You
brought him all the way up here?"

> We have arrived at the reservoir
> where we camped before, listening
> to coyotes while we discussed God.
> *I knew this was where he'd want to be.*

# No One Ever Told Me

The details of Ethan's death
and burial. I never asked. Wasn't
strong enough to hear. I'm not sure
I am now. But I really need to know.

> *He died on impact,* Kevin says.
> *They said he felt no pain.*
> *He didn't suf—* He chokes
> on the rest. And I do, too.

We dismount, leave the horses
to graze, and Aunt J leads me
to a small mound of granite
rocks, adorned with a simple
cross made of willow branches.

> Kevin continues, *When Ethan's*
> *mother died, we buried her*
> *in a fancy casket, laid her in*
> *a grave between strangers.*

> *Ethan told me then he wanted*
> *to be cremated and left in*
> *the company of the mountain.*
> *I never expected the task*
> *would be left to me to accomplish.*

# He Turns Away

Aunt J follows him and they set
up camp, leaving me here to
grieve alone. I'm grateful for
the chance to mourn privately.
I sit cross-legged on the small
mound of meadow covering

Ethan's ashes and as the sun sinks
below the mountain's rim,
painting the sky mauve, I ask
out loud, "Are you here?" and
I swear, I hear him on the wind,
or on wings of memory,

*Well, of course.*

I lie facedown on his little grave
and our night together here soaks
into the grass on a flood of tears. I
cry until dusk becomes night and
there is nothing left inside to cry.
It has grown cold with the dark.

Just over there is a campfire.
But I can't quite pull myself away.

# Smoke Rises into the Evening

Trailing the scent of burning
juniper. The breeze carries
its exotic perfume across
the meadow, rich with memories
of this place. Caliente, where
love first came looking for me.

Aunt J and Kevin sit close
together in silhouette. Her head
tips against his shoulder, and
in that small gesture, I feel
the sadness lift. People aren't
meant to carry sorrow alone.

And joy? Well, that is something
best shared. I found happiness
here. Right here with Ethan,
and woven from threads of
family I barely knew existed.

Thin plumes of smoke climb toward
the heavens. I send my questions
with them and as they stretch,
ghosts, into the hinterland of night,
murmurs of hope float back to me.

# Finally, I Whisper

Toward the lake of stars,
blinking on, one by one, in
the black velvet Nevada sky,

"I will always love you,
Ethan. You are my forever
love. But I think Aunt J was
wrong. I think real love can
find you more than once.
I hope so, or why go on?

I'm not sure yet if Angel
is the one, but I won't know
if I don't give him a chance.

I'm glad I'll always be here,
so close to you. But there has
to be room in my heart
for another. And this land
demands to be shared. It's time
for me to move forward."

In the distance, a coyote howls
and the wind picks up and
the moon's pale face shines light.
I find Ethan in all those things.
And in none.

## Journal Entry, June 21

*Summer solstice. The longest day*
*of the year, and it could be longer*
*yet. There's so much to do here.*
*Horses. Cattle. Chickens. Geese.*
*Feeding livestock. Tending garden.*
*Angel can help with those things,*
*and he does, despite his weak arm.*
*He has become a part of the family,*
*and we're such a ragtag bunch.*

*Aunt J and Kevin. Angel and me.*
*Jackie and Gavin come to visit.*
*He decided on college in Reno*
*so he can be close to her. I'm grateful*
*for that. His love is building her up.*
*Douglas and Gerard have been out,*
*too. "Exploring the vast nothingness,"*
*Gerard says. One day I convinced*
*him to ride Old Poncho. Priceless!*

*I no longer look for signs of Ethan,*
*or wait for some message from*
*the beyond. Jackie returned my locket.*
*It still has his picture inside, plus*
*one of Angel. I wear it constantly,*
*a reminder that real love absolutely*
*can find you more than once.*

# Author's Note

A huge story thread in *Burned* and *Smoke* is physical abuse. It is something I know personally, having lived in a physically abusive relationship for three years. At times, this man was charming. At times, he was a monster. I should not have stayed as long as I did, but like many women, I thought if I only did the right things, I could fix him. It rarely works out that way.

If you are in an abusive relationship, my heartfelt entreaty is to get out. Right away. You may need help to escape it, but help is available. Ask for it if you aren't able to leave on your own. The problem may be fixable. But you are not equipped to fix it, and the longer you stay, the likelier it becomes that the abuse will escalate. Whether it's a parent or spouse or boyfriend/girlfriend who's the abuser, tell someone you can trust. And don't wait.

Here are some statistics to consider. According to teensagainstabuse.org:

- One in three teens say they know a friend or peer who has been hit, punched, kicked, slapped, choked, or otherwise physically hurt by their partner.
- One in four teenage girls who have been in relationships have been pressured to engage in unwanted sexual acts.
- More than one in four teenage girls currently in a relationship (26%) experience repeated verbal abuse.
- 73% of teens said they would tell a friend if they were abused by a partner, but only 33% who have been in or known about an abusive relationship told anyone about it.
- Nearly 80% of girls who have been physically abused by an intimate partner continue to date their abuser.
- 30% of the women ages 15–19 who are murdered each year are killed by their husbands/boyfriends.

And, according to childhelp.org:

- A report of child abuse occurs once every ten seconds.
- Every day more than five children in the US die because of abuse.
- Child abuse occurs in all ethnicities, cultures, and religions, and at all levels of education and income.
- Roughly 30% of abused children will grow up to abuse their own children.
- Children who have suffered abuse are 25% more likely to experience teen pregnancy.
- Abused teens are less likely to practice safe sex, which puts them at greater risk of getting an STD.

It's up to every one of us to help turn these statistics around and break the cycles of abuse. If you or someone you know needs help, please ask for it. Not next week or tomorrow or even later today. Now.

A Reading Group Guide to
# Smoke
By Ellen Hopkins

## About the Book

Blamed for her abusive father's death and haunted by the loss of her boyfriend and their unborn child, Pattyn Von Stratten is on the run. Aboard a bus destined for California, she makes friends with Adriana, a young girl whose family helps her find work as a housekeeper for the Jorgensens, a wealthy ranch-owning family. Pattyn sets out to build a new life under a false identity, but she is overwhelmed by feelings of loss and guilt and questions her ability to build new relationships and establish a new existence. Back home, her younger sister is the sole person who knows what happened in the shed that day, but Jackie is haunted by troubles of her own. Her mother, for one, refuses to accept reality and the role Caleb played in the death of the girls' father. *Smoke*, the much anticipated sequel to *Burned*, brings closure to one girl's heart-wrenching journey.

## Prereading Questions

1. Why is abuse (both physical and emotional) so prevalent in society?
2. Discuss what you would do if you knew a loved one was in an abusive relationship.
3. In your opinion, why do individuals stay in abusive relationships?
4. What responsibility do we have when we know a loved one is in a dangerous relationship?

## Discussion Questions

1. The story opens with Pattyn having run away from home and Jackie in the hospital. What event has occurred?

2. Pattyn, bound for California, meets Adriana on a bus. Why does Adriana open her home to Pattyn and how does Pattyn prove to be useful to Adriana's family?

3. Angel, Adriana's brother, helps Pattyn secure a job as a housekeeper for a ranch owner. Describe the family and Pattyn's feelings about working for them.

4. When Jackie returns home from the hospital, her mother begins making new plans for the family. How does their life change? Why does Jackie's mother turn a deaf ear to Jackie's story about Caleb? What reaction does Jackie have to her mother's denial?

5. How does Angel help Pattyn adjust to her new life? What does he know about Pattyn's past and why does Pattyn give him limited information about why she is on the run? How does she feel about Angel not having the right facts?

6. Religious convictions play an important role in the Von Stratten family's responses. How does faith impact Ms. Von Stratten's decisions and her responses toward her daughters? How does their religious upbringing impact the way Pattyn and Jackie respond to their lives?

7. Pattyn nurses María and her baby, Teresa, through the measles. María and her family are poor, yet "María lives in hope of the future, a more precious gift than she knows." Why might Pattyn hold this belief?

8. As Pattyn becomes more acquainted with Adriana and Angel's family, what does she learn about the life of migrant workers and the plight of undocumented workers in the United States? In what way does she feel connected to their plight?

9. Pattyn is surprised to learn that Adriana knows she is on the run for murder but has never approached Pattyn about what happened. Adriana says, "[G]uilt—is more punishment for you than jail." Do you agree or disagree? Would this be true for everyone? Explain.

10. Pattyn believes that to embrace courage, two things are required: "unshakable faith that death is no more than a portal to some

Shangri-la reunion. Or zero belief at all." Is her argument accurate? Does she view herself as courageous? Does the author present her as a courageous character? What about Jackie? Their mother?

11. Jackie believes that truth is a product of perception. Explain what she means. Is her statement accurate? Why or why not?

12. Mr. Jorgensen and others are surprised to learn that Pattyn can tame Shoshone. What previous experiences with horses does Pattyn have? How does working with Shoshone bring Pattyn peace?

13. After returning home from the hospital, Jackie decides to focus on school and seeks out a tutor—Gavin. Is Gavin good for Jackie? Explain. How is he different from Caleb? What strengths does he have as a friend?

14. Ms. Von Stratten invites Caleb and his father to a holiday dinner and Jackie is outraged. Why does Ms. Von Stratten invite them and how does Gavin come to Jackie's aid?

15. Pattyn goes Christmas shopping with Angel. In some ways, the holiday is satisfying, but in others it is not. What mixed feelings does she have?

16. Why does Ms. Von Stratten send Jackie to clean out the shed? Is this decision a good one? Why or why not? How dottes Jackie respond to the task?

17. Deirdre, the Jorgensens' older daughter, is an angry and dangerous teen. What warning signs does Pattyn see and why doesn't she share those with Deirdre's family?

18. Describe the scene in which Jackie speaks up against Caleb in church. Why does Jackie speak out? What does her action say about her character? Is her mother's response expected?

19. Who are Aunt J and Kevin and why does Pattyn go live with them in the end? What does the reader learn about their past? Is this arrangement in Pattyn's best interest?

20. As a sequel to *Burned*, how is *Smoke* a fitting title for this latest Hopkins novel?

## Questions/Activities for Further Discussion

1. In addition to physical and emotional abuse, what other strong themes are apparent in *Smoke*? How do these themes evolve throughout the story?

2. Ms. Von Stratten seems worried about image and perceptions. Find a scene that supports such a fear. In what way is her behavior damaging to her family? Is she likeable? How does she serve to advance the plot?

3. Identify an especially compelling scene, rich with imagery, and discuss the language the author uses to make the scene effective.

4. Pattyn and Jackie both develop new relationships over time. What do Angel and Gavin have in common? Keeping their personalities in mind, describe a short scene in which Angel meets Jackie for the first time and Gavin meets Pattyn, or describe a scene in which Angel and Gavin meet.

5. Physical abuse is a central theme in *Smoke*. Using Hopkins's suggested site, teensagainstabuse.org, as a starting point, gather five additional facts (not identified by Hopkins) from other websites or informational texts related to physical abuse. Share your points with a small group.

Guide written in 2013 by Pam B. Cole, Professor of English Education & Literacy, Kennesaw State University, Kennesaw, GA

This guide has been provided by Simon & Schuster for classroom, library, and reading group use. It may be reproduced in its entirety or excerpted for these purposes.

Turn the page for a look at

by Ellen Hopkins

# In the Narrow Pewter Space

Between the gray of consciousness
and the obsidian where dreams
ebb and flow, there is a wishbone
window. And trapped in its glass,
a single silver shard of enlightenment.

It is this mystics search for. The truth
of the Holy Grail. It is this believers
pray for. The spark, alpha and omega.
It is this the gilded claim to hold
in the cups of their hands. But what

of those who plunge into slumber,
who snap from sleep's embrace?
What of those who measure their
tomorrows with finite numbers, cross
them off their calendars one by

one? Some say death is a doorway,
belief the key. Others claim you only
have to stumble across the threshold
to glimpse a hundred billion universes
in the blink of single silver shard.

# Have Faith

That's what people keep telling me.
Faith that things will get better. Faith
that bad things happen for a reason.
Implicit in that ridiculous statement
is the hand of some extraterrestrial
magician. Some all-powerful creator,

which, if his faithful want to be totally
frank about it, would also make him/her/it
an omnipotent destroyer. Because if
some God carefully sows each seed
of life, he is also flint for the relentless
sun beating down upon his crops until

they wither into dust. Zygotes to ashes
or some other poignant phrase. And why
would any of that make someone feel
better about snuffing out? The end
result is the same. You get a few
years on this sad, devolving planet.

If you're lucky, you experience love,
someone or two or three to gentle
your time, fill the hollow spaces.
If you're really fortunate, the good
outweighs the bad. In my eighteen years
all I've seen is shit tipping the scales.

# Case in Point

I've been abruptly summoned to
the front of the classroom at the urgent
request of my English teacher, the oh-so-
disturbed, Savannah-belle-wannabe
Ms. Hannity, emphasis on the Mizz.
She pretends sympathy, for what,
I've no clue, and like she gives half

> a damn about anything but clinging,
> ironfisted, to her job. *Mr. Turnahhhh.*
> Fake "South" taints her voice and
> her eyes—no doubt she'd describe
> them as "cornflower"—are wide
> with mock concern. *Would you*
> *please come he-ah for a minute?*

I think she thinks she's whispering,
but twenty-seven pairs of eyes home
in on me. I straight-on laser every one
until they drop like dead fly duos.
"Yes, ma'am?" The feigned respect
isn't lost on her, and she doesn't bother

> to lower her voice. *Mistah Carpentah*
> *wishes a word with you. Please see*
> *him now. And the rest of y'all, get back*
> *to work. This doesn't concern you.*

# Why, Then

Did she make it exactly everyone's
concern? The ends of my fingers tingle
and my jaw keeps working itself
forward. Backward. Forward. I force
it sideways and audibly, painfully, it pops.

For some messed-up reason she smiles
at that. I really want to slap that stinking
grin off her face. But then I'd get expelled,
and that would humiliate my father,
everyone's favorite science teacher, not to

mention the coach of the best basketball
team this school has seen in a dozen years.
Then Mom would bitch at him for not kicking
my ass and at me for turning him into such a wuss,
until I had no choice but to flee from our miserable

termite-ridden shack. And I'd have to live in
my fume-sucking truck, eating pilfered ramen,
drinking Mosby Creek water until I got the runs
so bad I'd wind up in the ER, hoping Dad
hadn't had time to dump me from his insurance.

And, despite all that, Mizz nose-up-my-ass
Hannity would still be a rip-roaring bitch.

# As I Wind Up

That extended interior monologue,
I notice everyone is once again staring at me,
waiting for some overt exterior reaction.

Expecting, I'm sure, one of my infamous
blowups. More fun to keep 'em guessing.
"Can you tell me why he wants to see me?

Have I done something I'm not aware of?"
I'm pulling off As in every class. Maintaining
the pretense that all is well, despite everything

being completely messed up. It would be nice
to have some idea of what I'm walking into.
But Hannity gives nothing away. *Just go.*

Don't flip her off. Don't flip her off. Don't . . .
I flip her off mentally, sharp turn on one heel,
head toward the door. Laser. Laser. Laser.

Pairs of dead flies drop as I pass, anger obviously
obvious in the death beam of my eyes. What now?
All I want is to be left alone. All I want

is to cruise in radar-free space. Scratch that.
What I really want is to disappear. Except,
if this in-your-face place is all I'll ever

get to experience, I'm not quite finished
here. "Live large, go out with a huge bang,"
that's my motto. Too bad so many minuscule

moments make up the biggest part of every
day. Moments like these. A familiar curtain
of fury threatens to drop and smother me.

I push it away with a smile, hope no one
takes a candid photo right now, because
I'm as certain as I can be that I resemble

some serial killer. Tall. Good-looking.
The boy next door, with near-zero affect.
Totally fine by me. Keep 'em guessing.

I swear, I can hear the collective breath-
holding, all those goddamn flies hovering
silently at my back. I plaster a grin. Spin.

"Boo!" Audible gasps. Yes! Okay, screw it.
I flip off the lot of them, dig down deep
for something resembling courage, and skip

from the room, a not-close-to-good-enough
tribute to my little brother, Luke, deceased
now one hundred sixty-eight days. Exactly.

# A Tribute

So why do I stop just beyond
the door, assess the scene . . .
what am I waiting for? A sign?
The hallway is vacant. Silent.
No one to bear witness to . . .
what? Some ill-conceived
testimony? "Fuck you, Luke."

Another pointless statement,
echoing. Echoing. Echoing
down the corridor. Luke. Luke.
Luke. You selfish little prick.
My eyes burn. No, damn it!

If the vultures see me cry,
they'll swoop in, try to finish
me off. And I'm just so tired
of fighting, they might actually
manage it this time. Screw that.
They already got my brother.
It will be a cold day in hell
before I give up, give in, allow
them to claim another victory.

# I'm Not Quite

To Mr. Carpenter's office when the bell
rings. Okay, technically it's a blare, not
a bell. Some new-wave administrator
decided to replace the old *buuurrrriing*

with a blast of music so we don't feel
so much like we're in school, despite
the off-white cement walls and even
offer-white linoleum, lined with

not-quite-khaki lockers. Doors slam
open and out spills noise. Lots of it.
Laughter and curses and screeches
echoing down the corridor. I scan

the crowd, as I always do, hoping
for even just a glimpse of her. There,
on the far side of the counselors' offices.
She's hard to miss, my amazing girl—

a whole head taller than her pack
of loser friends, with perfect slender curves
and thick ropes of honey-colored hair.
"Hayden!" I yell, though it's impossible

to hear in this obnoxious swell. Yet
she turns, and when those suede chocolate
eyes settle on me, her diamond smile lifts
my mood. She gestures for me to come there.

I shake my head, tip it in the direction
of the counseling offices. Even from here,
I can see the way concern crinkles her eyes
at the edges. I shrug a silent, "No worries."

That's one thing I love about Hayden—how
we can communicate without words. It's not
the only thing I love about her, or even close
to the most important. But it's really special,

sort of like Heath bar sprinkles over the vanilla
cream cheese frosting on top of the very rich
red velvet cupcake. Ultra extra deliciousness.
Sometimes it's hard to believe she's mine.

But knowing that—trusting it—helps
me tilt my chin upward, straighten
my shoulders, and put one foot in front
of the other, toward Mr. Carpenter's lair.

# FROM THE *NEW YORK TIMES* BESTSELLING AUTHOR
# Ellen Hopkins

**CRANK**
"The poems are masterpieces of word, shape, and pacing . . . stunning."
—*SLJ*

**GLASS**
"Powerful, heart-wrenching, and all too real."
—*Teensreadtoo.com*

**FALLOUT**
"*Fallout* is impossible to put down."
—*VOYA*

**BURNED**
"Troubling but beautifully written."
—*Booklist*

**SMOKE**
"A strong, painful, and tender piece."
—*Kirkus Reviews*

**IMPULSE**
"A fast, jagged, hypnotic read."
—*Kirkus Reviews*

**PERFECT**
"This page-turner pulls no emotional punches."
—*Kirkus Reviews*

**IDENTICAL**
★"Sharp and stunning . . . brilliant."
—*Kirkus Reviews*, starred review

**TRICKS**
"Distinct and unmistakable."
—*Kirkus Reviews*

**TILT**
"Graphic, bitingly honest, and volumious verse."—*SLJ*

**RUMBLE**
"Strong and worthy."
—*Kirkus Reviews*

### PRINT AND EBOOK EDITIONS AVAILABLE
From Margaret K. McElderry Books | Published by Simon & Schuster

For anyone who loves **The Outsiders**, this is a powerful, gritty story about standing up for what's right, even when you're living on the wrong side of the neighborhood line.

**A lot of the stuff that gives my neighborhood a bad name, I don't really mess with. The guns and drugs and all that, not really my thing.**

PRINT AND EBOOK EDITIONS AVAILABLE
TEEN.SimonandSchuster.com

GRAPPLING WITH GRIEF IS HARD ENOUGH

WITHOUT REPEAT VISITS FROM

THE RECENTLY DECEASED.

PEARL DEALS WITH DEATH, LIFE, AND FAMILY

IN THIS HAUNTING, HUMOROUS,

AND POIGNANT DEBUT.

PRINT AND EBOOK EDITIONS AVAILABLE
From Margaret K. McElderry Books    TEEN.SimonandSchuster.com

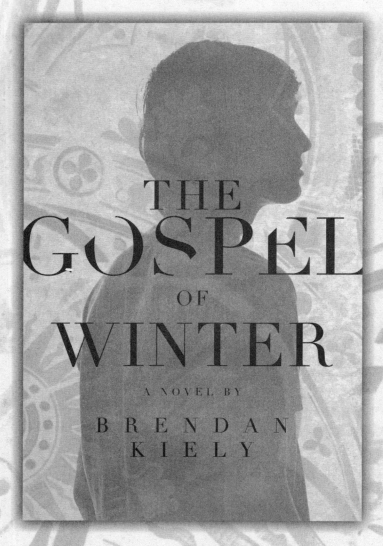

A fearless debut novel about the restorative power of truth and love after the trauma of abuse.

"Unflinching and redemptive."—Colum McCann, *New York Times* bestselling author of the National Book Award winner *Let the Great World Spin*

PRINT AND EBOOK EDITIONS AVAILABLE
From Margaret K. McElderry Books
TEEN.SimonandSchuster.com